A Shores Mystery

COD
ONLY KNOWS

I0642845

A Shores Mystery

COD
ONLY KNOWS
Hilary MacLeod

The Acorn Press
Charlottetown
2017

Other books in the *Shores Mysteries* series...

Hilary MacLeod

"Hilary MacLeod is a terrific writer with a sly wit."
—*Anne Emery, author of Sign of the Cross*

REVENGE OF THE
LOBSTER LOVER

MIND OVER
MUSSELS
A Shores Mystery

CBC Bookie award-winner
Hilary MacLeod
author of *Revenge of the Lobster Lover*

ALL IS CLAM
A Shores Mystery

CBC Bookie award-winner
Hilary MacLeod
author of *Revenge of the Lobster Lover*

SOMETHING
FISHY
A Shores Mystery

CBC Bookie award-winner
Hilary MacLeod
author of *Revenge of the Lobster Lover*

A Shores Mystery
BODIES
AND SOLE

CBC Bookie award-winner
Hilary MacLeod
author of *Revenge of the Lobster Lover*

ACORNPRESS

P.O. Box 22024
Charlottetown, Prince Edward Island
C1A 9J2
acornpresscanada.com

Edited by Jane Ledwell
Copy edit by Laurie Brinkley
Cover illustration and interior design by Matt Reid

Library and Archives Canada Cataloguing in Publication

MacLeod, Hilary, author
    Cod only knows / Hilary MacLeod.

(Shores mystery)
Issued in print and electronic formats.
ISBN 978-1-927502-91-4 (softcover).--ISBN 978-1-927502-92-1 (HTML)

    I. Title.

PS8625.L4555C63 2017   C813'.6   C2017-905349-3
                                               C2017-905350-7

 Canada Council Conseil des Arts
for the Arts du Canada

The publisher acknowledges the support of the Government of Canada, The Canada Council for the Arts Block Grant Program and the Province Of Prince Edward Island..

To the two friends who sparked my imagination:
Henry Mead and Virginia Van Vliet.
Without you, there might have been no stories.

And God sighed in the sunset; and the sea
Chanted the soft recessional of Time
Against the golden shores of mystery;

—From Progress of Love by Alfred Noyes

Chapter 1

The fish leaped in the air, yanking the line, tugging the dory across the waves.

It was a small boat. It was a big fish.

Bigger than me, thought Seamus O'Malley, looking at the photo. That was saying something, because Seamus was three hundred pounds on a good day.

The fisherman's back was to the camera. He was wearing a hat that obscured his head. There was no telling who it was, or how old he was. Then or now. Must be old, because the photograph was. So was the hat.

The fish was a cod. They usually weighed around ten to twenty pounds these days. The record was about two hundred pounds, but never this heavy. It was a cod, that was clear, even though it was difficult to see all of it, twisted around in the air as it was, leaping and plunging to escape the line. It was mossy green, with the characteristic chin whisker, the barbel, of the cod. It had dorsal fins, the spotted back, and the telltale lateral line. It was interrupted, smudged in the middle, as if a part of it had been erased, making it hard to tell if it was a genetic or photographic error.

It was a cod, all right. The biggest he'd ever seen. You couldn't spread out your arms to show how big it was. Sometimes fishermen held up catches like this by the tail to demonstrate how long they were next to the man – five, six feet. In this case, thought Seamus, the fish would have to hold the man. If it were riddled with worms like the small cod, one giant cod worm would make a Sunday dinner. He paused to think a moment. A new industry? Cod worms? Taste just like the real thing. They would, wouldn't they? You are what you eat.

O'Malley had heard of big cod in the deep Atlantic, but not this huge. Here on Red Island? Never.

Until now.

Or then. Years before when the picture had been taken. Today, that photograph would have been all over Facebook. Then, it was just a curiosity to the inhabitants of a tiny village the world had never heard of.

Until the last few years.

All those murders.

O'Malley was sitting, feet up on the desk, in his office at the Red Island fisheries department in Winterside. He'd been staring at the photograph of the man and the fish on and off for the past half-hour. It was torn, shredded on one corner. It had been stuck in the back of a file cabinet drawer he'd been cleaning out. It came from a book, but he couldn't find the book anywhere. He knew that it was local because a patch of the photo credit remained: ...*Red Island, courtesy of...* Who the photographer and the fisherman were had been lost when the page was ripped from the book.

Probably it was one of those community vanities. There were several of them in the cabinet drawer, books that villages across the island self-published, detailing founding families, community firsts, faded and damaged old photographs of the hall and the school, the first automobile and its owner and so on. He'd searched through them all. None was missing a page, nor contained any other magnificent shots like this one, with the fisherman being dragged out to sea by a fish.

The one that got away? Along with the book that told the tale? Had the cod been reeled in? Or freed because it was too big? Had it been eaten?

Seamus smirked. It would take a village to eat that cod.

It must have gotten away. If it had been caught the story would have been told. He had scoured the *Guardian* newspaper files with no luck. One way or another, the fish would be dead now. The oldest cod he'd heard of had lived twenty-seven years.

But the man might be alive to tell the story.

If he were, Seamus would surely be able to find him.

If he could find out more about the big fish, where it came from, it might take him off this godforsaken island and onto that other one. The other might be godforsaken, too, but it was *his* godforsaken island. Home. Where cod had once been currency, Newfoundland currency, until the bottom fell out of the bank. The Grand Banks, that is. Codforsaken. If he could find a fish like this, he might return home a hero.

Could more such fish exist? Here?

***

Brock Ferguson tossed a bottle cap into the massive Nebuchadnezzar wine bottle, three times the size of a Jeroboam, filling the corner of his den. He'd found the cap in his jacket pocket and remembered he'd picked it up off the bottom shelf of a cupboard and slipped it into the pocket. It was careless of him to have forgotten it. *Care less.* He'd once been fonder of the collection than he was of his wife Letitia – that was before she became a lottery winner three times over. A record in itself. How could he not love her for that?

Their meeting was no coincidence. After her first lottery win, Letitia had given up her job at a snow crab processing plant in Nova Scotia and tried to hide from celebrity in a small village in northern New Brunswick. She became its most notorious inhabitant, the front-page story in a regional magazine. Ferguson had his own reasons for wanting to get out of Nova Scotia. He followed her, wooed her, and married her. He didn't take long to put her money to his own use, engineering a move to the obscurity of Red Island.

The move was in process, happening in stages. He had come ahead to supervise the installation of the cat litter removal system for Letitia's strays and his own trio of massive fish tanks, all of them engineered by him. He'd had his collection of fish and all the comforts he required transported here, to his den at the back of the big old barn. Letitia, her cats, and the rest of their furniture would follow.

He placed the last item from the last box, their wedding photograph, on the desk, slumped down in his chair and looked at it. She was wearing a Vera Wang dress that hung on her frail body. He was wearing Armani. The bridal bouquet burst with white lilies, obscuring the bride's face. There was no reception, because they had no friends, but there was a honeymoon – the two of them sipping margaritas on a golden day with sunshine spilling across the neat, cropped lawn at Dalkeith, a massive nineteenth-century summer home with stone exterior and detailed wood interior, built by an American industrialist and later sold to a rum runner. The stay had given Ferguson a taste for Red Island and the ammunition for his latest obsession. It was a photograph. A photograph he came across quite by accident.

The expensive wedding gear and the honeymoon stay at Dalkeith had been paid for by Letitia's first lottery win and organized by Ferguson, although she would have preferred something more modest. If there hadn't been a lottery win, there wouldn't have been a marriage. Ferguson had married Letitia for her money. Then she won twice more. Was it she who was lucky, or he?

He frowned again. It had been a trade-off. He hated asking her for money, hiding his needs inside her projects. For instance, the cost of building this den with its adjoining aquaria had been tucked into the price of the litter-removal system for her cats, a marvel of engineering, and his own brilliant invention.

The three fish tanks, built to accommodate freshwater, brackish, and saltwater fish were the combined size of a four-car garage – ten-thousand-gallon tanks that had cost hundreds of thousands of dollars to construct. Ferguson was hoping to establish it as the largest in-home system of its kind in the world.

The fish had been pricey. He'd spent fifty thousand of Letitia's dollars on them. There were the discus, beautifully patterned circles of red, blue, turquoise, and other exotic colours. They were fish with personality, who would come and greet him when he walked over to the tank. The tigerfish, who liked to stalk and hunt, acting and looking like tigers with their thick black stripes. The freshwater stingrays, big and flat, some three feet across.

There were black ghost knifefish, archer fish, lung fish, African butterflyfish, solo fish, fish in schools, so many species Brock sometimes found it hard to keep up with them. He had at least a hundred fish. It cost him two thousand dollars a month to feed and maintain them.

Or rather, it cost Ferguson's wife, Letitia, and was the cause of strife within the marriage. They were worth it, or so Ferguson thought, but it wasn't his money he was spending.

"I have to have something that's mine," he had argued when she found out that he'd traded up from his hundred-gallon tank, bought these monsters, and had them installed in their new home right next to her cattery.

It would be an odd juxtaposition, no doubt, the cats and the fish. It wasn't that Letitia didn't like fish. They were beautiful, but she felt that, unlike her cats, the fish should be in the wild, not captive and nosing up to the glass of the tank that enclosed them.

The tanks took an entire wall of Ferguson's den, and a great deal of his interest that wasn't devoted to the pursuit of the world's fattest Atlantic cod, the only fish that would set a world record for him. This system wouldn't hold that fish, but that pond might, that pond outside the back window, perched like a tadpole above the shore. It had turned out to be saltwater. Could it be a home for a massive cod? Maybe.

His eyes fixed on the wall opposite where there was a print of a woodcarving that had hung in Boston's state chambers since 1784. It was a codfish, just shy of five feet long, nick-named "The Sacred Cod," because it was a symbol of the state's former dependence on the cod fishery, before it died, there and everywhere else on the east coast of North America. The woodcarving had been "codnapped" twice by students. Who wouldn't want a big cod?

Ferguson did. He wanted a real one. Bigger than the sculpture's measly eighty pounds. He wanted a record-setting fish.

He'd come to the place he thought he'd find one.

***

The old man slipped out the back door, his form illuminated by the moon, but almost no one in the village would know who he was. They might recognize his bow-legged gait, but few remembered his face. If they did know who it was, the pink knapsack might throw them off.

He wheeled the bicycle from inside the building and eased onto it. It wove erratically as he drove across the lawn and along the driveway before executing a wide right turn onto the Island Way, the road that led to Big Bay.

He was anxious to get there, but he wasn't going fast. He'd never been able to ride a bike with skill, not even as a child. Stubbornness was etched across his face. If you couldn't see his face – and it was hard with that hat on – you could see his determination in the set of his body on the bike, the hard push on the pedals.

It was a fifteen-minute ride to his destination – but, wheels wobbling, it took him more than twice as long. He knew where he was going, but he wasn't sure what he was going to do. Not yet.

Hidden behind a fishing shack, he scanned the harbour. Seeing no sign of life, he leaned the bicycle against the shed and climbed aboard a lobster boat. Was he going to take it? Now? In the middle of the night?

He slipped down into the cabin.

Four hours later, as dawn came on, he emerged, eyes heavy with sleep, a pair of binoculars in his hands. He shimmied up onto the bow of the boat and brought the binoculars up to his eyes, peering out to the west of Big Bay where the tall dunes and dangerous currents were.

When he brought the binoculars back down, he smiled.

Circles.

The circles were back.

The conditions were the same as thirty years before: the circles; the unusual height of the tide; the deep colour of the moon, its size, and the fact that it had risen smack in alignment with the "chimbley" of old Ethan Cooke's wreck of a house. The second time only in thirty years.

They were here.

He hauled the bicycle up and cycled toward the village. As first light rode in on the waves, he pedalled into the blinding glow, through the village toward the causeway. He felt the way an infant does; if he couldn't see, he couldn't be seen.

His mind was blind, too, a white emptiness. He was in a fog of forgetfulness, with glimmers of remembering. He knew who he was, more or less. He didn't know if it was now – or then. Nor what he was doing.

The circles turned in his head, making him dizzy.

Chapter 2

"Abel's missin'!"

Gus Mack came flying out of the house, faster than she'd moved in forty years. She almost smacked into Hy, who was coming up the front steps.

"Abel? Missing? How can you tell?"

Hyacinth McAllister wasn't being unsympathetic to her old friend, but everyone knew Gus's husband Abel was never around. Hy wasn't sure when she'd last seen him. She'd begun to question if she ever had.

The energy that had propelled Gus from the house drained out of her. She suddenly looked every one of her eighty-plus years, her face a map of worry wrinkles, deep set.

"Don't you think I'd know if he wasn't here?"

Hy kept silent. She'd always wondered when Gus ever saw him.

"His coffee mug is missin'."

The only proof Hy had ever seen that Abel drank coffee, every morning, at home, was the empty cup. A duck cup. Big yellow head. Abel drank out of the bright orange beak.

The sound of a screen door squeaking shut, being eased to a close and not slammed, told them that Gus's neighbour, Estelle Joudry, had slipped out onto her stoop. They looked up. Estelle was slightly deaf. She was cocking her head in their direction, the better to hear what they were saying. When she saw them looking her way, she turned her back to them, pretending an interest in a murder of crows pecking at a dead fox on the road. She began to speculate about who had hit the animal.

It couldn't have been her husband, Germaine. He was still in bed. Moira's man, Frank? No, he always went on about roadkill being the result of bad driving. Abel? Abel was ninety-plus. He wasn't supposed to drive at all. There was his car, though, parked in the backyard for a quick getaway onto the Shore Lane, if he fancied a drive.

Hy guided Gus up the steps and back into the house. She sat her down in her purple rocker recliner and went on the hunt for the missing coffee cup, sure that it must have been put down somewhere.

"You're on a wild goose chase," Gus called from the kitchen. "For sixty years he's been putting that mug down on the table here."

The table had not one clear inch of surface. It was covered in quilt patterns and patches, newspaper clippings, family photos, and odd bits and bobs of this and that.

"Never misses a day. Only the once, I didn't set out the pot for him, I was in such a flap to get to the hospital. Dot was that quick coming out."

Dot was Gus's eighth – and last – child. Gus had been in her forties when she had her. After that, there was no more evidence of that kind that Abel was around.

Dot wasn't around anymore either. She'd left The Shores as soon as she could and become a doctor. Gus did not approve. She thought it would have been more fitting for Dot to be a nurse. Doctor Dot, as the villagers referred to her, had travelled the Third World, taking her medical skills to those most in need and photographing the misery she encountered. Then she had given birth in the Antarctic to Gus's only grandchild, and spent the last year here at The Shores. Then she'd "up and left," as Gus put it.

Dot had disappeared the day before Abel had, but not as mysteriously. It was no surprise to Gus to see her come down the stairs, hauling her oversized backpack with Little Dottie casually slung under one arm.

"You're off, then." Gus barely looked up from her knitting.

"Yes." Dot put Little Dottie down on the floor, where she grabbed a ball of knitting wool and stuffed it in her mouth.

"Where to?"

"I don't know."

"Just not here."

"Not here, for now. No."

"And himself? Himself can't keep you here?"

Dot shrugged her shoulders. What could she say?

"I guess not." Finn had been fun, but it was no big romance. They both had known that. But the way she was leaving – without telling – wasn't fair. She knew that. She hoped he'd understand.

"And the little one?"

"Dottie?"

"What other little one is there?" Eight children she'd had, and only one grandchild. A grandchild she was aching to hold, now that she was about to lose her.

Dot sensed Gus's yearning and picked up the child. She placed her on Gus's lap.

"She could stay here."

Gus opened her eyes wide. They shone with expectation. Hope. Desire.

"Here?"

"There's no other here than here." Dot smiled.

Gus hugged the child close.

"No," she said, finally. "It wouldn't do. A child belongs with its mother." She kissed the top of Dottie's head and held her up.

Dot scooped up the child. She never would have left her. They both knew that. What Gus also knew, in that moment, was that she was too old. Too old to be a grandmother of one so young. Certainly too old to be a mother and give her what a mother could give her, wherever in the world they were. Old enough to know that you couldn't change someone's ways once they were set. All her adult life, Dot had been travelling to remote places, taking photographs.

Gus resumed her knitting.

"Don't be so long away this time."

"We won't, Ma."

Finn, when he returned to Gus's house later that day, was hurt, confused, and then angry. Angry that Dot had not thought better of him, that she couldn't have told him it was time for her to move on. An odd glimmer of relief underlay that anger. He couldn't deny that his attractions and attentions were straying from Dot. It had bothered him, because he cared for Dot. But now Dot had done this...

He moved out the next day – back to his half-sister Hy's – so that by the time Abel disappeared, Gus was alone.

Quite alone.

***

Hy scoured through "the room," the one that was never used except for company and putting up quilts in winter. She inspected the dining room and back porch and peeked into the downstairs bedroom. No coffee cup.

It wasn't easy to miss, that bright yellow duck, its lip decorated with an orange beak that delivered the coffee directly to the drinker. Ceramic mouth-to-mouth resuscitation. Perhaps that was the secret to Abel's longevity.

Hy returned to the kitchen and shrugged.

Gus looked smug, in spite of her distress.

"I told you. The mug's not here. Didn't have his morning coffee. Not here, leastwise. You find that mug, I 'spec you'll find Abel."

"How long has he been gone?"

"I don't rightly know. I was asleep all night, like usual. Then when I woke, he was gone. I knew afore I saw his cup was missing. I could feel it in my bones."

"The same bones that predict the weather?"

Gus nodded.

"The bones that know if a pregnant woman's going to have a boy or a girl?"

Gus nodded again. "As long as she's close kin."

"Did you check the building?" The building was a large shed that housed the lawn tractor and the place where Gus put up her quilts in summer. Friends and neighbours would drop by to help with the stitching and to gossip.

"Yes, and the well house, though what he'd be doin' squeezed in there I don't know…"

"Let's wait and see if he comes back. If he doesn't, we'll call Jamieson in."

"What's she going to do?"

"I don't know. Whatever it is Mounties do to get their man."

***

RCMP Constable Jane Jamieson was at a loss as to what that might be, when she responded to Hy's call later that morning once Gus had convinced Hy that Abel really was missing.

"He can't have gone far," was her first response. "The man's over ninety."

Ninety had been the age on his last driver's license, the one she took away from him. Not in person. He was as hard to find then as now, but he always left his license on the dashboard of the car, and Jamieson, strolling by one day, had snagged it through the open window.

It hadn't stopped Abel from driving.

"Did he take the car?"

"I don't think so." Hy hesitated. "I'll look."

"Okay. I'll be right over."

Gus, at first, didn't want to let Jamieson look around, because, she assured the Mountie, she'd already "looked everywhere."

People always said that kind of thing, Jamieson knew that much. But if someone were missing, they had to have gone somewhere, and that must be somewhere no one had looked. Jamieson had insisted on a thorough search of the whole house, including attic and cellar, and was about to check the outside buildings.

"I've looked there, too," Gus's words were punctuated by the creak of her rocker recliner, underlining her certainty.

"It would help if I knew what he looked like."

"He'll be the man holding the bright yellow coffee mug shaped like a duck," said Hy.

Jamieson shot her a look that warned this could be a serious matter. Hy's grin turned upside down.

"Do you have any photos?" Jamieson asked Gus.

Gus shuffled through the photos on the table. She'd found a whole new stash after putting together *Time Was,* the anecdotal history of The Shores that had been published the year before to commemorate the village's two hundred years.

"Wouldn't you know I'd find these when it was too late to use them," she'd said to Hy at the time.

"You could use them still," Hy had replied. "For the second edition." The first had sold out as soon as it was published and Red Islanders were clamouring for more. Many of them could trace their roots back to The Shores, named for three once busy villages that had dwindled into one. It was an isolated area, cut off by a storm surge and rejoined to the rest of Red Island by an unreliable causeway, but it had supplied the main island with no fewer than five provincial premiers, several federal government ministers, – and could lay claim to the Island's famous author, the literary mother of that irrepressible redhead who'd captured hearts around the world. She'd had family in The Shores and loved to picnic there. A descendant had commemorated that fact at the 200th anniversary celebrations the year previous, by making a gift of the author's cat carrier to the hall. Or, at least, a cat carrier she was said to have used. The red-and-black-checked cage now stood on proud display, centre stage at the hall, with a plaque that described in full detail whom the carrier had belonged to, or been used by, and the names of the cats it had carried. Lucky, Pat, Brownie, Duffy, and Smut.

"Here." Triumphant, Gus pulled out a black-and-white studio shot from the pile and handed it to Jamieson. Gus and Abel.

The bridal couple. A winsome woman with long light brown hair and an apple-cheeked bridegroom, already balding and looking pleased with himself.

"Me and Abel, afore our wedding. An hour later, we wuz man and woif."

Woif? Jamieson frowned. Then her expression cleared. Wife. Of course.

"Very nice." Jamieson handed back the photograph. She produced a thin smile. She'd been working on her people skills. "Have you any recent photos?"

Gus shuffled through the photos again. There were few with Abel in them, and of those –

"His face is shadowed." Jamieson dropped one back on the table. "He's turned his head." She rejected one after another.

"He never did like having his photograph taken."

Jamieson tossed another photo onto the table. "The brim of his hat is pulled down over his face."

It was a Tilley hat – a strange hat for an island farmer and fisherman to be wearing, although it was designed to be worn at sea. It had been given to him years before by a grateful tourist he had taken deep-sea fishing. Abel knew the quality of the hat. Best one in the village. He put the guarantee on the left-hand side of his bottom drawer, as advised by the Tilley people. It stayed there for twenty years. He wore the hat everywhere. It was knocked off his head many a time, because he refused to use the wind cord. The hat would float on the water a while, then sink, then show up days later, tossed onto the shore by the strong gulf currents. Seagulls had shit on it when they found they couldn't eat it. Traces of their beaks were visible on its brim. When it finally wore out from such treatment, Abel sent it to the Tilley people and demanded a replacement. They sent it back, with a new hat. Free. It was a lifetime guarantee, after all. Most lifetimes didn't last as long as Abel's. Not active ones. And most people who wore Tilley hats were not outdoor workers. They just wanted a stylish sunshade, one they treasured and protected.

Gus picked up the photograph, her eyes misting.

"He allus wore that hat. He said it could drive him to Charlottetown." She shocked herself. She was talking about him as if he were gone. Gone gone. Surely he wasn't gone like that. Gus looked up at Jamieson, fear and a question in her eyes.

"You'll find him?"

"I'll certainly try. There can't be that many ninety-year-old men wandering the village." Then she remembered, looked at Hy. "You checked? He didn't –"

"Take the car?" Hy shook her head.

"It's in the backyard as usual." Gus eased out of her chair, to confirm that the car was there.

Jamieson went ahead of her, through the pantry, and looked out the dining room window. There it was, a brown 1964 Cadillac, long, and shark-like. A farmer's car. She had tried to chase it down numerous times. She hadn't been able to see Abel, only the hat. She knew he drove without a license. Other hats belonged to other eighty- and ninety-year-olds in the village, all of them driving without licenses. There were many offenders, but none as slippery as he.

She was relieved that, wherever he was, Abel was not in the car.

The relief was short-lived. Where was he, if not in the house or the car? She was convinced that wherever he was, at his age, he was probably nearby and undoubtedly dead. Still, she had at least to put on the show of a search, and the sooner they got to it the better.

Chapter 3

"Fisheries." He spoke through gritted teeth, gnawing at his fingernail. "Seamus O'Malley speaking." He was tapping one foot against the other on the top of his desk. He felt like bolting, stomach churning.

He was off his meds. It made him feel powerful. Like he could do anything. But it made him shaky and nervous, too. Impatient.

Brock Ferguson was on the other end of the line, leafing through The Shores' 200th anniversary book, *Time Was*. It had brought him here. He'd found the book in the built-in shelves of the library at Dalkeith, meant to look at it, but never did. When the honeymoon was over, Letitia had mistakenly packed it, thinking it belonged to him. It sat hidden in a stack of books in their bedroom, and it was only months later that he came across it again. When he saw the photograph and the fish, he was seized by a desire to capture it, a record-breaking fish, a fish that would make his name. Over time, he managed to convince Letitia that a move back to fresh ocean air would be good for her. He reminded her how happy she had been at Dalkeith. She gave in. And Ferguson had preceded her to Red Island.

While he was waiting for Letitia and her annoying cats to arrive, he had been keeping a low profile, but he was itching for the hunt to start. And, unlike the guy in the photograph, once he caught the cod, he would not let it go.

"The Old Man Out to Sea" he had dubbed the photograph. The fish dragging the dory and the old man clinging to it. Had he landed it? Obviously not. If he had, there would have been a photo of that, most certainly. Unless, as often happened "time was," the photographer had run out of film. The photo credit said: "Abel Mack and the one that got away. Three-hundred-pound cod drags Mack out to sea."

"Brock Ferguson here. I'd like to speak to the man in charge." The fact that it might be a woman never crossed his mind.

"She's away at the moment. Can I be of any help?"

"I'm interested in…interested in…" How much should he give away?

Seamus himself was staring at that photograph of Abel and the giant cod, as he did several times a day, feeling a greater sense of urgency as the time for his boss's return grew closer. He could do anything now, order out boats and crew as he wished. Maybe he'd have to answer for it later, but he was hoping he wouldn't have to answer for anything. He'd be packed up and on his way to Newfoundland with a giant cod. Exactly how he'd accomplish that, he wasn't sure yet. Seamus wasn't a biologist. It just said he was on his resumé.

"Ye-es." Seamus drew out the word, fuelling it with impatience and a dash of sarcasm.

"I'm looking for a fish."

"Plenty of fish around here. Any particular fish?"

"A particular fish. A three-hundred-pound cod."

Seamus inhaled, a deep inhalation that burst down the phone line. Then silence. *Someone else was after his fish? Damn.* Then: "No such thing."

"Oh, but there is." Ferguson's tone was insinuating. "I'm surprised you don't know of it."

Seamus paused again. What did this man want with the fish? He better find out. "Well, and I do, as it happens. So what of it?"

"I'm a collector," Ferguson put his feet up on his desk and leaned back in his chair.

"You collect fish?" Seamus could imagine them stuffed and mounted on Ferguson's walls. Dead fish, bought and paid for on some charter in the Gulf of Mexico. Well, he wouldn't be catching or collecting this fish, not if Seamus could help it. This fish was his. Out there somewhere, he hoped, off the shores of Red Island.

"Yes, but that's not what I'm talking about. I *have* an aquarium, but I *collect* things, like bottle caps and tabs from cans, with the intent of setting and breaking records. I'm sure I have more tabs from cans than anyone in the world." When he said it, Brock thought, it sounded pathetic. Not good enough. "I have nothing special yet. Except maybe my lottery-winning wife. Three times she's won it."

Seamus whistled, his interest piqued. He was talking to money.

"Now," Ferguson went on, "now I'm looking for the biggest cod in the world. I think it could be right here."

"Off Red Island?"

Ferguson grunted. "Not too far, in fact, from where I sit right now."

Seamus's eyes lit up. Desire and greed. Did this man know where the fish was…were?

"Maybe we can help each other." Seamus sat up straight, gripping the telephone receiver, interest sparking in his eyes.

Seamus was thinking of the imminent return of his boss and his inability to play fast and loose with the taxpayers' money after that. But this man had money – and the same desire he had: to catch the big one.

"Ye-es." He drew out the word again, but this time peppering it with curiosity.

"Don't know if you've seen this local book. Recent. About The Shores. It has a picture of a fellow battling a massive fish."

"You mean…" Seamus paused, not sure how much interest to show.

"*Time Was.*"

"Yes, of course." Seamus wrote it down.

"I want that fish."

Seamus surprised himself with his response.

"So do I."

"Of course, it won't be that fish. That was thirty years ago."

"No. It probably won't be that fish, although you never know…"

"It's the size I care about. I want to find if there are any more where that came from – and where, in fact, it came from."

"We're on the same page there."

"I want it alive."

"Of course. I can understand that." Seamus wanted a live one, too. He could bring it back in triumph to Newfoundland. He had left in disgrace, having lost a lot of people's money with a failed hatchery scheme. He'd promised his investors big cod. Instead he delivered dead ones. Food for the fish is eighty per cent of the cost of running an aquaculture operation, and he hadn't been able to afford to feed them. Now, if he returned with a giant like this, he might be singlehandedly responsible for reviving the industry on the Rock. It might surpass anywhere else in the world. And this guy Ferguson could maybe help him, provide the backing, all the while thinking Seamus was catching the cod for him to keep.

"I want to set a world record. A three-hundred-pound cod would be a record for its species, if we could get hold of one."

"I may be able to help you there." Seamus stroked the photo with a thumb, contemplating. How would this Ferguson fella be able to help him? He'd liked the sound of the money. No matter how much he was able to exploit the department's resources, he was going to need money.

"Then perhaps we should meet." Ferguson smiled. Seamus smiled. They were both after the same thing. Each thinking he would get the better of the other.

Chapter 4

Jamieson had to turn a blind eye to several octogenarian drivers who showed up to search for Abel and parked on the lawn beside the hall. The Women's Institute phone chain had whipped into action and the villagers had gathered there, excited by the news and by the chance to tear themselves away: the women from watching soap operas and the men from tinkering in their sheds after the lawns were cut. Armed with binoculars that usually hung by their big picture windows, they were prepared to comb the area for Gus's missing husband.

Some were concerned that they might not recognize him if they found him – dead or alive.

"Last time I saw Abel? Can't say really. The centenary year… mebbe. Canada, that is. Not The Shores." The villager – Jamieson couldn't put a name to him – was toothless and so wrinkled that she thought he must be even older than Abel, perhaps a hundred years old or more.

"Don't know as I seen Abel in the last twenty years," said Abel's near neighbour, Germaine Joudry. "Not since he retired from fishin'."

Abel's much younger brother, Ben, reminded them that, twenty years before, everyone had seen Abel when he took a stand against Canada Post. The corporation had sent him a letter, informing him that it was going to use a triangular piece of his land by the road – where the General Store used to be – to put up a community mailbox.

Abel never read the letter. Didn't open it. He couldn't see why

Canada Post would be sending him mail. Wasn't their job just to deliver it?

So, the first he knew of the community mailbox was when a big truck drove down the Island Way, past his house, past the hall, past Toombs's, and screeched to a halt at that triangle of land where Abel's General Store burned down. Two workers jumped out of the truck and painted a big orange square on the grass, one wielding the brush, the other holding the can.

"I was with Abel in his kitchen," said Ben. Everyone knew the story, but they loved hearing it again, especially from Ben, who could spin a good yarn when he broke his habitual silence.

"We was looking out his big pikcher window when they come. He hustled out, taking the shortcut behind the hall, fast as his bowlegs could take him, with me behind, wanting to see the action." Ben imitated a few of Abel's bowlegged steps.

They all remembered Abel's battle with Canada Post, and each added detail as the story unfolded.

Abel had got there just in time, as the driver was circling round to go back onto the road. He stopped the truck.

"What's goin' on?" Abel had called up, his authority diminished by the height of the truck and his squat stature.

"Didn't you get a letter? This here" – the driver pointed at the gleaming orange lines – "is for the community mailbox."

Abel had never heard of such a thing. He went marching straight home and scattered papers, family photographs, and quilt patches off the kitchen table onto the floor. He swept the ducky mug off the table, too, and it became the first of its kind to smash on the floor. Abel later ordered several more from the Sears catalogue. "Coffee don't taste the same," he claimed, unless it was from the duck's beak. Why? "Cools it to just the right temperature," said Abel.

He found the envelope from Canada Post, ripped it open, and read it. With difficulty. Abel had never got beyond the eighth grade, and what he had learned, he had sloughed off after one season of fishing. He passed the paper over to Gus, who read it, her brow wrinkling.

"Says here they're using the spot for a community mailbox, whatever that is."

Abel soon found out, and didn't like it.

"Everyone's going to come tramping all over my property to get their mail. They'll be snooping in my box, too, I'll bet," Abel complained to customer relations in Winterside. Customer relations weren't then what they are now – synthesized recorded voices and accents from countries far away. Customer relations then was the Island Telephone Company's lone receptionist, Sadie Beirsto, a cousin of Abel's several times and generations removed. Like practically everyone on Red Island – family.

"You'll have a lock and key, Abel."

"A lock and key? In The Shores? We don't lock our homes, we don't lock our cars, why would we lock our mailboxes?" Abel didn't see the contradiction in his argument. He did realize the scheme could put him out of pocket. The letter hadn't said anything about compensation.

"Are they going to pay for that land?"

"I can't rightly say. You'll have to take that up with someone else."

Who that was wasn't clear. Abel never did find out who was responsible. One morning while he was bringing in lobster, someone came and dug a big hole in the patch of land. There were two mounds of dirt on either side of it.

He was so mad he fetched a shovel and spent the afternoon in the baking sun, filling the hole back up, muttering complaints with each shovelful.

Gus tried to stop him several times, warning that he might "take a heart attack," but, as she told others after, he was "bound and determined" to undo what Canada Post had done without his permission. All Gus could do was bring him lemonade to cool him down and towels to sop up his sweat. Even then, his face was bloated and red, and his shirt soaked.

When the earth was back in the hole, Wally Fraser and Germaine Joudry came by. They'd been watching from Joudry's house, right next to Abel's own.

"Nice job." Germaine looked with admiration at the rectangular patch, Abel's boot marks on it as he continued tramping down the red clay.

"You watched?"

Germaine nodded.

"You could of helped."

Germaine put his hand over his heart.

"Oh, right." His heart. Germaine had been begging off physical labour practically all his life with that excuse.

Wally Fraser nodded. "Good work," he said. "Someone has to show the bastards." It was a word he couldn't use in his own home. His wife Gladys, president of the Women's Institute, wouldn't allow it. So he exercised it everywhere else, whenever he could.

"The bastards" returned the next day with the intent of erecting the box. They no longer had a hole to put it in.

Abel watched with satisfaction from his window as the crew turned and left. They'd be back, he knew, to dig the hole again, but he wasn't finished.

He went out the next morning with a lawn chair, a lemonade in his ducky mug, and his Tilley hat pulled down low against the sun on his head and face. He planted the chair smack in the middle of the dirt patch and sat there until nightfall in the sweltering heat. Each time he took a swig from the mug it looked as if a duck was wearing the Tilley hat "ass backwards," said Wally, with almost as much delight as he said "bastards."

This was in the days long before cellphones, or there would have been a plethora of shots of Abel. There was not even one photograph of his triumph. Local videographer Lester Joudry was still in diapers.

Abel sat there the next day, and the day after that. He sat there for seven days, at the height of fishing and farming season, until the men returned in the truck, saw him, and turned and left.

Then nothing. For days, nothing.

Abel got a letter – in his roadside mailbox – from Canada Post. This one, he did open. It said the corporation had reversed its decision for a community mailbox in The Shores.

Abel was triumphant, looking out the window at his patch of land. Then his face clouded over. A truck pulled up. Two men got out, began levelling the mound of earth, and rolled fresh turf onto the scar on the land. When they'd finished, they left the spot better than new, disciplined urban grass laid down next to unruly meadow grasses.

"They needn't have bothered," Abel turned to Gus. "It gave me an idea. I'm going to put a little building there to sell your jam and some campfire wood by the roadside."

That's what he did.

Apart from those few days twenty years ago, there had been almost no sightings of Abel.

"The only other time I saw him for more'n a couple of minutes would have been at my wedding…thirty years ago." That was Ben. If he'd hardly seen his own brother in thirty years, then who would have?

So not seeing Abel didn't mean he wasn't there. It was status quo.

How it had become so, Hy couldn't figure out. Was no one curious?

Chapter 5

They were curious now. Curious to find Abel. Most of them; Wally and Gladys Fraser slinked off, though. Moira Toombs, who lived right next door to the hall and had been peeking out her kitchen window, disappeared when she saw that Jamieson was organizing people in groups. In their backyard, her husband Frank had been oblivious to the gathering at the hall, in a reverie that grass mowing and riding a lawn tractor seem to inspire in some men. Away in a world of their own. Or the best of both worlds. Working and not working at the same time. The tractor stalled and Frank came back to the real world.

He saw something was going on. He strode over to offer his help. Frank hadn't forgotten how folks had helped him with his heritage project – half a dozen wigwams formed of metal poles and parachute silk, standing on land adjacent to Moira's house. The wigwam village was the most unusual tourist accommodation in The Shores – indeed, on all of Red Island – and was listed in the top ten "Places to Stay in Canada" on several tourism websites. As long as it wasn't windy. It was, most of the time. That made the accommodations even more desirable. Risk-taking for the jaded.

It was in one of these wigwams, the hole in the apex of its roof open to the starlight, that Frank and Moira had finally consummated their marriage, long after the ceremony. It had cemented their union and made them, to everyone's surprise, a happily married couple, in spite of Moira's sour ways and Frank's philandering gaze. But now it was a gaze only.

Frank was grateful for the villagers' help in sealing his marriage to Moira, and so, he was always happy to "give back." He volunteered to lead a group into the potato fields along the capes. Other groups prepared to comb the shore – around the run, Vanishing Point, and Mack's Shore. Finn said he'd go where he was most needed. Jamieson said that would be right here with her. He raised a quizzical eyebrow.

She flushed. She hadn't meant anything by it.

"I want you…" she paused, flustered, "to map out the entire area between the causeway and the dunes on the west side of Big Bay. That way, we'll know where we've been and where we have to go."

He saluted and smiled. She almost smiled back.

"We have to start small from here at the centre and fan out. When you get where you're going, do the same thing from there. Fan out from a central point, so that every square inch is covered. When you're finished, report back to me. I'll keep track of where we've been, so we don't duplicate our efforts," Jamieson instructed.

"Don't skip a thing. We are looking for a man, but anything you see, anything unusual, may be pertinent."

Some eyes had already glassed over. They were ready to search but unwilling to listen. Hadn't they found missing people before? Children gone astray on the shore. Tourists who lost their direction cycling down one of the lanes that led nowhere. But the eyes came alive at the unfamiliar word. Pertinent. Some looked confused; others, angry.

Pertinent. Was that the same as impertinent? Like regardless – and irregardless?

Jamieson saw she'd hit a wall.

"Anything that you see may have to do with Abel's disappearance. Anything."

She checked her groups again, conferred with the leaders of each.

"Now don't overtax yourselves. The forest fires in Quebec are sending us some dirty smoke, and though it only looks hazy, we are all inhaling that stuff, so, if for any reason, you feel breathless, sore, or thirsty, stop."

Jamieson frowned. She didn't need the complication of Quebec forest fires invading her turf. The search would get in the way of checking the elderly and asthmatic to see how they were coping. She'd been doing that all of August. A blazing sun had seared the forests mercilessly all summer, drying trees and leaves so that they were like matches waiting to ignite. The smoke filled the air above the woods, a grey cloud smothering the sky, and the winds blew it to Red Island, and even farther down the eastern seaboard. People were cursing and coughing, their summer fun destroyed. In Quebec, the fires showed no sign of letting up, and the winds blowing the smoke to The Shores showed no sign of veering off. New fires were sparking to life each day, and the old ones were taking time to run their course, burning, burning, until it seemed everything was ash, then reigniting and moving on. Authorities, who should have known, had no idea when it would end.

"Gus is serving tea and lunch for anyone who needs to take a break," Hy put in, using the word the way the locals did, meaning biscuits and cheese and squares. On Red Island, "lunch" usually came after supper, a little snack at the end of the day. Dinner was the midday meal. Gus had no intention of feeding the whole village dinner but had agreed to provide a little "lunch."

"I can't sit there and do nothing," Gus had said, when Hy suggested even that might be too much for her.

Hy and her close friend Ian Simmons were in a group going to the shore. They naturally paired up. They made a good team when it came to solving mysteries. Ian, a retired high school science teacher, had used his computer several times to solve murders. Hy had a knack for falling over or bumping into bodies, and a keen need to satisfy her curiosity about how they got that way.

The group would be taking the bridge over the run. The run had once been a comma of fresh water that flowed from the pond across the sand and into the salt water of the Gulf. It changed the way it flowed each year, depending on how winter storms carved out the shore. This year's changes had been dramatic. A vicious storm had carved a deep trough along the full length of the stream, right up to the bridge where the muskrat lived and the pond began. It was as if a dredger had been through. The run had gone from being knee deep to shoulder high, five times as deep and twice as wide as it once had been. The land was tilted so that the ocean ran into the pond, not the other way around, and it was now salt water. Access to the far side of the shore was tricky.

"Be careful on that bridge. It's not safe. Worse every day." Annabelle, Ben Mack's wife and Hy's best friend, was getting ready to lead a group into the potato fields that lined the cape below the hall. She and all of April Dewey's six children prepared to crawl down the rows of potatoes under the harvest-thick foliage, oblivious to the potato spray saturated deep into the soil.

Ian and Hy walked down Wild Rose Lane to the shore, in what should have been the easy companionship of a long friendship. It wasn't easy. It almost never was. There had been romantic moments, even a few days over Christmas several years back. There had been that kiss on the beach last August during the fireworks for the village's 200th anniversary. But no more than that. Neither of them could have said why not. Perhaps they feared romance would get in the way of a friendship they depended on, both being "from away" in this close-knit village.

But there was something between them. Their shoulders touched while they were combing the rose bushes that lined the clay lane for a sign of Abel. They both felt it was more than chance physical contact. It wasn't clear who pulled away first.

Ben Mack climbed onto his huge fertilizing tractor. The tractor looked like an alien life form or an oversized mosquito with wings closed at its sides. When open, they spread out over the rows of potato plants and sprayed death into the earth. Spray that smelled on the air and seeped into houses with windows open – even though the farmers claimed the spray went right into the ground. They sprayed because there had been too much rain. They sprayed because there hadn't been enough rain. They sprayed every chance they got when the wind was twenty kilometres or less. They sprayed sometimes when it was more than that, as long as no one complained. A legitimate complaint could stop the spraying. Usually.

The tractor towered above the land, and gave Ben a vantage point from which to watch the searchers in the field, to see that not a row was missed. It was fortunate the Dewey children were in the hunt. So close to harvest, the potato plants, deep green and lush, spilled over into each other from row to row, forming a thick carpet across the field. The children tunnelled under the plants in the furrows between the rows. Ben could watch their progress in the movement of the leaves like waves, as the children hustled down the rows.

If Abel were there, they'd find him.

Would they find him dead or alive?

***

The summer sun shone only as a faded outline, obscured by the smoke from Quebec, drifting in a constant canopy. The air smelled of fire, heavy with particles that coated everything with a smoky residue.

Somewhere, obscured in the filmy grey that choked the villagers and had sent tourists scurrying for home, leaving their cottages lined along the cape, deserted and desolate, somewhere was Abel Mack. He must be. Most likely dead. Jamieson became more convinced of that with every report back from each location. A man in his nineties, exposed to the elements – they were bound to stumble on him somewhere.

She gave a wry smile. Not they. It was Hy who was bound to stumble on him. She came across all the corpses in The Shores. She'd tripped and fallen on Lance Lord, dead and dressed in his Jimi Hendrix outfit. She'd been knocked off her skis by a corpse swinging from a tree in a winter storm. Running on the beach a few years back, Hy had discovered a woman flattened by a massive chunk of sandstone, broken off the cape. The woman was splayed out underneath, only her plump little hands and feet showing.

Hy hadn't found Abel. Not yet. Was there a reason for that? Was Gus right?

"He ain't dead," she kept insisting, as she presided over the teakettle in her kitchen, feeding and watering the searchers when they came for a break.

"How do you know?" the villagers asked again and again. And always the same answer:

"I know he's alive. Just as I would know if he was dead."

Odd, thought Jamieson. Gus didn't seem especially worried. Did she know something she wasn't saying? Or did she know deep within her, as she claimed? Jamieson found herself being carried away on that thought for a moment, feeling that Abel was alive somewhere, seeing his hat pulled down on his head against the wind, as he…as he…She pulled herself out of the vision. Her pragmatism took over. He would be found. He would most likely be found dead.

***

Ferguson's relationship to his fish was deep, stronger than his feelings for his wife. As their colours and shapes glided by his peripheral vision, he would close his eyes, his forehead would smooth, his jaw relax, his muscles soften; he would give himself up to their soothing company.

The bond had become weird.

It had started with him going into the tank to clean it. Plenty of aquarium owners did that. It was the easiest way to do the job.

It became an experience. Daily. Clothed. In a wetsuit. Then unclothed, except for a Speedo.

He would lower himself into the biggest tank, wearing a snorkel attached to a long hose so he could descend, and he would swim among them. The water was warm for the tropical fish, and there was no reason to wear a wetsuit. Much too uncomfortable. To get into. To get out of. To wear in the meantime. With his naked skin he had the delight of fish brushing up against him, some taking a small peck to see if he was food, and the discus especially trailing him around, weaving in and out of his arms and hands.

He became one with the fish. Shivering with delight at the sensation of being with them, in their environment. Sometimes so besotted that he forgot he was in the tank to clean it.

In spite of the trouble and expense of bringing these fish to Red Island, Ferguson was already losing interest in them. The proximity to his prey – the record-setting giant cod – had altered his focus, his interest, his obsession. He couldn't stop thinking about the giant fish. About acquiring it. And watching it. Owning it.

Chapter 6

Hy and Ian hurried down to the shore. Their group of searchers had spread out around Vanishing Point and over to Mack's Shore. They headed in the opposite direction – over the rickety bridge to the sea rock, a chunk broken off the cape and worn away by the waves and the wind so that it became smaller each year. And changed each year. Cape and sea rock now looked like two old men, staring each other down, one with a white crewcut formed of cormorant excrement, a solvent that was eating away the top of the rock. The other, like most of the village men, bald.

No one could hide on the shore – unless he'd drowned. Even then, the body would soon be tossed up onto the sand.

The run, that was different, now that it had been carved out to its new depth. Abel could be dead in the run or the pond, drowned.

Hy and Ian scoured the length of the run. They navigated the spongy marshland around the pond, but could see nothing. Would it have to be dragged?

What about the cookhouse? Maybe he had found shelter there.

The door creaked open. Unlocked. The place was a mess. It had once been the dream kitchen of a French chef, with granite counters, tile floor, and, in the back, a grotto, an indoor pond constructed to keep lobsters happy and healthy until they were killed and eaten.

There was red sand all over the white tile floor and counters.

The state-of-the-art appliances had been sold. The door to the walk-in freezer had been removed. Inside it, a lobster rights activist had nearly died of hypothermia.

Abel wasn't there, he wasn't in the indoor pond, and there was no sign that he had been. The footprints were all their own.

Outside, Hy and Ian scanned the sand, looking for evidence of a ducky mug. They found nothing and kept walking, plodding along the shore together, but separate.

"That way we'll cover more territory," Hy had suggested. She walked, barefoot, in the shallow water; Ian combed the capes. Together but apart. The story of their relationship. It was low tide, and so they were able to go from beach to beach, around the capes that jutted out into the water. At high tide, they couldn't get around them, but at low tide, they could scale the slippery rocks to move onto the next shore.

This went on for miles, and so did they, mile after mile with nothing but sand, rocks, and sea.

No Abel.

They were the last on the shore. Heading back, they could see the full length of the beach, wisps of smoke drifting across it like dirty fog. But it didn't smell like fog. Deserted. The searchers at the other end had given up. If they couldn't walk any farther, how could a man who was more than ninety?

Hy and Ian stopped again at the cookhouse, staring down at the dory behind it. The dory and the cookhouse belonged to local scumbag Jared MacPherson, Hy's near neighbour.

The boat didn't look as if it had been used in a long time. Not since Jared had been poaching lobster five or six years before, stealing out of the fishermen's traps at night. The dory was covered in sand and seaweed, shells and rocks. There were a couple of gashes in the wood. Not seaworthy.

Jared was in Sleepy Hollow, the provincial jail, serving time for fraud. Online fraud. A step up on the criminal ladder for Jared. Usually it was possession, dealing drugs, operating a grow op.

Not this time.

It was Ian who had found him out.

This past winter, when The Shores was snowed in for weeks, and he was bored of his other online pursuits, Ian had come across an Internet site, slugged *Murder, He Sells*.

The seller was cashing in on the notoriety The Shores had gained from the number of murders and deaths that had occurred there in the past several years.

The items offered up were beach stones and shells upon which, the claim was, Lance Lord's body had lain, after someone had killed him with an axe to the head, right through his Jimi Hendrix wig. The murder had happened down on the shore, five or six years before.

Why would anyone be interested in buying the stones? Lance Lord had been a minor Canadian celebrity. His dubious claim to fame had been his role as an Anglo on a French TV show. He had become a cult figure among Francophones, not because he was so good, but because he was so bad.

Ten bucks. For a small bag of stones and shells. With a certificate declaring the items genuine.

"You didn't go for it, did you?" Hy had asked Ian at the time.

"Not yet, but I'm thinking of it."

Hy had examined the onscreen image of the stones and shells. They could have been picked up anywhere on Red Island.

The certificate of authenticity was hardly convincing – something anyone could have produced with a computer and printer, ignoring spell-check.

"There should be only one 'r' in guarantee." Hy had pointed at the offending word. "Must have it mixed up with warranty."

"And this…" Ian had tried to say the word as spelled, but had a hard time. "Authentica…authentica… authentica-city."

A few days later, Ian had found more offerings on the site:

"Glad I waited. Now you can get the bag of stones for only five bucks, if you spend twenty-five on the weights Big Ed used."

Big Ed Bullock, owner of the fitness operation Mind Over Muscle, was famous for having used the power of his mind to build back his strength after his head was sliced open with a machete in Vietnam and part of his brain left lying on the jungle floor. He'd built a dome-shaped structure on the cape some years back. Hy had almost died there. Jamieson had almost died there, too.

"I wonder if they weigh anything," Hy had commented wryly. Big Ed's barbells didn't weigh a thing – and yet they had managed to kill.

"Who do you think is behind this scam?"

Ian had shrugged. "You got me."

Ian had bookmarked the site. A few days later, packs of Tarot cards were on offer. Cards that could, like the original set after which they were patterned, reliably predict the outcome of a murder investigation.

The next item made it clear who the perpetrator was.

Fish that had fallen from the sky. Cooked at the time, frozen now.

When Ian showed her, Hy knew.

"Jared." She had whispered, stunned at his gall.

"Exactly."

Jared had tried to sell the fish before. When they fell from the sky a couple of years back, he'd collected a freezer full.

"Do you think they're the same fish?"

"I don't know, but the rest is certainly a scam. This has told us who it is. Now I'm going to prove it. I've ordered the full set. To my post office box in Winterside, so he won't know who it is. He's got a P.O. Box on the site. Two can play the same game."

"Don't you think we ought to tell Jamieson?"

"When did you ever do that?"

That had silenced Hy. It was true. Whenever she stumbled on something, she tried to solve it herself first.

A week later, Ian had gone to Winterside to check his post office box. He stopped at Hy's on the way home. The package was open, and he was beaming when she answered the door.

"I got a bonus," he'd said. "Bits of the blade from the wind turbine."

The turbine had nearly wiped out the village's children. Some claimed it was evil and had done so with intent.

"I can get a special deal on the next item – pieces of plasticized flesh from Vera Gloom's husbands."

Hy had winced. Vera Gloom, the serial widow.

Ian presented his evidence to Jamieson – and his suspicions. She had flushed with anger that he'd conducted an investigation without filling her in, but she agreed that Jared was likely behind it.

She had busted him, and found all the evidence she needed in his house: the stones, the weights, the fish, and the fake flesh, laid out on the kitchen table to be packaged, should anyone other than Ian order them.

"Fraud?" Jared had looked genuinely shocked when Jamieson used the word. "Them stones are from this shore, you can't say they're not." He gave her a sly look.

"No, but I can say they are not the stones Lance Lord's body lay on."

"How can you?"

"Because the winter before piled so much sand onto the shore, there was barely a stone or a pebble to be found that year."

Some of the stones and shells had splotches of red paint on them.

"Is that meant to be Lance Lord's blood?"

Jared shrugged.

It was the fish that had sealed it. It was herring that had fallen from the sky. Jared had cod.

He'd tried. "You don't know if there wasn't a patch of cod. Yes, it was cod that came down at the cookhouse, I could swear it."

"Save your swearing for court."

Jamieson would rather be booking Jared for murder, but settled for fraud. Jared had been implicated in at least one of the killings in The Shores, but she'd never been able to pin it on him. Now she'd got him, for taking advantage of the great interest in the killings in the tiny village. There had been so many. And such good media coverage. Lucky Lester Joudry, videographer son of Gus's nearest neighbour, Estelle, had been on the scene for most of them and was able to disseminate the news rapidly and photographically, with video and online presence. The whole world knew about The Shores. That's why it had been getting so many tourists lately.

So Jared had figured a website to sell items associated with the murders and deaths would be a great scam.

The judge thought it was a scam, too.

Jared was behind bars now for a good long while.

His dory was still there.

"No luck, then?"

They were startled by her voice.

Jamieson. In full uniform, hair neatly scraped back into a bun.

"This boat hasn't been used in years," said Hy.

Jamieson looked over the expanse of sand to the water.

"Even if it could be, I can't see how a ninety-year-old man would drag this into the water."

"Not even at high tide. But none of us knew…knows…him… or what he's capable of."

"Gus would know. Maybe she could pick up a trail we can't see."

"She hasn't been to the shore in twenty years."

"Maybe she should." Jamieson turned and marched up Wild Rose Lane, leaving Hy and Ian in her wake, wondering: should they follow, or should they stay? Ian shrugged. Hy nodded. They followed.

Chapter 7

"Now what would I be doin' goin' down to the shore at my age?"

"Looking for your husband?"

"I never did go lookin' for him. That's one of the things Abel liked about me. Just stayed put and waited 'til he come home."

"This is different. You don't know where he is."

"Won't be the first time."

"Are you saying – ?"

"Not lately, not since he was a young man. Down to Charlottetown when the season ended. Bit of fun. Can't blame him."

Jamieson bet she couldn't. It seemed every time Abel had touched Gus when she was young, she got pregnant. Eight kids, thought Jamieson, who would likely never have any. What kind of life was that?

It had suited Gus, even though it hadn't been promising at the start. As the three visitors stepped out her door, Gus stared out the window. A wave of smoke drifted by. When it settled, it was clearer to see. Past times.

***

She was going home from the potato fields on a crisp fall day with her three brothers and a sister. Was it more than sixty years ago – or was it yesterday? It felt like yesterday. She had a spring in her step and her hair in a long fat braid, and it swung in rhythm to her hips. Child-bearing hips.

The truck wagon chugged up beside her, and he leaned out. "Fancy a lift?"

She did. Her back ached from a long day in the potato field.

She smiled when he shoved the door open and reached out a hand to help her in. She'd never been really pretty – especially not then, when she was so skinny. But her smile – in her eyes and her mouth – lit up an otherwise plain face.

"Room for a few in back, and one more up here."

Her brothers climbed in and sprawled on the sacks of potatoes. Her sister squeezed in next to her.

It was a tight squeeze – and, as she later told him – the closest she had ever been to a man she wasn't related to.

"I should hope so," he had replied.

There had been many more lifts home after that, with a decreasing number of siblings in tow, until, finally, even the sister chaperone disappeared with some excuse, and he asked her to marry him.

What else could she say?

No.

***

It was eerie how quiet the house was without Abel, how hard it was not to see his duck cup there on the table. Wherever he'd gone, he'd taken it with him. What did that mean – if anything?

The rockers on Gus's recliner creaked in his absence.

The clock on the mantel in the dining room ticked louder, marking the time since Abel had disappeared. Making it seem a long time. Forever.

Other people didn't seem to notice the strange silence of the house without Abel in it. They'd been in and out all day, sipping tea and chattering, none of them hearing the silence Gus heard. Nor did they notice when she thought she heard the tread of his foot, the familiar clearing of his throat. Were these sounds echoing through time, or was he here, somewhere, somehow here, but not visible?

He could not have simply disappeared.

But he had.

"Without a trace," Gus whispered as she tried to force herself to mend a pair of his socks.

Socks. Did he have socks there, wherever he was?

He would be needing clean socks by now.

Perhaps she should give some to Jamieson for when she finally found him. He'd want those right away.

There was a clam chowder simmering on the stove. She'd made it – his favourite meal – in hopes that it would lure him home.

It hadn't. She hated clam chowder. She poured it down the sink, not caring if it clogged and him not around to clear it, and went back to darning the sock, in the peculiar silence of the house without Abel.

***

No one had pressured Gus to go down to the shore on the chance that she would turn up Abel where they had not been successful. Somehow, she was here now – in the dark – stumbling along the shore in search of him. She was wearing her nightdress, and, thank God, her dressing gown. None of the neighbours could see her. There were no lights on in any of the houses up the Shore Lane. There were no houses. Not even hers.

A fresh breeze whipped her nightclothes around her ankles, and they billowed up with each gust. She shivered in the cold of the late August night.

As her eyes grew accustomed to the light, she saw a lump on the horizon, on the far side of the run, near the sea rock.

She panicked. Abel? How would she get to him? She stood at the edge of the run, peering into the dark, her eyes trying to make sense of the shape on the sand. She had no choice. She'd have to wade through. She had no idea of how deep the run had become. The cold salt water stung her, and the swift current twisted her nightclothes around her legs, threatening to pull her down.

She dragged herself out, wet cotton clinging to her and making it hard to walk.

"There he is!" A voice she knew. Gus looked behind her. Hy and Jamieson, wearing dresses and pushing bicycles through the sand. Jamieson shone a light down the beach. The beam appeared to be coming from the palm of her hand.

If she could have run, Gus would have.

There, just up from the high tide mark, was a pile of clothes, neatly folded and stacked, Abel's work boots beside them. Sitting atop the dungarees and striped cotton shirt was the Tilley hat.

Jamison and Hy trudged through the deep dry sand. Their bicycles had disappeared. Gus stayed where she was, unable to navigate the sand, but itching to grab up Abel's clothes; a part of him, at least, found.

Jamieson and Hy stopped and stared down at the pile.

Jamieson crouched down, looked at the clothes, out at the water, up at Hy.

"What do you think it means?"

"I know what it looks like."

"That he took off his clothes and walked into the water."

"That's what it looks like."

"Any other explanation?"

"None that I can think of right now."

Had he walked into the water?

"He ain't dead," Gus kept insisting.

"How do you know?" Jamieson asked again. And again, the same answer:

"I know. Some things you just know. This is one of the things I know."

"In spite of his clothes on the beach?"

"They don't matter. Those clothes ain't him."

"Surely they suggest..."

Gus cut her off. She didn't want to hear the "s" word, as she called it. Suicide.

"Only to some people as don't know Abel."

Gus stood up tall, in her "end of conversation" pose.

"'Sides, his long johns aren't here."

***

She woke to find herself standing on her stoop, Hy gently shaking her shoulder.

Gus was in a daze. It was dawn. She'd been dreaming. And sleepwalking. That hadn't happened to her since she was a child.

"Abel…" she murmured.

"What's going on?" Jamieson's voice rang out from the lane.

Hy looked over. "Nothing. It's…uh…nothing."

"It doesn't look like nothing." Jamieson marched over and up the steps. She took a close look at Gus. At her eyes. Unfocused.

Hy could see, too, that Gus wasn't quite with them.

"I wuz dreamin' about Abel."

"And?" Hy coaxed.

"I saw his clothes on the shore."

"You were at the shore?" Hy looked down at her old friend's feet. Bare.

"Can't say as I was, but I reckon I was walking in my sleep."

"I better check," said Jamieson. It was a long shot, but who knew where Gus had been in her nightie?

As expected, she found nothing.

Chapter 8

It was Gus's neighbour Estelle Joudry who spotted the body when she stepped out on her front stoop the next morning. She actually had to crane her neck to see it, but she was skilled at that, and the open door of the house across the road was just visible beyond the spruce trees that fronted it. Estelle made her way on tiptoes down her front steps and across the lawn.

She looked both ways before crossing the road – not to see if there were any cars, but to see if anyone was watching her. She continued on tiptoes up to the house.

When she saw him, it took a moment to register that she was looking at a body. A dead body.

She screamed.

Backed away.

Screamed again.

Turned and ran. No tiptoes now. Hard thumping on the wet morning grass. Her damp footprints fleeing across the road. Back to the safety of her front stoop.

She gulped in air, and with it, smoke. The smoke was so thick and her body so tense, she couldn't take a proper breath. She kept gulping. The gulping turned to hyperventilating, panic, and the sound alerted her husband Germaine, who polished off his morning coffee before he went to help his wife.

He thought it might be a heart attack. He knew about those, having had a couple himself, bearing the red scar from a quadruple bypass.

While Germaine knew about having a heart attack, he didn't

know anything about dealing with one. So it was handy that Estelle was not in cardiac distress.

Gradually she calmed down, and Germaine went back to the kitchen to pour himself another cup of coffee, leaving Estelle on the steps. She came in a few moments later, her face white, her eyes bug-open, her mouth opening and closing with no sound coming out.

Germaine thought that if it was a heart attack, she had poor timing. She hadn't made his breakfast yet. As if on cue, his stomach grumbled.

Taking the cue, Estelle cracked an egg into the toaster and popped two slices of bread into the frying pan.

Germaine looked confused. Estelle was confused by his confusion. Then she saw what she had done. Egg in the toaster and bread in the frying pan. She clutched her apron over her face. Dropped it down. Her world was upside down. Always looking for a choice piece of gossip, she had one now. Now she wasn't sure she wanted it. Or that she knew what to do with it.

"He's dead."

"Who? Abel?"

Her coughing drowned out his question and prevented a response. She shouldn't have run in that air. It was always worse in the morning, the smoke from Quebec. Germaine was watching the gelatinous egg white run down the side of the toaster. He could smell the bread, burning in the frying pan.

Germaine grunted. "How do you know he's dead?"

"Saw it with my own eyes. Over the road. Lying flat out right inside the house. Strong nor'easter musta blown the door wide open."

"How'd you know he was dead?" Germaine asked again, finding her answer unsatisfactory.

Estelle looked at Germaine with an edge of superiority.

"You'd know it if you seen it. Some things you just know."

"Then you better be phoning the Mountie." That's what most of the villagers called Jane Jamieson. They couldn't call her Jane. They couldn't get their heads around her surname. Jamieson. It was a man's name, wasn't it? At one time, the word "Mountie" would have meant a man. Times had changed.

The yolk of the egg had now slid down the side of the toaster, too, and was congealing on the plastic tablecloth. "Phone after breakfast," he added quickly, afraid his meal wasn't going to happen.

"No, it'll have to be now." Estelle had spied her neighbour Gus, out hanging clothes on the line. It gave her a sense of urgency.

***

"He was lying there, just like that." Estelle pointed down at the corpse splayed out in the tiny entranceway. She pointed at it, but turned her gaze from it. She couldn't bear to look.

Jamieson sighed at the intelligence of her witness. She should have been used to it. It had been some years now since she'd been assigned to this village in the back of beyond. Assigned permanently, a full-time police presence in a tiny village with a history of murders.

"Abel Mack," said Jamieson. So this is what he looked like. Thin. Spare, bones sticking out. She had not imagined him this way. A warm rush of anxiety overtook her. How would she tell Gus? Maybe she could tell Hy, and let her do the dirty work? She knew she couldn't do that. It was her duty to tell Gus her husband was dead. That was the problem with community policing. Getting to know people. Getting to…like people. It got in the way of the job.

"What'd you say?" Estelle looked confused.

So did Jamieson.

"Abel Mack," she repeated.

"No. No, this ain't Abel. This is Jimmi Dunn."

"Jimmy… Dunn?" What Estelle had said on the phone now made sense. Jamieson had thought that when Estelle had said "done," she meant dead. Well, he was dead. Dunn. Done. "Jimmy Dunn?"

"No. Not Jimmy." Having finished his breakfast, Germaine had strolled across the road to weigh in and pay his last respects to his old friend, Abel. But it wasn't Abel.

"It's not Jimmy with a 'y.' It's Jimmi with an 'i,' like his brother Billi," Estelle explained, as if somehow she could hear that Jamieson had been mentally spelling it wrong. In fact, she assumed come-from-aways wouldn't know, so she automatically corrected them. "Billi passed away a few years back. Same thing happened to him. Same exact door. Shoulda fixed it."

"Thought Jimmi died years ago." Germaine had overcome the shock of finding that Abel was not dead, at least not here right now. He gazed down at the body of Jimmi Dunn.

"No, no. That was his brother Billi." Estelle was the only one in the village who could tell one twin from the other.

"Never could tell them apart."

"Of course not. They was identical twins." And identical fools. They'd both changed the spelling of their names to end in "i" after smoking dope in the sixties.

"It's lucky we found him at all." Estelle was full of self-importance. "He never went out and no one ever visited. Weren't for that nor'easter that blew his door open, we'd never have known. For who knows how long."

She didn't stop to think that if the door had not blown open, neither twin would be dead, not from that, anyway.

Jamieson left the body untouched, until she got some forensic information on the manner of death from Finn Finnegan, Hy's long-lost half-brother. Hy and Finn had reunited last year, thanks to Facebook. He came to visit and stayed, mostly because he'd fallen for Gus and Abel's daughter Dot, who'd now dumped him and left the village. Finn was a forensic scientist who'd given up that career to focus on the environment, but he helped Jamieson occasionally.

This was surely a natural death? Hit by a door. Or perhaps a heart attack? Stroke? An old man. Jamieson found it disconcerting, that the death came hard on the heels of Abel Mack's disappearance. Were the two connected? Jamieson knew that anything unusual that happened around a death or a murder, perhaps also a disappearance, should be considered connected unless proven otherwise.

What was the connection between Jimmi Dunn and Abel Mack?

***

"Abel owns the mortgage to Jimmi's place." Gus was forthcoming when Jamieson asked her about the two men. "Owns the mortgage on a lotta places, come to that. Didn't ever make any money from it. Did it out of the kindness of his heart, helping people out."

"But the Dunns have money."

The Dunn family had produced a long line of doctors and undertakers in Winterside, keeping the business of the dying and the dead in the family. The senior Dr. Dunn was in his nineties, and still practising medicine. All those years practising and he hadn't got it right yet, Gus always said.

"Happen that's so. But Jimmi and Billi never went in for doctoring or dying. Their father disowned them. They shifted along as farm workers and fish-plant workers. They stopped working as soon as they got the old age pension. Then Billi died a few years back."

"So Abel held their mortgage. So they owed him?"

"Everyone owes Abel."

"And when they died, what was theirs became his?"

Gus looked up sharply.

"I s'pose it did."

***

What was theirs wasn't much, Jamieson discovered. Just the old house, in such bad shape it couldn't even be called a fixer-upper.

There was a shed, even older, and a patch of land carpenter Harold MacLean said "couldn't keep a rabbit alive." Hardly the killing fields.

Jamieson couldn't believe that the ninety-year-old Abel had killed Jimmi Dunn, but it bore thinking about, the disappearance of one coming so close on the death of the other. Had there been an argument? Some pushing and shoving? An old man losing his balance? A wound to the head? Manslaughter, if not murder? Or was Dunn collateral damage – ahead of the main event? Was there murder in the smoky air? Was this death a foreshadowing of more to come? Deaths never seemed to happen singly here.

Jamieson continued to toy with the idea of Abel as murderer – or guilty, perhaps, of manslaughter, an accident he had fled from. Jamieson used to get excited over the possibility of murder, cracking a big case, bringing the homicidal to justice. That was before it became a regular event in The Shores, of all places. She'd never had a murder case before she'd come to this tiny, sleepy village. Now it was an annual occurrence.

Unnatural.

"Natural causes," Finn's message said on the police-phone voice mail. The forensic people rarely came way out here to The Shores. Jamieson was glad to have Finn in the neighbourhood at times like this. That's what she told herself.

It didn't explain why she felt a sense of disappointment that she hadn't been there to take the call in person.

She brushed the feeling aside, and focused on what Finn had said.

What about the wound to the head?

It was as if the "voice-mail Finn" had anticipated her silent question.

"The door must have swung open and bashed him in the head. Same thing happened to his brother a few years back. Same door. Jimmi saw that happen, and Dr. Dunn was there at the time, visiting. That was before your time. Mine, too, but Dr. Dunn told me about it. Anyway, it works out mathematically and cerebrally. Should've fixed the door before it fixed him."

Said with a grin she could hear but couldn't see or respond to. Because he wasn't there, he also could not see something, something rare – the sudden, soft smile on her face.

The thought that produced it would have surprised him.

It surprised her.

Open and shut case.

It was the sort of thing Hy would have said. She must be rubbing off on Jamieson. Perhaps it was born of relief. Relief that this was not another murder, the traditional annual killing.

Fine. So they weren't looking for a murderer. Just a missing man. An old man who'd gone missing. *Gone missing,* the phrase they used in the media all the time. It did make sense in a curious kind of way, but did that mean if you found him he was here found? Gone found? Found missing?

Chapter 9

The hat was over his face, keeping the light out. There was a shade on the one window, but it had split with age and hung down, letting in a beam of light.

He had a pounding headache. A caffeine-withdrawal headache. He rolled off the cot, dumping the decades-old blanket on the floor, eyes squinting, adjusting to the play of the light and the dark in the tiny shack.

He searched for the ducky cup in the pink child's knapsack on the floor. The knapsack had been…whose had it been? He scrunched up his face in puzzlement. Someone. Someone close. Spot? No, that was a dog's name.

No mug. His face clouded, then cleared. He had three ducky mugs here, on the shelf above the sink.

He tugged a jar of coffee out of the knapsack. Water gurgled out of the faucet into a chipped earthen bowl shoved under it. The water came in burps, rusty at first, then clear. There was a single propane burner and a pot. He filled it with water, lit the burner, and soon was drinking his morning coffee out of the ducky mug.

He drank two cups. Put the cup he'd used back on the shelf and tossed an unused one into the pink knapsack.

Now he had to pee.

***

Seamus O'Malley's heart was in Newfoundland, where generations of the men of his family had fished cod. Until the moratorium. The mismanagement. The dismal days of no decent employment. The days that drove desperate men to desperate measures. His father was one of the most desperate. The first day he had gone to the food bank had been his last day. They found him late that night, hanging from a beam in the barn.

Like many others, Seamus emigrated to Canada. That's how he, and others like him, thought of it. Going to another country. He hoped to be going home soon, a triumphant hero, the saviour of the cod fishery.

He was looking down at the photograph on his desk, tracing the outline of the big fish idly, as he had been doing the past several days. His officemate, curious, came and looked over his shoulder.

"Man, that's some big fish," he commented. "Tuna?"

Seamus snorted dismissively. Brian Cobb was an idiot. How he'd managed to get a job with fisheries, Seamus didn't know. The feeling was mutual. Cobb thought Seamus was certifiable. That it was madness on the boss's part that he'd been left in charge.

"Tuna?" Seamus sneered. "No."

"Then what? That big?" Brian peered closer. It was hard to tell, because the fish was twisted around in its struggle to free itself, and he'd never seen any fish that big.

"Tuna could be that big – must be around two hundred pounds. Bigger than the man."

"Could be around three hundred pounds. Maybe more. Yes, I think more."

Brian whistled. "Where?"

Seamus suddenly realized he'd got sucked into this conversation all because of his own interest in the fish. He didn't want to talk about it. He didn't want anyone else getting ideas like he had. Not that Brian would know an idea if it hit him. Literally. Anyway, this was common knowledge. Or public knowledge, anyway. This photograph. He had to find the book. Or the fisherman. Or both. Before that Ferguson guy did. He wanted to have the upper hand.

When Brian left for lunch, Seamus picked up the phone and called his only contact at The Shores. Hy McAllister. She'd done a lot of work for the Red Island Department of Fisheries, through her website editing company, *Content*. She'd know.

"I'm looking for a fisherman," he said when she answered.

"Why?" she asked, suspicious. She had never liked Seamus O'Malley. He was pushy. She could tell that right now he was trying to contain himself. That must mean that whatever he wanted, he wanted it badly.

He ignored her question. "A certain fisherman."

She sensed he was pacing, because the line kept cutting out. He was on his cellphone, and he'd called Hy on hers. Hadn't used the landline because he heard they still had party lines in The Shores. Whether that was true or not, whether The Shores was really that backward, he wasn't willing to risk. What he didn't know was some of the women had bought police scanners when the party-line system ended, and they could listen in on cellphones.

A few were doing so now.

"Which certain fisherman?"

"I'm not sure of the guy's name. He was in the front photo of that community book, *Time Was*."

"Abel Mack?" She'd blurted out without meaning to. Still, it was no big secret. All the newspapers, radio, and TV stations had done stories on the book when it came out the year before.

She'd reached over to a pile of books on the harvest table, slipped it out.

Time Was.

She opened it up. There was the photo – and it clearly named Abel Mack. A typical photo of him. Couldn't see a thing. She wondered why Seamus wanted him.

"That's it." There was urgency in his tone. "I need to talk to him. Thought you might know how to get in touch with him."

Silence.

"Do you know how to get in touch with him?" Seamus persisted.

"Wish I did."

"What do you mean?"

"He's missing," she responded.

"*Missing* missing? Or just missing at the moment?"

"*Missing* missing."

He hadn't counted on that.

He might have to go searching, but he didn't know what Abel looked like.

He hung up and immediately phoned back, to ask what Abel looked like.

Hy could see it was him calling, so she let it go to voice mail.

He hung up without leaving a message, then rang back. There was something more important he wanted to ask.

Again, she let it go to voice mail.

She clicked to listen when the phone beeped the end of his message.

A desperate sound.

"Have you seen circles?" He knew they'd been seen elsewhere. But here?

She had. She had seen circles when she'd gone for a lobster lunch at sea with Ben and Annabelle, Ian, Finn, and Dot earlier in the summer. They'd seen the circles in the water west of Big Bay. She had no idea what they were or why Seamus wanted to know.

***

No one would have been able to identify Abel from the posters that now went up around the village, down to Big Bay, and east along the Island Way to the causeway and ferry crossing.

The causeway and the ferry were the slim links to what the villagers called "the mainland," the rest of Red Island. Five years before, a storm surge had sliced through the natural causeway, driving a mass of sea ice that crushed and buried five houses, threw cars into the water and boats up onto the road, and killed nine people – all in thirteen-and-a-half minutes.

The causeway had been shored up, but never well, with the result that an old river ferry from New Brunswick had been put into service nine months a year. Still, rain and snowstorms often isolated the village from food and services. There were no stores in The Shores. There had been some tourist operations over at Big Bay for the 200th anniversary the previous summer, but they had closed. Now there was only the coffee stand at the ferry, run by Nathan Mack, Ben's son and Abel's nephew. Nathan was also the village's volunteer paramedic, with a beat-up van he'd converted into an ambulance.

The unidentifiable Abel stared down from power poles throughout the village and from the salt-stained window of Nathan's coffee stand, a structure of various vintages, fashioned from recycled pickings from the local dump. Abel was unidentifiable because the hat obscured his face, the face no one except Gus had seen in twenty or thirty years.

They did recognize the hat.

They all said:

"That hat drove him to Winterside, many's the time."

Underneath the hat, in bold, black capital letters:

**MISSING:
ABEL MACK, 92,
COULD BE CARRYING A YELLOW AND ORANGE
COFFEE CUP SHAPED LIKE A DUCK.**

Not very helpful, thought Jamieson, looking at the poster on the hall door. She wondered who had made it.

Moira Toombs, who had not taken her husband Frank Webster's name on their marriage a year ago – she oddly preferred her own – came slithering over from her house, a proud smile on her often sour face.

"That's mine." She pointed at the poster with pride. She'd borrowed the photo from Gus, scanned it, and played around with layout and graphics, all on the new iMac Frank had given her for Christmas. She no longer cared if Ian Simmons found her computer skills clever. She'd been in love with him for years, thwarted by his dithering affection for Hy. Then Frank came into her life.

"Hard to see his face." Jamieson pointed at the hat.

Moira scowled.

"Everyone here knows what he looks like, anyway."

"Do they?"

Moira looked doubtful.

"Do you?"

Moira hesitated. "I think the hat tells a lot about his character."

"We're not looking for his character. We don't know if he's wearing the hat."

"Oh, he always wore the hat." Moira spoke in the past tense. She'd written him off. Couldn't see what all the fuss was about.

"That doesn't guarantee he is now."

Moira's attention shifted from Jamieson.

Jamieson turned.

The hat.

But not Abel.

Hy was wearing the hat. It covered her face, but the rest of her was unmistakable. Red curls nudging out from under the brim. Tall slim body, dressed in old jeans and an Irish cable-knit sweater Gus had made. Following her was the cat that parcelled itself out among Gus, Jamieson, and Hy. Gus called her Blackie, because that was her colouring from an aerial view; Jamieson called her Whitey, because her stomach fur was white when she rolled over, which she always did when Jamieson emitted an uncanny purr that sounded just like a cat. Hy called her Whacky, because she never knew what to call her otherwise.

The cat sashayed over to Jamieson, dropped down and rolled over on her back. Jamieson ignored her, eyes fixed on the hat on Hy's head. She recognized its pedigree. A Tilley hat.

"What are you doing with that?"

"Gus gave it to me."

"Gave it to you?"

"To use."

"In what way?"

"I suppose something like letting a search dog sniff someone's clothing. She thought if we took it on our search, it might help find him. If it took him to Winterside," Hy grinned, "it may take us to him."

Jamieson sighed. A deep sigh of exasperation. People were not taking this seriously enough. The man was most likely dead.

Hy wasn't finished.

"You know an elephant ate one of these three times. It survived."

Jamieson took the bait.

"What, the elephant?"

"No, the hat. I guess the elephant, too."

Hy frowned and removed the hat. Her curly red hair sprang out.

"I don't think it's such a bad idea that the hat might help us find him. Except it's his other hat."

"Other hat?"

"He never actually wore this one. This one's the new one – the one he got from the Tilley people when he wore out the old one. But he kept on wearing the old one." She pointed at the poster. "That's the one he'll be wearing. Not this one. Obviously."

She spun the hat on one finger. Jamieson grabbed it.

"Hey…"

"Evidence."

"Evidence?"

"I'm keeping this as evidence." Of what? There hadn't been a crime, had there? She hoped not.

Beside the poster was a sign-up sheet for the various searches Jamieson had organized throughout the community. Potato fields. The Shore. Sheds and outbuildings. The woodlots that ran south of the village. South, but on the high ground.

There was not one name written down.

"This is disappointing," she said.

"Oh, don't worry. Everyone's going. They don't need to sign up."

And some can't write, thought Jamieson.

"Joudry's potato fields today," said Hy, looking at Moira and Jamieson.

Moira looked panicky.

"I'll fetch Frank." She turned and hurried back to her house.

"I bet," said Hy, as she and Jamieson headed to join the crowd of people gathering in Ben Mack's field.

Moira had improved since she'd married her Frank, but Hy thought a leopard doesn't change its spots.

Or its hat?

Hy looked over at Jamieson, who had unconsciously put the Tilley on her own head.

"Now *you* look like Abel," she said.

Embarrassed, Jamieson whipped it off, and then was stuck, hat in hand, not knowing what to do with it. She thrust it at Hy.

"Here. Take it back to Gus."

Hy planned to return it, eventually, but not before she had tested if it would drive her to Winterside.

Chapter 10

The searchers had all gone home. It was dusk. Night falls fast in late August, and the dark this year was intensified by the veil of smoke still drifting down from Quebec. Hy could hear the seasonal chirping of the cicadas swell. They wake with the sunset and set with the sun. Some of their cousins, she knew, the southern cicadas, burrow into the ground as newborns and spend most of their lives there, waiting to emerge, mate, and die in a handful of weeks. Not much of a life, she thought, buried in the ground.

Something was up on the Island Way in "the holler" near Hy's place. Looking down the road, she could see a car parked in the driveway of the house next to Jared MacPherson's.

Three elderly sisters had lived there until last April, when they all succumbed to "the cruelest month," and died within three weeks of each other. The house had always been plain, a big, grey unpainted barn of a place that looked as if no one lived there, except in the summer, when the sisters planted a thin thread of annual flowers in a row, along the ditch at the roadside.

The house had been on the market for only a month. Someone – unknown, as yet – had scooped it up, cleaned and painted it, mowed the lawn, and done a lot of construction work on the barn – mostly inside. It had been the talk of the village – all that work going on in the big barn of a house and the big barn itself – until Abel disappeared and became the new topic.

There had been a moving truck there, the day before Abel disappeared, but no one had spotted the new people yet.

Hy was feeling exhausted, her energy spent as much by the worry as the physical search. Worry not for Abel, but for Gus. Hy didn't know Abel, but she did know he mattered to Gus. That made him matter to her, too.

A chilling damp was moving in with the dark. Hy shivered. Curious as she was about the new neighbours, she was more interested right now in a deep, hot bath with bubbles and a generous glass of white wine.

***

That "*the moon was a ghostly galleon, tossed upon cloudy seas*" was never truer. Dark clouds and wisps of smoke floated across its face, on a wind that was, blessedly, blowing away the fumes from Quebec, sending them back where they had come from.

Where was Abel, under the full moon? Gus wondered where he was, but didn't question that he was somewhere. All their married lives, he had been somewhere. Mostly somewhere else. Not right there with her.

Why should it be any different now?

He was not dead, but missing.

***

He kept asking her to marry him, and she kept saying no. She wouldn't say why. He couldn't understand. Of course he couldn't understand. He was older by nearly ten years and already balding, but he was a catch. He had land, a farm, a small fishery, and a canning factory. Or he would have when his father passed away. So why would a woman say no?

His mother and father weren't easy, but everyone had to deal with in-laws. His mother, particular in her ways and thrifty – too

59

thrifty, judging by the nearly inedible meals she served up. And his father, frankly, a drunk.

She drew away from him without even knowing these things. Some days, she refused the ride. On other days, weary from the day in the fields, she would climb in and sit beside him without speaking.

What had attracted him had disappeared into silence. No more of the funny stories of the day's happenings and stupidities, the smile that lit up her plain face, the laugh that came from deep within her that promised so much about the wife she would be.

If he could only get her to say yes.

And then one day it came to him.

***

Two old men. Jamieson kept going over it in her head. Two old men dead? Jimmi Dunn. And Abel Mack? Surely Abel wasn't merely missing. He must be dead. Exposure, if nothing else. The nights were cooling down as fire raged heat in the Quebec forests and rained ash on The Shores. Ashes to ashes. Dust to dust. A grim reminder of mortality. Smoke, drifting down over the village, enshrouding it, blurring the line between reality and another world beyond, slipping out on the tide.

Jamieson shook her head. Nonsense. What nonsense. She was prone to fanciful imaginings about her cases, but when she drifted off into one of them, like now, watching that moon rise along the chimney line over Ethan Cooke's old cabin, she briskly shoved it away. There was no smoke tonight.

Back to work.

From the picture window of the police house, she could see the light in Gus Mack's kitchen. Still up. What time? Nine o'clock. Late for some villagers, she thought, but not for Gus. It was at about this time of night, Jamieson knew, that Gus came alive, telling stories of the past, slapping her knees and laughing at the foibles of her neighbours – and her own. Everyone's favourite story was about the propane tank explosion at Abel's old General Store. He'd come flying through the window, preceded by a Coke machine that cleared the glass for him, and landed smartly on his feet, close to home, and in time for dinner. Gus had watched it all and had his meal on the table when he came through the door at his usual time, precisely at noon.

Jamieson pulled on her jacket against the chill night air. Fall announced itself in The Shores around the middle of August with crisp air and cool breezes and a dazzling clarity of light, giving what the villagers called "large days." Light that, this year, was often obscured by smoke that hung low over the capes, grey and dirty. Not tonight, but still Jamieson coughed. The smoke had been burning her throat and sinuses for weeks. Coughing didn't help. It only increased the pain – sharp daggers slicing through her throat and chest.

There would be more deaths, she thought, if this keeps up. The old folks would surrender to it, asthmatics could die, could be created. Jamieson wondered if that might be happening to her.

***

Finn stopped where he stood, on the cape where the dome used to be. The dome that had gone down in a fire two summers ago, a fire that had almost killed Jamieson. He had nearly lost her, he thought. But that thought was crazy. He'd never had her. He hadn't even lived here when it had happened. Still, like the proverbial phoenix, rising out of the ashes of the dome, was this feeling for Jamieson. It had come to him as a complete surprise.

It had come, he had to admit to himself, before Dot abandoned him, returned to her life traipsing around the world, photographing and healing, now with a baby in tow. He couldn't compete with her desire for that vagabond life, and he didn't want to join her in it. They'd made a good-looking pair, tall and slim, doing tai chi on the cape as the sun went up or down. He had a dark thatch of hair, as dark as Jamieson's, and he wore black almost like a uniform. His arms and legs were so long some people thought he looked like a spider.

He thought Dot might have sensed his pulling away, his growing attraction to Jamieson. Dot didn't need him. He wasn't sure if Jamieson did.

He noticed her everywhere, flushed when she found him staring at her, was, for the first time in his life, tongue-tied in a woman's presence. He usually had charm, and to spare. It didn't help that she rarely said anything to him. He couldn't know what her silence meant, how deep he reached into her, causing a discomfort she'd been trying to ignore.

Now he watched as she moved into the beam of Gus's outdoor light. Tall, slim, confident in her movements, with that tremendous black hair neatly tucked away in a bun at the nape of her neck. Porcelain skin, ethereal in the light.

He felt compelled by her. But he couldn't budge. He stood where he was, watching her, unable to move until she had gone inside.

***

The old man was stuck in the shack all day. When he'd woken up, it was light, too late to move without being seen. He stayed where he was for the day, ducked down each time he heard a car pass, hit the floor when a big vehicle, a loaded hay truck, whipped by on the road.

He'd wait out the night and move before daybreak. In the dark. Why, he wasn't sure. He had an urgent need not to be seen, not to have his plan uncovered.

He couldn't think of what the plan was right now, but it would come to him, when he got where he was going.

Where was he going?

He lay on the floor for several minutes, puzzling it out. There was nothing but a muddle of images in his mind. His Tilley hat. The ducky mug. The dory, with the yellow and red stripes.

And then the mix of images gave way to one clear, compelling thought.

The fog lifted. He saw Winterside.

He had to get to Winterside. For some reason. And so he sat up on the cot through the night, ducking out a few times to pee in the grass…and one time he visited the outhouse that was sliding down the hill.

Now he was preparing to clamber back on the bicycle and make his way to town.

Why? The reason continued to nag at him. So did the need to get up and get going.

***

Hy woke before dawn, as was her habit. She lay in bed and pondered. What if Abel were unable to see clearly? What if he had stumbled from home, ducky mug in hand, and gone…

Gone where?

From her bedroom window, Hy could just see the foam-tipped breakers on the shore, a pale unearthly blue catching a glimmer of the first light breaking on the horizon.

The shore. Of course, the shore. Not this shore. No, the other one, over the causeway, a small strip of land that belonged to Abel, a shore with a deep pond, a harbour that had been halfway dredged and was deep enough for Abel to keep his boat in the water. He had fished out of there for a number of years. Why would he want to go there? Abel hadn't been to the shore, any shore – as far as anyone knew – in twenty-six years, ever since he had given up fishing.

He'd been a fisherman all his life. He might be living in that past.

Of course.

That's where he would be.

She wouldn't go there alone. She was tired of being the one who stumbled over the dead.

She'd round up Jamieson. She should be in on this. If Abel was dead, it was about time Jamieson shared in one of the gruesome discoveries that always seemed to visit themselves on Hy.

It was early, but Jamieson would be up soon.

***

Two Mounties – novices from away stationed on the island during the busy tourist season to police the Cavendish tourist area – had not been alerted about a missing old man, because it wasn't their territory. They had drifted to this patch of the island on a haze of marijuana, smoked to make the early morning shift more palatable. They didn't think much about the old man pedalling the woman's bicycle down the road early that morning. Except that he shouldn't have been there. No lights on. A hazard to himself and any motorists who might happen by.

One moment he was there, the next gone. The officer driving had brought the car to a stop by the side of the road. When he looked up, the old man and bicycle were gone.

His partner looked at him, shrugged his shoulders. The guy had just disappeared.

With a heavy sigh, the cop got out of the car, waving for his partner to stay behind with the vehicle. He didn't like the feel of this. He crossed the road, peered over the embankment and began to gesture at the other officer to join him, with a frantic wave of his arms.

Not because there was someone there. Because there was no one there.

One shrugged his shoulders. The other scratched his head, and they returned to the cruiser and took off. This wasn't their patch anyway.

They went back to their regular beat – the young, drunk, drugged-up crowd they'd barely escaped being part of themselves. They never said no to a joint, and puffed away at one as they headed away from the deep island and its secrets.

Chapter 11

Hy sped up Shipwreck Hill, right past Ian's house. He was looking out his kitchen window, curious that she hadn't stopped in as she did most mornings. She was heading for Jamieson's at a clip. Must be something up. He stepped out the door.

What he saw next formed slowly in his vision, so unexpected was it. At the bottom of his lawn, where it sloped to the road. Yellow and orange. The ducky mug? He dove down the lawn, retrieved the mug and, holding it up like a trophy, headed for Jamieson's, where Hy stood on the stoop, pressing the doorbell. The only doorbell in The Shores, installed last spring.

She heard the lock click on the inner door. It swung back, and Jamieson appeared, framed by the metal storm door, which she proceeded to unlock. The only pair of locked doors in the village. Hy backed up to let the storm door swing open and burst into the house, nearly knocking Jamieson over.

Ian had just about reached the stoop, trophy in hand, but was not fast enough to stop the door from swinging shut behind Hy. It slammed in his face. He was close enough to hear her blurt out:

"His fishing shack. On Montgomery Shore. We haven't looked there." Hy was jumping up and down in excitement. She had a feeling about this…

Jamieson grabbed her jacket, shoved it on, signalled Hy to follow her, pulled the inner door open, and pushed the storm door wide.

It almost hit Ian in the face. He dodged it as she threw it open.

"Oops." Hy grinned. "Almost pulled a Jimmi Dunn there."

"That," said Jamieson, "is precisely why doors should be locked and visitors should knock." That it was more the opposite occurred to Hy, but she thought better of mentioning it.

"But I've found Abel's mug." Ian held it aloft, a big grin on his face.

Hy looked him up and down.

"And lost your clothes."

Ian looked down. He was still in his pyjamas. Not his best pair.

He flushed. But Hy and Jamieson weren't looking at him. They were staring at the mug.

"Where?" Hy and Jamieson asked at the same time.

"On the lawn. Near the road."

"How long had it been there?" Hy reached for it.

"How would I know?"

Jamieson snatched the mug before Hy could.

"I'm going to take it to Gus to see if it's the real thing."

"I'm coming," said Hy.

"Me, too," said Ian.

"Not dressed like that, you aren't," Jamieson threw him a look as she headed out the door.

Gus was not the least surprised when she saw Abel's mug. If anything, Hy and Jamieson were the ones surprised, at her composure as she identified it.

"I told you he wasn't dead. I'll agree, mebbe, he's livin' in the past. That could be why he's turned up at his gramma's."

"His gramma's? Ian's place?"

Gus nodded.

"He pretty near grew up there, as a boy. His mam lived with her mam; their men worked the water and the land. That was the way people lived then. Old folks, young families, all together."

"So Abel could have been going home, back to his childhood?"

Gus nodded and rocked back and forth, a wordless yes.

"What would make him go? What would make him leave?"

"The fog," said Gus.

Hy looked out the window. A new wave of smoke was rolling into the village. "That fog?"

"No. In his head." Gus pointed at her own.

"Gus," Hy hesitated. "Do you think Abel could have Alzheimer's?"

Gus looked up sharply, fear in her eyes. She didn't have to say a thing, but she did.

"Old timer's? I 'spec' he has it. I 'spec' for a long time."

And Gus herself? Did she have it? Hy wondered. It annoyed her when people said Gus was "sharp as a tack." Condescending, she thought. Implying there might be something lacking. Was there? Was Gus changing? Aging? She wouldn't go there now. Not even in her thinking. Focus on Abel. Abel, whom she didn't know, could not remember ever having met. Maybe it was she, Hy, who had Alzheimer's, she thought with an inward smile.

"Still 'n' all, he could of been passing on the road and dropped it."

"Do you mind if I hold onto it?" Jamieson was gripping the mug as if it might escape.

"Go ahead. Use it if you want. I got no need for it. Never did like it. Plenty of others."

"Ducky mugs?"

"Yup," said Gus.

"Where?"

"Somewheres. Just like Abel. Maybe you'll find him as soon as he knows where he is hisself."

Jamieson had never met Abel. She was more than willing to believe that he had wandered off in a fog of dementia.

***

The year that Abel courted Gus, there was smoke from Quebec, too. The lack of sun affected the potato harvest and islanders were resentful.

"This'll be smoked fish, time it's finished," she said to her sister,

as the two clambered on the roof of the house and laid the herring out flat to dry.

When they finished the job, they lay back for a moment and looked at the smoky sky. They heard the truck wagon pull into the yard before they saw him. But he had seen them.

"Hoi," he had called up. "Got a cup of tea for a hard-workin' man?"

She could hardly refuse him. Not especially when he hauled a sack of potatoes off his wagon. There were usually more potatoes than a person wanted this time of year, but they'd had a poor harvest, so they'd sold as many as they could and kept back fewer than they usually did. Not enough to last the winter. Their mother would be grateful.

"For your mam." He tossed the sack over his shoulder and waited for the girls to climb down, first from one side of the tall roof, onto a gable, from the gable onto the porch roof, and down the ladder. He held onto it with one hand, the other hand holding the potatoes.

They invited him into the kitchen, in the smaller, older part of the house. The two sides had been built at different times, and there was no way to get from the new bit to the old without going outside. Christmas dinner was a parade of people carrying hot dishes of food out into the snow from the kitchen and back inside to the proper dining room. That was one reason the room was almost never used. Most meals were served in the warm, homey kitchen, with its big pine table and wood range.

Getting inside didn't do him much good. Her mother wasn't there, nor her father. So he had his cup of tea and left, no wiser, and no closer to making her his bride.

His disappointment at the failure of his plan – to convince her through her mother – left him wanting a drink stronger than tea. He found it back behind the barn where a couple of her older brothers were ending a hard day with a hard drink. They passed the bottle around and soon were the best of pals. He confided in the two his desire to marry their sister, and how he'd hoped to convince her through her mother.

"Oh, no, that'll never work," said one.
"That'd be the worst thing you could do," said the other.

***

Abel's fishing shack on the Montgomery Shore. No one had thought of it, because it wasn't handy to The Shores and Abel hadn't used it in years. It was beyond repair, sliding crookedly down a secondary dune off Montgomery Shore. Not Lucy Maud's family. Other ones – or so said Bill Montgomery, who owned most of it and was the only person on Red Island by name of Montgomery who didn't lay claim to kinship with the famous writer. He was mistaken. Of course he was related. If not by blood, by a convoluted multi-branched tree of marriages. He was like an Irishman refusing to wear green on St Patrick's Day. Or King Cnut, trying to get the waves to roll back. A Montgomery on Red Island had to be one of those Montgomerys, especially as he owned this patch of land deeded in the family name. Montgomery land.

Through a convoluted succession of trades, purchases, and card debts paid off, a small parcel of Montgomery Shore had come into Abel's possession. He had planned to fish out of there – the pond and access to it had been dredged at one time, with the hopes of opening up a harbour. There was a fishing shack that belonged to him, now sliding down the sand. The trees, tilted by the wind, rising on a slope from the shore, appeared to be bending forward to hold the land in place. He'd built the fishing shack and an outhouse on a secondary dune.

That never would have been allowed now, although it still did happen. Tourists built summer homes on them all the time, and nobody, it seemed, was prepared to blow the whistle. There was too much money to be made in waterfront real estate. The closer to the sand and water, the better, preferably with a sunset over a cape.

Abel's grand plans came to nothing. True, it was inconvenient to fish out of The Shores, dragging boats in and out of the water by horse, but Montgomery Shore was too far away. He used it more as a retreat than anything else, disappearing there on the eve of Setting Day and downing a bottle of moonshine with his fishermen friends. They claimed it was a Masons meeting.

When the storm surge came and ruptured the causeway, tossing boats and cars around like Dinky toys, that began the erosion that was causing Abel's buildings to slip into Cousins' Pond.

The outhouse, a two-seater, was almost as big as the shack itself. The two buildings were picturesque in their decay, with morning glory and cucumber vine encircling them, appearing to hold them together as they crumbled into ruin. The doors of both buildings had been cleared of vines. Someone had been there. Recently.

Looking at the shack and the outhouse, Jamieson felt a chill run up her spine. That would be the place. That would be where he was. There could be no doubt about it.

Hy was thinking exactly the same thing.

So was Ian. Properly dressed, though unshaven, he'd caught up with Hy and Jamieson.

Would they find Abel, undignified, in the outhouse? Sprawled on the tilted floor of the shack?

They would find him, they knew. It seemed so certain.

Their feet dragged, their spirits low, as they trudged toward what they were sure was Abel's last resting place.

Here on the shore.

Where it should be, after all.

Chapter 12

Gus nursed a small hope that Jamieson would find Abel at the fishing shack. She'd felt her heart leap at the thought of it. Perhaps it wouldn't be long before they were reunited. She put in a load of laundry, full of his socks and shirts. They were clean, but he would have worn them if he'd been here. She'd have been doing the laundry, just the same. They'd be ready when he got back.

***

Her mother didn't want Gus to get married. She wanted her to be a teacher like she had been. It was a job she had loved. She'd had a sense of independence, of earning her own way in the world, and that's what she wanted for Gus, her eldest. She didn't accept that Gus had no interest, that she wanted to be a wife and mother, that she didn't think she was smart enough to be a schoolteacher. Her copybook had won first prize at the annual fall exhibition, but only because her penmanship was so neat.

Abel was a catch, and he knew it. Gus, winsome as she was, wouldn't do better, and she knew it. Then why had she refused him? And why could he not talk to her mother? He was sure he could get her to agree. He had a way with women, especially older women. So, in spite of her brothers' advice, Abel decided he would speak to her. He knew exactly when he would find her home, when she wouldn't be in the fields or milking in the barn.

Monday, "warsh" day, she'd be home. It was a day with as regular a function as Sunday, church day. There wasn't a woman on Red Island who wouldn't be hanging out her wash on Monday. This particular Monday was a day when the wind blew so hard that the sheets shot out parallel to the ground, dried and ready to be taken down almost as soon as they'd gone up.

"Good morning, missus." Abel doffed his hat and had hardly finished forming his ingratiating smile when the sheet she was hanging swung around and enveloped him.

He felt at a distinct disadvantage, struggling to extricate himself from the wet cotton shroud. He finally managed, without any help from her. She knew why he had come.

"No," she said, before he could get a word in.

"No?" he repeated, dumbly.

"No." End-of-conversation tone. A tone her daughter Gus inherited and would use many times in her long life, to good effect.

"No," said Abel, his shoulders slumping.

That was the end of it. The conversation. Neither could have said much more, without raising their voices above the flapping of the laundry.

No.

Abel turned and left, almost ready to accept the answer. He was in need of a wife, and his mind turned to the charms of other women he knew. But he kept coming back to Gus. She was the only woman he knew with the practical good sense he wanted in a wife; with the household skills that were disappearing in their generation; with the good child-bearing hips and nature that would make her an excellent mother and wife.

Perhaps he should speak to her father.

Gus's father knew his daughter. When Abel went to speak to him, he could see a good match. He advised the couple to elope.

They did. Abel arranged everything, but it wasn't until they were standing in the parlour of a minister Up West that Gus had her chance to say "yes."

Gus's mother never spoke to her again.

Her mother-in-law more than made up for it.

She never stopped talking.

***

The bicycle wheels slipped on the thick morning dew coating the road. The old man hidden under the Tilley hat lost control, and for the second time that morning went sliding into the ditch. He jumped up and tried to retrieve the bicycle, which had one wheel still spinning around. He stopped it and hauled the bicycle up out of the ditch.

And he forgot. Forgot what he was doing. Where he was going. He didn't even recognize the piece of road that he was on, the Island Way that he'd known all his life. The spruce trees lining the asphalt on either side loomed over him, threatening. He felt a sharp jolt of panic in his gut, spreading to his chest. He felt dizzy. His ears rang with the high pitch of tinnitus that had nagged him for forty years. Felt like he was somewhere he'd never been before. He hauled the bicycle out of the ditch, raising it high to skirt the tall grass.

Ears still ringing, one of them deaf to everything but the tinnitus, he was unaware of the car that pulled up behind him. Its driver had been trolling the Island Way in the smoky dawn.

As Seamus came closer, the old man disappeared, down into the ditch, and back up again. Seamus caught onto the rhythm of the hat the man was wearing. Up and down it bobbed, in and out of the ditch. It was semi-concealment. He may have wanted to catch a ride, but he didn't want to be seen.

It was when the man, with his back to Seamus, heaved the bicycle up in the air and tossed it down into the ditch, that he realized who it might be.

Abel Mack. The man he was looking for. In that instant of physical movement, he had struck the same pose, topped by the same Tilley hat as in the photograph in the book. Seamus sped up as the hat bobbed along in front of him at the side of the road, luring him as if he were a donkey chasing a carrot on a stick. Every time the hat bobbed out of sight and into the ditch, Seamus felt a grip of panic that it might not reappear.

Finally, he pulled up beside the cyclist.

"Going my way? Want a lift?"

The man stopped, tilted his head down, so the hat covered his face. He grunted.

He yanked the passenger door open and climbed in, so Seamus assumed the grunt meant yes. The man sat without saying anything more, nor making any move. It was clearly his intention not to buckle his seat belt. That was the bane of law enforcement in places like The Shores. Jamieson, for one, could never convince the older folks to buckle up. They "weren't used to it," a phrase they often employed as an excuse not to step into the modern world. Seat belts made them feel unsafe. They wanted to be thrown clear of the car going up in a ball of smoke.

The two spoke not at all, Seamus wondering what he was going to do with this old fellow now that he had him.

Was he a kidnapper?

Not intentionally. Certainly not intentionally. He just wanted the man to tell him where the fish was. The guy had dropped right into his lap.

What to do with him?

Take him to Winterside, for starters. Mr. Tilley Hat did not seem in the mood to chat.

Perhaps later in the day.

And perhaps tomorrow Seamus would have another talk with Ferguson, now that he held the high card.

The Ace of Spades.

Abel Mack. The man who'd almost caught the big one.

***

Inside, it was like a funhouse. A room that sloped down, low on one end, high on the other, the walls crooked, window bulging in, door off one hinge.

Jamieson felt dizzy, the way a funhouse with a sloping floor made a person feel. No Abel. Was that a good sign – or a bad one?

Abel's Mason's apron was hanging from a hook on the door.

There was the photo of Abel, trying to reel in that big fish. It was a yellowed black-and-white shot, thumbtacked to the wall. Three corners were bent up, the fourth was cracked off. There was a series of tiny holes in the white borders, as if a woodworm had chewed at it, where it had been tacked, undone, and tacked again to the wall.

There was a…ducky cup. Jamieson seized on it, but as she did, saw another. Two ducky mugs. That made three in all, with the one in her car.

The cup in her hands had been used. Recently. There was a slick of coffee in the bottom, and still some warmth to the cup. She handed it to Hy. There was a spent match on the small counter, the smell of burnt propane on the air.

"He's been here." Hy looked triumphant.

"Somebody has." Jamieson burst her bubble.

"Who else could it be?"

"Some vagrant."

"There are no vagrants in The Shores."

Hy frowned and held the mug up to Jamieson. Jamieson was regretting she and Hy had handled it. Should have dusted it for fingerprints. But there hadn't been a crime committed. Had there? Maybe she should get Finn to take a look. Finding Abel's fingermarks wouldn't prove that he'd been there recently, though someone had.

Hy nudged her with the mug.

"Better put your duckies in a row." She grinned.

The other mug had never been used. It was covered in dust.

Jamieson found a box and put them in it.

"To avoid confusion," she said to Hy and Ian, as if she must explain herself. "The next time I see a ducky cup, I want to see it attached to Abel."

There was still the outhouse. Please, no. Let him not be there.

With a sinking feeling that he was, Jamieson crawled up the crooked floor to the outside door and clambered out, Ian carrying the box for her, and Hy following behind.

They stood for a moment, the three of them, staring down at the outhouse.

***

The suite was in an apartment building opposite the Department of Fisheries building. An ancient elevator clunked its way down to the lobby at the press of a button, floor by floor, stopping and opening at each one no matter the button you pressed, agonizing in its slow progress.

When it arrived, the doors creaked open and Seamus had to push his companion into the elevator. He didn't know that Mr. Tilley Hat had never been in one.

The man tensed as the doors scraped closed and grabbed onto his hat as the elevator began to ascend. He was out the door in a flash when they reached their floor.

Inside the apartment, he went straight to the bed, sat on it and tested the mattress with a few bounces. He stood up and played with the blinds, opening and closing, opening and closing, until Seamus stopped him. It wouldn't do to draw attention from the outside. All of Winterside knew this was a government suite. With the curiosity born and bred in Red Islanders, people tended to keep an eye on the place, whether it was occupied or not, speculating about who was staying in luxury on their tax dollars.

Seamus now thought he'd made a critical error in bringing the Hat Man here.

It might have been better to take him to his own home. No. There was no room on his couch for a visitor, no spare room, no space anywhere. Couch, tables, chairs, and even his bed were covered with marine artifacts, including dozens of buoys scoured off island shores in springtime.

Books about Newfoundland and the cod fishery were in messy stacks on the floor, everywhere there was a space to be found. There were paths barely wide enough for Seamus to walk through, which led to the bathroom, and kitchen, and the mattress that was his bedroom.

No. Much better to have brought him here.

Seamus showed his guest the fridge and cupboards, opened them, still full of staples from the last visitor five days ago. Mr. Tilley Hat took a great interest in the contents and was soon snacking on crackers and cheese, washed down with orange juice straight out of the container.

Seamus had to at least show his face at work.

"Have to leave for a few hours. See you later." Seamus left without another word being spoken by either. Hopefully, the old man would be chattier the next day, once he got used to his surroundings.

Seamus closed the door behind him, and the sound of the lock engaging triggered the question again:

Am I a kidnapper?

***

Jamieson frowned as she yanked at the door to the outhouse. The putrid smell wafted on the smoky air. Even after all this time, tilted off its base, its connection to its former use was pungent, redolent of decay. Not the decay of a corpse. And not old decay. New rot.

The outhouse had been used. Hy leaned over Jamieson's shoulder and held her nose.

"Fresh." She said. "Can you get the DNA off that?"

Jamieson supposed she should examine it more closely, but she couldn't bear the smell. She shut the door, and the movement caused the little building to shift. It wouldn't be long before it fell right over – or the morning glories ensnared it and pulled it down with them to the pond. Looking back as she returned to the shack, Jamieson could have sworn that the morning glory had resumed its job, its tendrils growing as she stood there wondering, what next?

She returned to the police house, discouraged. There was a voice mail from detachment offering to send reinforcements for the search. Offering reluctantly. No one wanted to go out to The Shores, the back of beyond, now made worse than ever by the grey mist of smoke from away dusting the village and the lungs of its inhabitants.

She returned the call to her superior officer with the ridiculous name. Superintendent Constable. People believed that, though inept, he had been promoted because of his name, because Constable Constable sounded even worse, as if the Mounties were a group of stutterers.

"I could spare a few men," he said, his tone suggesting it would be onerous.

Jamieson bristled. They could use some help, but The Shores belonged to her. She could take care of things. Now that it was offered, she wouldn't accept any help from outside.

"That's okay," she said. "We can take care of our own."

She hung up, wondering when – and how – she had come to sound like Gus Mack.

Chapter 13

I know where they are.

That's what he'd said.

I know they're there.

With such conviction it was hard to disbelieve him.

They're hiding. Watching.

Could he really believe that? Anything the man had said? He clearly had lost a few marbles. Seamus had returned to the apartment in the afternoon and was happy to find the old man more talkative. More talkative, but not making much sense.

Looking out the window, the old man said: I can see the ocean from here.

He had a disposable camera in his windbreaker pocket. He kept taking pictures through the window. He'd show them to Seamus. There was nothing there, the camera used and useless.

Seamus had looked out the window. What he saw was the hospital, the fisheries building, and a great big parking lot, full of cars in the day, abandoned and floodlit by night.

Christ, someone might see them. The newspaper had printed the photograph of the man in the Tilley hat, under the bold, black headline: MISSING. Someone might recognize him. He had to get rid of the hat. He reached out for it but fumbled when the old man turned and slipped by him. For a moment he was out of his line of sight, as if invisible. Seamus felt his heart leap with fear, fear that the old man had disappeared, disappeared on him.

He was standing in the shadows, beyond the pool of light.

Seamus stepped out of the light. The two men stared at each other in silence.

My God, what have I done? Have I kidnapped this man – or has he come willingly?

Seamus was struck by the enormity of what he had done.

He wasn't certain that the man was suffering from dementia. If he knew that for sure, then, yes, he could be accused of kidnapping. Since he didn't know, not for sure, perhaps it was a simple collaboration, a way to get what they both wanted.

The giant cod.

He's out there, he had said. *Waiting. Watching. The cod are there. I know they're there.* He kept repeating it, like a mantra.

Could a man who saw the ocean from this inland window be trusted to know where the cod were – and what they were doing?

Seamus had to take that chance. It was his only chance. He had to know what this man knew.

If that made him a kidnapper, so be it.

If it made him a fool, it would not be the first time.

***

Hy thought Jamieson should have been more grateful for her idea about Abel's fishing shack. It hadn't panned out, but it wasn't "a wild goose chase," as Jamieson had called it. Ian had pointed out that it was early in the season for goose hunting. That had earned him withering looks from both Hy and Jamieson. Jamieson thought it was not a matter for joking. Hy thought it was a bad joke.

So her spirits lifted when, driving down into "the holler," she saw a large moving van approaching the driveway of the house next-door to Jared MacPherson's.

Plumbers, carpenters, roofers, even a welding company had been in and out of the house and the big barn for weeks. A black Mercedes SUV had been parked in the driveway, but no one had seen the new owners. That didn't stop the villagers from speculating about the new people. What they usually came up with could only be described with accuracy as alternative facts. This time, however, the villagers had forgotten all about the new neighbours because of the fuss over the missing Abel. One moving truck had come and gone, and no one had noticed. Now there was a second.

Hy pulled over to the side of the road, where she had a front-row seat.

***

He opened his eyes.

Closed them.

He had no idea where he was.

That wasn't unusual. It had been happening a lot lately.

But this place was different. He'd never been here before. He'd never been anywhere like it.

It was like a hotel. He'd never been in a hotel. Fancy furniture. Everything black and white. Leather and chrome. Everything new and shiny. Except that big old wardrobe. Not a quilt anywhere. Could use a quilt.

With eyes closed, he tried to conjure up home.

Home.

Where had it gone?

Where had he gone?

I'm gone missing, he thought, his heart sinking. It did exactly that, lowering in his chest, fogging his breath.

To lift his spirits, he thought about the circles. And the moon in line with Ethan Cooke's chimbley. He remembered that. He smiled, keeping his eyes closed, the better to picture them.

The chimbley. The circles. This man – where was the man? – would take him to them.

Or was it the other way round?

Had he come here alone? Or was someone with him? Had someone brought him here?

No, he'd come alone. Hadn't he? How? And where? Where was this?

He remembered striking out in the shadows and the smoke, rolling his bike down the road, toward that bay. That big bay. That's right. Big Bay. That's where he'd spent the night before. Or was it the one before that?

What had happened then?

He'd forgotten.

He'd had a purpose. He knew that. But he couldn't find it in the puzzle that was his mind, a jumble, no straight edges, no connecting pieces. Thoughts like threads of smoke, wisping away on the air.

He knew who he was. He didn't know what he was up to.

***

Letitia Ferguson was tiny, with straggly dark blonde hair and a grey complexion. When she finally followed her husband Brock to The Shores, to the home he was already settled in, she did not look well, and she was not. By contrast, Brock was big, handsome, with salt-and-pepper hair and flashing dark eyes.

They were standing at the open doors of the barn when Letitia's van arrived, full of them. Grey. Ginger. Black. Black and white. Long hair. Short hair. No hair. Cats. Crates of cats. Her movers unloaded the furry, squealing, hiding, trembling, hissing, yowling cargo into the barn. Letitia followed them in. Ferguson returned to nursing a beer at the kitchen table. At ten in the morning. His family was from Glasgow, Letitia would tell people, as if that explained it. In a way, it did.

He'd thrown the tab in a bucket full of them beside the sink. He scratched a mark on its side. Almost one thousand, and time for a new bucket.

Letitia counted the cages, one by one, and released those cats she knew could safely explore the massive, multi-storey cage within the barn without first being confined. The space contained everything a cat could possibly want. Climbing trees, sleeping hammocks, even a "bowling green" – a large, hard surface, contained on all sides, full of tinkling plastic, bouncing foam balls, and catnip creatures to bat around. It was enclosed in Plexiglas, so the balls couldn't get out, but had platforms to allow the cats to jump in and out. There was already an intense game going on. Gingers, who seemed always to stick together, against a variety of black, white, and tabby cats.

Seventy-nine. She finished the count. She was happiest in this small feline universe, happy that her good luck had given her the money to be able to provide for these helpless creatures.

But her heart was broken over and over. Rescue cats had much shorter lives than domestic cats, and death happened weekly, monthly, too many times a year. With infinite financial resources, Letitia did everything she could to keep an ailing cat alive, until it was obviously suffering. Then, with difficulty, she would let it go, weep, recover, and carry on.

They'd come here because of Letitia's health. Brock had said the fresh ocean air should clear out those lungs of hers. So far, it was worse, thought Letitia.

She hadn't known about the smoke. Had he?

Ferguson hated cats. He was back in the barn, a sour expression on his face. He hated everything about them. Their good looks. Their fussy ways. Their grooming habits. Their ability to look comfortable all the time, no matter what position they were in. All the things other people like about them.

He had indulged Letitia when they were first married and allowed three or four cats in the house. He stroked them when she was around, but when she wasn't looking, he'd kick them aside or let them out of the house.

Once she'd won the money, the second and third times, he'd had less say about what went on. He negotiated the move to The Shores by agreeing to a cat shelter and sealed her approval by coming up with the litter-removal system.

The number of cats they now sheltered was no record, and he wouldn't have cared if it were. He had other fish to fry. He smiled at his own pun.

His fish and he were well away from the cats at the back of the barn, where he couldn't hear Letitia's wheezing and coughing. In fact, he'd had his den soundproofed so he wouldn't have to listen to the cats, either.

The barn housed not only them, but also Ferguson's bitter resentment and a grand plan for fame and fortune, as yet unrealized. Money and a name of his own. Other than fish, his possessions at the moment consisted of bottle cap and soda can tab collections. Dismal, disappointing preoccupations that had stuck with him from the age of six. He hated the caps and tabs, too, but he still couldn't stop collecting. He'd long surpassed the record in both categories, but he didn't want to announce it publicly. It wasn't good enough. He wanted something unique.

He was about to need a lot of money, and there was no way he could think of to hide it from Letitia, but it was for something of which she would not approve. She hated the idea of keeping wild animals in captivity. He had pointed out that her cats were in captivity. She said that was different, that they were domesticated. That it was for their own good.

It was an argument he couldn't win.

But Letitia was winning fewer arguments these days. She had not the breath to sustain them. She was constantly on her inhaler. When she lifted it to her mouth, he tensed with irritation.

She noticed, and sometimes out of deference to him, when she really needed the relief the puffer provided, she didn't use it. Inevitably, this resulted in a coughing attack and Ferguson charging out of the room.

She couldn't win. The lottery, yes. Married life, no.

Ferguson spent most of his time in his den, soothed by the elegant swimming of his pricey tropical fish, thinking of better things, of luxuries he could afford if the money were his and not hers. He'd flip open his laptop and check on his favourite car, the Rolls Royce, in any and all of its manifestations. Sixty-five per cent of Rolls cars ever made were still on the road today, he mused, as he opened a link on the first one, the Rolls Royce 10, built in 1904. In those days, the company only provided the chassis; it was up to the owner to put on a body. They'd built sixteen of them, and four still survived. Now, *that* was a marvel of engineering. His talents, meantime, were going to waste. Literally.

One of the old cars had sold for five million at auction not too many years ago. Five million. It could have been his, if he had the money Letitia had.

At least he had Letitia. That was a start.

And there was the fish.

Chapter 14

It was Murdo Black who provided the first information about Abel. Murdo was Jamieson's work partner and the one who had engineered their posting in this backwater. It was self-serving in part. He'd fallen for the village's best cook, plump and pretty April Dewey. Her cheating husband, Ron, had squealed out of the village leaving behind deep tracks in the clay driveway, and six children. He was, as Gus put it, "living the life of Reilly in Winterside." She said it a lot, but if someone asked who Reilly was and how he lived, she'd hum a few phrases from an old vaudeville song:

> Is that Mister Reilly, can anyone tell?
> Is that Mister Reilly that owns the hotel?
> Well, if that's Mister Reilly they speak of so highly,
> Upon me soul, Reilly, you're doing quite well.

Murdo had fallen for April's family, too – a half-dozen tributes to über-domesticity that had swelled his heart.

Now his belly was swelling, as he gobbled April's tasty offerings. He was out of shape, and Jamieson couldn't remember the last time he'd done a lick of police work. He'd lost the temperament for it.

Murdo in love was like a toddler, fascinated and delighted by everything around him. Waking up with April in the morning was a new thrill each day. Sinking into the cozy bed with her beside him and the warm duvet wrapped around them was sheer delight at night. He gloried in the scent of sausages, pancakes, and eggs cooking on April's old wood range in the morning. The whole world was a constant distraction to him, as if it came new every day. Living in such thrall to the joys of the world made him useless for most things. So for him to come up with a piece of evidence in Abel's disappearance was remarkable.

Jamieson had stopped by April's in the faint hope that she could dig up some new clue. She had abandoned any possibility that Abel might be alive, but they must track down his body. April might have been the last one to see him; the only one in the village, apart from Gus, who ever had any idea when he was around. He would follow the scents wafting from her kitchen and beg for scraps at her back door, with Toby the beach dog and Newt, the small terrier mutt who lived nowhere but ate at every house in the village. The dogs were his cover. April actually never saw him. A shadow maybe, that was all.

"I really can't say…" April responded to Jamieson's query if she knew where Abel might be.

Murdo was roused from his reverie watching dark clouds scudding across the sky, mingling with the tendrils of smoke still fingering The Shores from the north. He looked surprised, eyes open wide.

"Abel's missing? Since when?"

"Tuesday."

"Tuesday. Tuesday." He rolled it over in his mind. "Now when was that?" He brushed some cake crumbs off his shirt. "I seen him that day."

Jamieson's expression, clouded at the state Murdo was in, brightened. Then fell again at Murdo's next words.

"Or maybe it was Wednesday…"

Unlikely, she thought. Gus had reported Abel missing on Tuesday. The search had begun. They'd have found him if he'd been wandering around the village. It really didn't matter what day Murdo thought it was. It mattered what he'd seen.

"Okay… Tuesday… Wednesday…no matter. Where was he?"

"On a bicycle, heading for the causeway, round about six in the morning."

The road was clearly visible from April's bedroom window.

"Why didn't you say?" Jamieson's cheeks flushed red with anger.

Murdo looked confused.

"At the time. Why didn't you say so at the time?"

"I didn't know then, did I? That he was missing, I mean. This is the first I heard of it."

"You knew about it. You searched with the kids." April looked confused.

Murdo looked confused, too. He thought they'd been playing a game.

Jamieson thought Murdo was far gone.

***

Seamus pulled up, as directed, at the second white house on his right in "the holler." Ferguson had used the local word with disdain.

He was outside to greet Seamus and led him back to his den behind the cathouse. Seamus tripped over his feet as he stared at the contraption that housed the cats – and at the many cats. This guy was interested in fish?

Apparently so. Seamus stared at the massive wall aquarium, and the fish that came right up and nosed the glass when he entered the room. As he sat down opposite Ferguson, he spied the wood sculpture of the giant American codfish.

Ferguson tossed his copy of *Time Was* across the desk. He propped it open at the page with the picture of Abel and the fish. "You've seen this."

"Of course," said Seamus. *No. Not this. Not the book.* He wanted to snatch it.

Ferguson gave it a small shove, tempting Seamus with it.

"Do you know this guy?"

Seamus grabbed the book. His eyes feasted on the photo cutline, only part of which he'd ever seen. *Abel Mack.* He knew that now, but he had a number of other names for him. Mr. Tilley Hat. Sometimes just The Hat Man or The Old Man.

"Yes and no."

"What's that supposed to mean?"

"Well, I know who he is, but I've never met him." Seamus wasn't prepared to show his cards yet. Not until he knew there was a deal to be made.

"He's alive?"

"Yes, but –"

"But?"

Might as well stick to the story all over the village.

"He's missing."

Not anymore, thought Seamus, but that was his secret, for now.

Ferguson leaned forward and thrust a finger at the book.

"I want that fish."

"Who knows where it is…or might be? That man's the only one who could know." Seamus smiled, secure in the knowledge that he had the best shot of finding that fish.

He had the fisherman. He would tell Ferguson when – if – he needed him.

"There's no reason we can't both have this fish, if it exists." Ferguson leaned forward, a glint in his eyes. "I want to set a record with it. And you?"

"I want to restore the fishery. In Newfoundland. Not here."

"So you want to breed it?"

Seamus hadn't thought it all through. Did he want to breed it? Was he looking for a mating pair? When he thought this way, he realized how much he didn't know. How little time he had to play fast and loose with the fisheries department's resources. How much he might need to join forces with this guy and his money. Then find someone with the know-how. It might not be in the right order, but it was the only direction he could go in. He did know that the first thing was to find the fish.

He was beginning to see items on the Internet that led him to believe that there were other people, like him, who had their eyes on the same prize. He had seen sites, too, that dismissed them as "kooks," these adherents to the growing worldwide movement of "Gigantisms," as it was being called. It had its roots in the giant vegetables grown in Findhorn, Scotland, in the 1960s. One site claimed to have found water circles containing giant cod off the Isle of Skye. The site, ignoring copyright, used the slogan "Feed the World," as its rallying cry, along with the song of the same name. Seamus wanted to be in the forefront of the movement – or would be, if he could get ample backing.

"We'll keep each other informed." Ferguson stood up to usher Seamus out. At the door, they shook hands, each thinking he would get the better of the deal.

***

Seamus was no sooner out his door than Ferguson left the house, headed in the opposite direction.

He knew precisely which house to go to, to try to find out what he wanted. He knew that in a Maritime village the person who knew everything would live in the house with the best view of the place.

Ferguson knocked on the door and stirred Gus from a light snooze in her recliner, her knitting needles, hands, and yarn in position to take the next stitch.

Who would be knocking at the door? It must be a stranger.

She dropped her knitting on the floor, straightened her apron, and shuffled to the door.

By the time she got there, Ferguson's nose was pressed up against the screen, trying to see if anyone was coming to answer.

When she opened it, he stuck a hand out to shake hers, and all she could do was rub her hands up and down the sides of her apron. She wasn't used to shaking hands.

"I'm Brock Ferguson."

She nodded. "The new fella. The cat place up the road. Come in."

"Oh, I don't want to bother you. I just want to talk to Abel Mack."

"Me and all," she said. Did this person know anything about Abel going missing?

She pointed to a jacket hanging from a hook.

"He should be wearing that, day like today."

"Does he live here?" Ferguson couldn't believe his luck.

"Usually he does."

"But not now?"

"I never know where Abel is." Gus was backing off being honest with this man. What if he had something to do with Abel's disappearance? What if he wanted to know that she was alone in the house, with no Abel to protect her?

"Hasn't been around a lot lately. Reckon you should check at Wally Fraser's."

After finding out from Gus where Wally Fraser lived, Ferguson went and knocked on that door. Gladys answered, face like a bulldog.

"I'm looking for Abel Mack," he said.

"You won't find him here." She slammed the door on him.

It was the same everywhere – no one was willing to tell a complete stranger where Abel was or wasn't. They didn't know, did they? So why should they say anything?

***

Murdo went with Jamieson along the Island Way and pointed to the precise spot he'd seen Abel. Jamieson got out of the cruiser, and kicked around the side of the road, but it seemed a trivial pursuit. She jumped back in and drove to the causeway, where they got out.

The ferry had just landed, with a full load of eight cars. One of them was Ian's. Ian had bought yet another iMac. He got a new one every two years. Even the disappearance of Abel couldn't prevent him from going into town when it was shipped. Hy was with him. She wouldn't have minded using Abel as an excuse to avoid going to the dentist, but she'd lost a filling that had to be replaced.

"Just the person," Ian said. On spying Jamieson, he had stopped his car next to the cruiser. "How'd you like my old iMac?"

She would love it. Of course she would.

"Can't afford it," she said.

"Not selling," said Ian. "I'd be happy to give it to you."

Ian always gave away his old computers. It was a personal mission to get his friends up to speed with the best equipment. Well, not the absolute best. That was whatever he had most recently acquired. He gave away the next best thing.

A few years back, he'd even given an iMac to Gus. He'd set it up in her kitchen while she was napping, with a screen saver of swimming fish. When she woke and saw "that contraption" she first thought that she'd had a stroke, and then that someone had installed an aquarium.

Gus used the computer to Skype her daughter Dot when Dot was in Africa or Antarctica or other remote places of the world. It was on a computer screen that she first saw her granddaughter, Dottie, just hours old and half the world away. It was a strange and beautiful sight, Hy often thought, to see Gus, born in the opening years of the twentieth century, putting a finger to the onscreen image of the infant born in the opening years of the twenty-first. A communication across time and space.

Gus's computer had been relegated to the back room when Dot had come home for the year. The back room was a former porch that housed Gus's quilts and quilt patches. So now it was also a computer room. Another strange and beautiful juxtaposition, the piles of quilt blocks and patches illuminated by the cool glow of a computer screen. Two preoccupations, separated by a century or more.

The computer was for Dot – and Abel. Gus didn't use it

anymore, but Abel was all over it. Like everything he did, largely unseen; he spent hours on it at night. Dot, as her father began to remember what hadn't happened and forget what had, would follow the Internet trail of where he'd been, interested in what his interests were. She couldn't make sense of it at first, but it soon became clear.

She said nothing to anyone. They'd think he was crazy.

Chapter 15

Seamus had a smile on his face.

The old man was going to take him to the fish.

In return, Seamus had promised everything Abel would need to catch the cod himself – including, of all things, a dory. Dories had a history as the workhorse of the east-coast fishery, the tiny twenty-eight-foot dory with high sides and a flat bottom, used in all weathers to transport boatloads of cod, hundreds of pounds at a time, to be sliced, gutted, and salted on the mother ship. When the mother ship was full, the dories were stacked up, one inside another, for space-saving transport to and from the harbour. People thought that dories could be tippy, because of their flat bottoms, but they weren't. They gave a bumpy ride over the waves but in high seas were remarkably stable.

At first, they were rowed by oar, and then powered by one-cylinder engines, never more.

There was a dory revival going on – among people with more money than sense, rich people who spent their summers on the east coast of the United States and Canada. Old fishermen could never have afforded the new dories with their custom features, beautiful woodwork, and bright colours. Except for some catches from sport fishing, there was rarely an actual fish on their shiny flat-bottom decks.

No, the old man would not be getting a dory – new or old. You couldn't put even one of them aboard a Red Island fisheries vessel. But Seamus had promised he would provide one – after The Hat Man showed him where the fish were.

Kidnapping and lying.

He'd let him have an inflatable if he insisted on going after a fish himself. Seamus was hoping the old man would be happy if they caught one on the fisheries vessel. He could stop feeling guilty then. And maybe let him go.

Or maybe not.

***

Jamieson was tempted by the thought of an iMac, but right now it was finding the bicycle that was on her mind.

"We'll talk about it." She hesitated. "We're on Abel's trail," she added, uncharacteristically offering up information.

"I thought the trail had gone cold." Ian leaned farther out his window, his interest piqued.

"Maybe not," said Jamieson. She indicated that he should park at the side of Nathan Mack's coffee stand.

"What are we looking for?" Hy jumped out of Ian's car. It wasn't often that Jamieson invited her into an investigation. She spent more time discouraging Hy from sticking her nose into police business, but four people could get more accomplished than two.

"Either Abel…or his bicycle." Jamieson was betting bicycle. She expected he had cycled here and got on the ferry, but the ferryman denied seeing him. So where had he gone? Where was he headed?

They spent about a half-hour searching through the brush on either side of the ferry launch. Then they crossed the causeway and tried the other side.

No luck. Not surprising. The darkness from Quebec had created poor visibility. They were about to give up when the sun peeked out, shimmering on the sooty clouds, and Hy caught a glint of silver in the tall grass. She didn't say anything to the others, who had their backs turned to her.

She dove into the brush and triumphantly tugged it out.

"Got it!" she yelled, wheeling it out onto the asphalt.

"Sure that's his?" Ian looked skeptical. "It's a girl's."

Hy shrugged at Jamieson. "Ask Gus. She'll know."

***

"I couldn't rightly say." Gus scratched her head. "All I know is he kept it there in the building. I got so I didn't notice if it was there or not."

"Let's see if it's there," said Jamieson.

"Or not," Hy chimed in, unhelpfully.

"There should be two over there." Gus pointed to the far end of the building. "Right there." She was pointing straight at an empty corner.

"Nothing there," said Hy.

"Well, I'll be." Gus turned to Jamieson. "They're both gone."

"So then we don't know if the one we found is his?"

"I reckon not."

It was, perhaps, a clue to where Abel had gone. Across the causeway. He'd spent some time, an overnight maybe, at his shack on Montgomery Shore. Jamieson still had no clue where he was now.

Why had he headed for the causeway? Where had he gone from there, without the bike? Was it another wild goose chase? A hunter in his youth, Abel knew all about that. But he'd always been the hunter, not the hunted.

***

Be my guest.

The man had said: *Be my guest.*

But was he a guest? Or was he a prisoner?

He didn't know where he was, or how he'd got there. He didn't find that particularly unusual. It seemed to be happening to him more and more. Nothing was clear, defined. Everything happened in a haze he couldn't see through or think through. So, here he was, and he didn't know why.

It was a comfortable enough place. He sat on the bed. It was much better than his bed at home. There was a reason for that. He and the missus had lain on that mattress for fifty years. She'd always been heavier than he, so it sloped in one direction, no matter how many times it had been turned or flipped. He was always rolling into her. Perhaps that's why they'd had so many kids.

The apartment was a suite acquired forty years before by the federal government as a place to house visiting personnel working on medium-term projects on Red Island. Back then, you couldn't hope to find a place to stay on the island from the start until the end of summer. Everything was booked, down to the last farmhouse, where farmers and their wives would vacate their summer bedroom, the living room sofa bed, and sleep in the kitchen, to give desperate tourists a place for the night. Abel and Gus had done it many times.

Now was different. Too many rooms. Too many resorts and high-end accommodations. The fear was no longer having enough beds, but having too many.

It all made this place look shabby, not that he cared. It was comfortable enough. He plunked himself down in an armchair, swung his boots up onto the glass table, and wondered again – what was he doing here?

Did it have something to do with the fish? Had he brought that up himself? Or had the other guy? Where was he, that man? Who was he? What did he want? He kept asking himself the same questions, kept getting no answers.

He pulled the ducky cup out of his pink knapsack. He wondered again where the knapsack came from, but it was familiar. At least he had the mug, something solid to grasp, to hold onto, a reminder of home, even if home was blurry in his mind at the moment. What had happened to his mind?

He knew what would clear it out. A cup of coffee. There was plenty of that. He wasn't used to making it himself, but he thought he knew how. He poured coffee into the well on top of the machine and water into the jug. He put the jug on the hot plate, turned the machine on and turned his attention to the food. There was lots of it, on the table and in the mini-fridge, including his favourite cinnamon rolls, the ones made with lots of cinnamon. He ate two of them before he realized he couldn't smell the coffee. He looked over at the machine. The jug sat on the plate, still plain water. He got up, but couldn't figure it out, so he put a couple of tablespoons of coffee in his mug and poured hot water into it out of the tap. He sat down, smug. He wasn't supposed to have coffee this late at night, after 6:00 p.m. Both his wife and his doctor said so. They weren't here now. Only he was. And he was here, because – he didn't know. He went back to the questions. Was he a guest? Or a prisoner?

He took a swig of the coffee. Spat it across the room; dots of brown splattered on the cream broadloom.

***

The posters of Abel were becoming tattered and torn, wet from the heavy dew that fell in late August, the ink from the jet printer streaking, making it appear as if the search was long over and had failed. New posters went up, but not for the missing Abel. They were offering work at the cat shelter.

Billy Pride yanked one down and went to fetch his girlfriend Madeline. Madeline was Moira's browbeaten younger sister. She and Billy were trying to save to get married, and to get Madeline out from under Moira's thumb. Billy was glad Moira wasn't home and couldn't make an objection.

The two set off for the cattery on Billy's lawn tractor, his mode of transportation. They pulled down all the cattery posters along the Island Way.

They were shoo-ins. Letitia liked them right away for their youth and energy, two attributes she did not possess. She looked up at Billy, tall, strong, impossibly handsome. She looked down at Madeline, tiny but cheerful, with an aura of willingness.

"I'll show you around, and you decide if you can do the job. It's not really that hard, but I don't have the strength to do anything." She took them into the barn.

The cat shelter occupied almost the full size of the barn, three storeys high, surrounded by pet screening and built on top of an enclosed space.

"Why's it so high up from the ground?" Madeline and Billy climbed the stairs after Letitia, who was out of breath by the time they reached the top.

"That's to accommodate the litter-cleaning system." Letitia pointed at what appeared to be a series of sandboxes lined down the middle of the shelter. Several cats were scraping around inside them. Others were doing their business outside, in corners and on sleeping pads.

Madeline pointed at the sandboxes. "What are those?"

"Automatic composting cat toilets."

"They look clean for cat boxes. For this many cats." Billy observed.

"My husband, Brock, is an engineering wizard. He designed them and we had them built."

"They slide out every half hour." Ferguson had come up behind them, beaming at his own cleverness. "They sift the clumping wheat litter, undergo a cleaning and refresher, and slide back fresh. The waste drops under the floor and then slides into a chute that delivers it to a container where, over time, it breaks down into compost. Usable compost."

"Wow." Billy's eyes were full of admiration.

"The only thing humans have to touch is the bags of wheat litter to fill the chutes." Ferguson pointed to dozens of large bags on the upper storey of the barn, around a balcony. "There's a dumbwaiter to get the bags up there. The removal is like pulling out a drawer, after it's become clean, usable compost. The most expensive compost in the world." Bitterness edged his tone of self-satisfaction.

"It's not perfect." Letitia jumped at the grinding sound coming from the mechanism as it prepared to begin its half-hourly job. Cats went flying in every direction.

"They hate the sound." There was despair in her voice. "I've asked Brock if we can do something about that."

"They'll get used to it," he frowned. "You can't have every-thing." He turned and stomped down the stairs.

"I would have preferred something less high-tech," Letitia whispered, watching to see that Ferguson was out of range. "Some of the cats want nothing to do with it, and I've had to put out regular trays of litter for them. Then there are those who are so upset by it, they won't use any litter at all. I guess it's a problem in all shelters, though. So you'd have to deal with that. I hope you're not squeamish."

They visited the cats, most of whom disappeared at the arrival of the strangers. Letitia took Billy and Madeline into the house and kitchen and outlined their duties and hours. Letitia was generous because she wanted her helpers to have every reason to be good to her cats. Billy and Madeline did the math on how soon this new source of money would allow them to get married, and smiled.

"I'm hoping to make this a chain. I've certainly got the money to establish a large, far-reaching charitable organization. I'm thinking of a name for it. It will have an endowment of course. A sizable endowment." She reached into the fridge and pulled out a couple of cans of soda, offering them to Billy and Madeline.

"You never said anything about this to me," Ferguson's booming voice preceded him into the room. The word "endow-ment" had brought him in.

"It came to me recently, dear. I haven't thought it all out."

"Obviously not. What about your health?"

"I'm hoping that will improve here."

"In spite of the smoke?"

"When the smoke goes."

Madeline frowned at this exchange. She wasn't the brightest of lights, but she knew when someone was undermining someone else. Her sister Moira had been doing it to her all her life. She couldn't imagine Billy being mean to her like that, and she'd never dream of being that way to him.

Billy popped his soda and reached over to toss the tab in the garbage he assumed was under the sink. Ferguson grabbed it out of his hand and growled:

"We don't throw those out here." He indicated the bucket.

"And we keep track." He indicated the felt marker tied to the bucket handle.

Billy shrugged, tossed the tab in the bucket, and left it to Ferguson to strike a mark on the bucket.

Billy was a big boy with a prodigious appetite and thirst. He emptied the can in one huge gulp.

Then he squeezed it.

"Hope you don't save these, too."

Ferguson stalked out of the room.

"Only for the recycling," Letitia said, taking the can from him with a kind expression.

Chapter 16

As the old man squeezed into the helicopter, the wind brushed off his Tilley hat. His hand went flying to the top of his head, and panic etched across his face as he turned and watched the hat bounce across the tarmac. He tried to get out, but Seamus pushed him in and shoved a sou'wester onto his head, wondering if he should go chasing after the Tilley hat to prevent it from being found, from being recognized, from becoming bait for law enforcement. He was too fat and lazy to do it. Besides, what distinguishes one Tilley from another? The fact that this one looked like it had been eaten by an elephant? The hat might be found, but the link to the old man might not necessarily be made. He watched with satisfaction as the hat nestled at the base of a stand of spruce, their branches, raised by the wind, now descending and almost entirely covering the hat.

But not entirely.

Not so much that a pair of sharp eyes couldn't ferret it out. And did. She scooped up the hat as she watched the helicopter fly out of sight.

Moments too late. Moments.

Where were they going?

The circles. They'd be going to the circles.

***

Billy and Madeline turned out to be perfect caretakers of the cats. If they had any faults, it was that they were too fond of them. Madeline would have taken them all home with her, but she couldn't adopt even one. Moira complained when Madeline came home, that she smelled of those "filthy creatures." Moira swore that her house still smelled of cat years after a tourist had brought two with him.

"A wonder that woman up there can take a breath. You can hear her coughing out on the road. She'll be allergic to the cats, that's what. I've seen it plenty of times. I know what I'm talking about. You don't need a doctor to tell you that."

Madeline shrank away from Moira's sour comments, kept her head low, and escaped to her bedroom.

"At least she'll be earning her keep," Moira had said to her husband Fred. She was planning to take Madeline's pay and give her a small amount back each week as pocket money.

The truth was that Madeline's "keep" was covered, as was Moira's, by the money their father had saved and invested over the years, a man careful and clever with his cash. He'd been a garbage man, or "sanitation expert," as Moira preferred to say. Actually, in his last years he'd been demoted to what the villagers called a "garbage picker." He was one of the guys who rode around in the Waste Watcher van, opening people's big black bins to check that they were sticking to the rules and not throwing out recyclables as waste. He'd leave a "ticket," indicating where they'd gone wrong, and, if not, a colourful card that cried out, "Good Job!" Moira had a basket full of the good tickets on display in her mudroom. She considered her father had played a vital role in protecting the island environment, and she was proud he'd had to know how to read to do it. He was also good at math and totting up the dollars in his bank account so his daughters would never go wanting. They had a joint interest in the house and the bank account, but still little Madeline could call none of it truly her own.

***

Seamus wasn't sure how it had happened, how they had come to the agreement, but somehow, they had, with so few words between himself and The Hat Man, as he had begun to call his hostage. Hostage. He'd begun to call him that, too, because that's what he was, wasn't he? A hostage. At least until they found the fish. And then what? That was bothering him more, the more he thought about it. Then what?

After all these years, he didn't imagine that it would be the same fish. Of course not. He wondered what the chances were that the conditions that had created that massive cod existed at all – or only had for a brief time. What sign would there be of it? The Hat Man seemed to think there was a sign, a sign in the water that the fish were there. Circles, he'd said. The same as those websites. Circles of giant fish. How difficult would it be to find them?

Seamus shrugged his shoulders. A three-hundred-pound fish would have a hard time hiding.

It had to be done in a hurry. The boss would be back any day. Just like her to say she wasn't sure when she'd return. Seamus knew, they all knew, that it was a tactic to keep them on their toes.

***

"She's a fish-plant worker as won the lottery. Him, I don't know."

The monthly meeting of the Women's Institute had gone off the rails even before Gus had made that comment. Somehow, it had turned into a town meeting, with men present, unsure as to exactly why they had gathered there.

Gus had brought a copy of *The Guardian*, Red Island's number one newspaper: "covers the island like the dew."

An article headlined "She Caught The Big One – Three Times!" told the story of Letitia's record-setting three consecutive lottery wins, each in the millions, and the fact that she and her husband now resided in Red Island and ran a cat shelter.

The women passed the paper around.

"I don't care how much money they got, or where they got it

from, it's not right, bringin' all them cats as don't belong here, here." Gladys Fraser, President of the Women's Institute, spoke first, as she usually did.

Hy nudged Annabelle. "Coals to Newcastle."

"And she's the head collier," Annabelle whispered back.

It was a stretch for anyone to support Gladys, but they were all cowed by her pugnacious attitude, her fists balled up like rocks, her chin thrust forward, determined to get her way. The fact that she had a barn full of cats of various pedigrees – none of them noteworthy – didn't escape them. They were all well aware of it, the overflow often spilling into their own barns and sheds. None of them dared say anything about it.

Besides, she was right. These new cats were "from away."

Hy scooped up Whacky, who'd come in on her heels. Gladys gave them a belligerent glance, then softened slightly, when the obvious Fraser pedigree showed itself in the all-black back, all-white front that made Whacky into what Hy sometimes called "two, two, two cats in one." Like a breath mint. Whacky's breath more often smelled of fish than mint – except when she'd been into the catnip that grew behind the police house. Hy found it amusing. A drug for cats on law enforcement property.

"The municipality can't allow this."

"What municipality?" Hy challenged.

Gladys looked offended. She took disagreement, and many other things, as a personal affront. Like the time she smashed her car into the historic site sign in front of the hall. Hy had watched the whole thing, finding it hard not to laugh. When the sign had reared up in front of Gladys, Gladys had looked insulted. It was obviously the sign's fault, not hers.

Just like now.

"Well, this one. This municipality."

"This is not a municipality."

Dead silence. Even Whacky seemed uncomfortable, squirming in Hy's arms, then digging her claws into Hy's breast, so that Hy, with a wince of pain, let her go. Unafraid of Gladys's bellicose demeanour, the little cat trotted up to her, sniffed her shoes, made a spraying motion, then turned and breezed across the room and out the door as Billy Pride and Madeline Toombs came in. They were late as usual, having grabbed the chance for some snuggling while Moira and her husband were out.

The silence continued, until April Dewey coughed. Moira Toombs cleared her throat. Gladys started up again.

"It's a rural municipality."

"No such thing." Hy was wondering why she had got into this ridiculous war of words with Gladys. The woman was wrong, but she'd never admit it.

"What do you mean, no such thing...?"

"Rural municipality. It's an oxymoron."

Gladys turned bright red.

"There's no need to call names."

"I said *oxy*-moron." Hy emphasized the first part of the word, but she should have known that wouldn't explain its meaning to Gladys. It was like shouting to communicate with someone who didn't speak your language.

"And I said rural municipality. What's wrong with that?"

"Municipality means city, town, borough, burg, if you will."

"Burger? What's this got to do with food?"

There was a giggle, a few titters, followed by one outright laugh from Ian, who now began to feel peckish.

Hy sighed.

"You're either rural...or...a municipality. You can't be both. The Shores can't be a municipality. It's a village. It probably should be a hamlet."

Ham. Ian was definitely hungry now. His stomach grumbled. April Dewey smiled from a few seats away. Perhaps she'd invite him to lunch. There was enough for him and Murdo both. Both big eaters. Who wouldn't love the products of the best cook in a village of culinary goddesses? April took the cake, when one of hers killed a man. He'd died eating it, half a slice clutched in his hand. Having lived a happy life, his only regret may have been not getting to eat the last half. April's white cake, with the thick butter icing, was made with cream from the cow Murdo kept in the barn and eggs from the six chickens that had free range of their backyard. It was cooked in an old-fashioned wood stove. No one else could be bothered to do that anymore, but April claimed the even penetration of the heat kept all her cakes and pies and roasts moist as a baby's bum. It was an unfortunate comparison, but nobody could argue with the product.

Ian was thinking about that cake now, his eyes and concentration locked on April. He was becoming hungrier by the second and didn't know how much more he could stand of this meeting that was going nowhere.

"I say we don't want them cats, with all their fleas and disease, said Moira. "I think we should take a vote."

"Should the vote go in your favour, what would you do to get rid of them?"

To everyone's surprise, Ben Mack had stood up and spoken up, challenging Gladys. A gentle bear of a man, he was more inclined to keep in the background, but the villagers knew he could be roused. They'd seen it years ago, when that storm surge had sliced through the causeway and the province had decided to evacuate the area permanently rather than go to the expense of fixing the link.

That had woken up the gentle bear, and he'd roared into Charlottetown, backed up by the local fishing fleet and Shores descendants from all over the island. The Macks had always lived in The Shores, and Ben determined that wasn't going to change.

The campaign was a success. The evacuation never happened. Neither was there a good job done on the causeway, so it remained, to this day, an unreliable connection to what the villagers had begun to call "the mainland." Some of them liked it that way.

Ben was moved to speak on this occasion because of the plight of the poor helpless creatures. Well able to take care of himself, he had a deep pity for those who could not.

Ben's question had a peculiar effect on Gladys. She had no answer.

"I said, what would you do to get rid of them?" He repeated the question into the stunned silence it had created.

"If there's going to be a vote, please allow me to speak on our behalf and that of those poor creatures we are sheltering." Brock Ferguson's deep, booming voice bounced off the walls of the hall. He had just walked in to hear the last of the argument. Everyone turned to get a good look at him.

He was tall, slim, and handsome with salt-and-pepper hair.

And that voice, now they heard it again as he spoke, not just deep and powerful, but smoothed with cream and spiked with whisky.

As they prepared to vote, two things resonated with the villagers – the first, like an echo, that deep voice, so deep it must be honest, assuring them that "We turn no cat away." Ferguson would come to regret that, when the next day, one after another, the villagers, felines in hand, lined up at his door to offload them.

"We turn no cat away." It was a powerful message given great consideration.

The other thing...well...the other thing was the famous author's cat carrier, the pride of the hall. There it sat, in state, front and centre on the stage, right below the ancient photographs of Queen Elizabeth, slim and serene, and her handsome husband Prince Philip, hand on his ceremonial sword.

The carrier tipped the balance. They imagined the island's beloved writer would never have picnicked here with her aunt, who was a villager, if she thought The Shores unfriendly to cats. The slips of paper went in, some showing their "yes" or "no." Gladys frowned when she saw the last vote: "yes." She was overruled. By one vote.

"That'll be his." She glared at Brock Ferguson.

"He's a member of the community, too." Hy stared at Ferguson, but found his expression unreadable. Neither pleased nor displeased. Guarded.

"It'll be his and someone's else's," Ian added. "Otherwise it would have been a tie."

And so it began.

"If my Lester was here, it would have been two votes more in favour." Estelle Joudry had a couple of cats in her barn she was hoping Ferguson would take.

"Harold had to go to town today, but I know he would have voted against it." Olive MacLean looked round the room, daring anyone to contradict her.

On it went, until Jamieson called them to order.

"The vote has been taken," she said. "Not that I think it has any authority one way or the other, but it seems the Fergusons can keep their cats in The Shores."

The decision made, Ferguson broached the subject that had brought him into the hall when he saw the crowd there.

"Is Abel Mack here?"

Silence. Didn't everyone know Abel was missing?

"Abel Mack? Does anyone know where he is?"

One more try. "Is Abel Mack still alive?"

Jamieson frowned. What was going on that she didn't know about?

"What do you know about Abel Mack?"

"Nothing. I know nothing. I was just looking for him."

"So are we all."

"He's alive then?"

"We don't know that. Do you know anything about that?"

"Absolutely nothing. I'm just looking for the guy. It's business."

"Abel Mack is over ninety. How much over ninety, I'm not exactly sure. But over ninety. What business could he possibly have?"

Ferguson bristled. "I don't think that's your business."

"It is, if you know anything about where he may be."

"I don't. That's why I came asking here."

"If you do know anything, you'd better not be keeping it from me, because I will find out."

"Just asking." The booming voice grew quiet.

Everyone looked at the man, curious. Most curious of all were Jamieson, Ian, Hy, and Gus.

What did this man have to do with Abel Mack? Why did he want to know about him? Jamieson did not plan to question him in full view of the entire community, but she would be catching up with him. Soon.

The continuing silence throughout this exchange exploded into chatter once it was clear that the Mountie and her prey had ended their exchange and moved out of range.

The meeting had turned out far better than any of them expected, what with the vote, the appearance of their newest neighbour, Ferguson, his looking for Abel, and the invitation to dump their cats on him.

At least that was how they'd heard it.

Jamieson, meantime, had collared Ferguson as he left the hall.

"I'm asking you again, privately, what business is it you have with Abel Mack?"

"As you said yourself, it's not really business."

"Do you know where he is?"

"If I did, I wouldn't be looking for him."

"He's an old man. He's been gone for days. He could be dead."

"I'd be sorry about that."

"Sorry? Did you know the man? What did you want from him?" For surely he had wanted something. He hadn't just picked the name out of a hat. A mental smile. *Certainly not a Tilley hat.*

"It's personal."

"Personal? I ask again – did you know him?"

A long pause.

"No, I did not."

It occurred to Jamieson that they were talking as if Abel were dead. She thought he was, but that wasn't the official position yet.

"How was it personal then?"

"He had something I wanted."

In Jamieson's experience, that was never a good thing. It often led to everything that was wrong: theft, assault, murder, kidnapping.

Kidnapping.

Now there was an angle she hadn't thought of. Who would want Abel? For what purpose?

Ferguson smiled, trying to lighten things up.

"It's a fish story," he said. "You wouldn't want to hear it."

"Wouldn't I now? Try me."

"Another time, maybe," he turned away and climbed into his Mercedes G-Class SUV, leaving her speechless, lips sealed by fury, fuming at his lack of regard for her uniform.

That she wasn't wearing at the moment.

Chapter 17

Ferguson was at the cat-barn door, eyeing, with an expression of displeasure, the line of villagers, carrying cats and cat carriers, all hoping he'd accept their unwanted felines.

It was obvious that a majority of the cats were of the same lineage – and that their birthplace was Gladys Fraser's barn. That was the home base of the giant ginger Ralphie, a huge, amiable thirty-pounder, with a perpetual smile on his face. No wonder, he'd had every female feline in The Shores. Including all of his descendants. The only plus for population control was that there were fewer female cats in the village, as they gave birth to more and more gingers like Ralphie.

Gingers – with few exceptions – are male.

There were lots of gingers in that line-up – big, with that smile, amiable nature, and unneutered state.

Ferguson was thinking fast. He held up his hands.

"I'm sorry, but we can't accommodate all these cats now…"

There was mumbling, some grumbling, a handful of "but he saids," until Ferguson held up his hands again and commanded silence with a deep booming voice that sounded like thunder rolling up the coast.

"Please." He made it sound like a command, not a plea.

"Please," he repeated, this time a growling threat, a sound that made the cats perk up their ears. Danger?

"I know I said we turn no cat away, but it's my belief that most, if not all, of these cats have homes."

Hy arrived and couldn't help butting in. "Not good homes," she yelled. "Or they wouldn't be trying to get rid of them."

A few of the villagers looked shamefaced.

"I will listen to anyone who thinks they have a truly legitimate case, but otherwise, give it time. Please, unless you absolutely cannot care for your cat, leave us to get on with caring for the many rescues we do have."

Reluctantly, grumbling, darting looks at one another to see who would stay and who would go, one by one they all turned, taking their cats with them.

All but one. Eighty-nine-year-old Sadie Robinson was clinging to a scruffy longhaired tabby. The two, woman and pet, were equally thin, bones sticking out of their backs, faces a skeletal mask with skin or fur stretched over it. The cat had lost its whiskers. The woman had sprouted some.

She could hardly move as she shuffled forward. Hy leaped forward to help her, taking her arm by the elbow.

"I can't care for him anymore. My Geordie." The old woman stroked the cat, and tears spilled down her face. Geordie licked them. "I can't bend over to feed him. I can't scoop out his litter."

Brock Ferguson appeared ready to cave in to the sad case, but Hy jumped in. It tore at her heart to see this woman having to part from her cat.

"I'll come and do it for you. When I can't, I'll make sure someone else does."

The offer set off a fresh flow of tears, as Hy guided the woman away.

It would not be a burden for Hy. She could do it a couple of times a week and pay the Dewey children to take care of the other days. The youth, the activity, the people coming into her life would rouse the old woman. Both she and Geordie would begin to eat. They would be seen walking together in the village. Sadie, bent over; Geordie limping. Both smiling.

But Hy's action did not stem the flow of tears.

Every time she saw Hy, Sadie cried.

***

In the close quarters of a coast-guard helicopter, it was almost as if he weren't there, his hat obscuring his face as he looked down on the waters below.

Looking down at the immense stretch of Big Bay and its dots of islands, Seamus realized that the best way to find what they were looking for was by helicopter. The coastline stretched in both directions, closing in on itself in a crescent. In places, red clay bled into the shoreline, the land quietly, but surely, melting into the vast waters around it. Someday, global warming would split the island into five. If predictions bore out, this cold windy province might become a string of low-lying islands. Finally, they would all slide into the sea.

In peril on the sea. The expression took on new meaning when applied to today's environment. The words had popped into Seamus's mind as he stared down. He could see everything that was going on in the water. They were flying over the great stretch of sandbar that protected Big Bay harbour, allowing boats in and out only at high tide, sheltering them when the tide was low, the sandbar raised up against the angry sea.

Of course. It had to be this part of the north shore. These were the old man's waters. It must be somewhere around Big Bay, home of the world-famous oysters. Soon to be famous for its giant cod?

They are there. That's what he'd said. That's what he kept repeating, as if the repetition would make it so.

This must be there. They must be here. Somewhere in this vast expanse of sheltered water, tucked in close to the shore of one of its islands, hidden in one of the small bays of the bay.

I know they're there.

Seamus looked over at The Hat Man, the nickname sticking.

He was hoping for a nod, a grunt, a definitive gesture.

An arm raised. A finger pointed ahead. Past Big Bay. Not Big Bay? Where then?

Circles, he had seen circles, then and now. This was the place, he knew. Those circles meant the fish was here again, after all these years he'd been waiting for it. The cod would be there, where the sand dunes rose high, and the currents ran cold and deep. He stared, fascinated by the circles, the circles he had seen back then. The big cod must be there. He could remember it clearly now. Now that he was here. They were here.

Seamus wondered, had the old man lost it? He wasn't moving and appeared to be staring with glazed eyes, not seeing. But he stabbed the air again, and Seamus saw the circles. Huge circles. Circles of cod?

He knew that cod circled when they mated, but he didn't think they had any impact on the water flow. Unless they were giants.

There must be giants there below.

***

"I hear you have a parrot."

Ian looked with surprise at Ferguson, at his front door, holding a box of canned soda pop.

He edged the door open and let the man in. Ferguson dumped the box on the kitchen table.

"I should say, I *see* you have a parrot." Jasmine, a young African grey Ian had rescued years before, was perched on Ian's shoulder. She was preening herself as she often did when male visitors came.

"Can she open soda pop cans?"

"As a matter-of-fact, yes. I don't encourage it."

"How many?"

"How many?" Ian looked puzzled.

"Twenty, thirty, more…?" Ferguson lifted his eyebrows, cocked his head, and smiled at Jasmine, as if a smile meant anything to the bird, other than a threatening baring of the teeth.

She was staring at the pop cans with interest. She hopped off Ian's shoulder, landed on the box of cans, inserted her beak in a tab and popped it off. She went for a second. And a third. She liked doing it, partly because she knew that humans found the opening of one can amusing, but more than one, annoying. Jasmine liked to be annoying.

"Enough, Jasmine." Ian reached over to pluck her off the box. Ferguson stopped him with a hand on his arm.

"No, let her go. Let's see how many she can do."

Realizing the man wanted her to keep going, Jasmine stopped. She also liked to be contrary.

She flew up and perched on Ian's shoulder again and resumed preening.

"What's this all about?" Ian stroked Jasmine's beak. She groomed him, pecking behind his ear.

"I was wondering if you had a world record setter."

"World record setter? Jasmine?"

"For most soda cans opened by a parrot. The number is thirty-five. In one minute. Speed is of the essence. Surely not hard to achieve, with a little training."

Ian snorted. "Jasmine can't be trained."

"Does she talk?"

Before Ian could answer, Jasmine repeated "does she talk?" in Ferguson's tone and cadence. His eyes lit up.

"Marvelous. Simply marvelous."

"Marvelous. Simply marvelous." Jasmine repeated, excelling this time at capturing Ferguson's deep baritone.

"You see, she can be trained."

"Jasmine says what she wants, when she wants. As for popping pop cans, I'm sure it's not good for her beak."

"Her beak is built for it. Imagine – setting a world record…"

"I'm not interested. Neither is she."

Ferguson smirked. "Surely she can speak for herself."

Jasmine swooped down and tugged another tab. The top came flying off and soda spewed all over Ferguson's face. Ian grabbed a tea towel and shoved it at him.

"I think she's spoken. Eloquently."

Ferguson wiped his face, frowned, and left. He slammed the door behind him.

"Not even a goodbye," said Ian.

"Goodbye," said Jasmine, sounding just like Ferguson.

"The guy's a nutcase," Ian said later, when he told Hy about Ferguson's visit. "He was obsessed with the Guinness Book of World Records and getting Jasmine in it."

"I'm sure Jasmine would have something to say about that."

"You bet," said Jasmine. "You bet."

***

The Hat Man, now in the sou'wester, was pointing down, finger stabbing at the window of the helicopter. There, west of Big Bay, in an area boats generally avoided because of the dangerous currents, was circle upon circle carved into the water.

Around, around the circles went, sucking everything in, fish, lobster, seaweed, bloodsuckers, delivering their prey as if on a cafeteria conveyer belt into the depths of the ocean. The ocean should not be that deep there, but Seamus had a feeling it was going to prove to be.

Were the circles being created by giant creatures below? By the fish this old man had almost caught? Or by its children or grandchildren or nieces and nephews? Were the giant cod spawning now, this time of year? This could be even better than Seamus had imagined. Multiple breeding seasons?

Imagine. The average female cod netted for market or aquaculture carried about half a million eggs per kilogram of body weight. So, say, on average, a million and a half. Would a three-hundred-pounder be true to the same rule? The math, and its implications, was staggering. Seventy-five-million eggs, at least. You'd only need one pair, a male and a female, for a whole industry. To breed by natural or artificial means.

That's why they were here. That's how Seamus planned to return home a hero. The price for this multi-million ova information was so cheap, what his informant wanted, so little, he had to laugh.

He did. It startled both the pilot and The Hat Man.

Chapter 18

Jasmine was missing. Ian knew it the moment he stepped into the house that afternoon. He always felt her presence wherever she was. There was no presence now. He stumbled over his feet as he raced through the house, upstairs, into all the rooms, opening and closing cupboard doors, looking under beds and dressers, calling for her.

He was hot with panic, the blood rushing to his head. He realized he cared about Jasmine's disappearance more than Abel's. She'd been his constant companion for over five years. She was a young bird. He often worried that she might outlive him. Then what would happen to her? All the depressing thoughts he'd ever had about terrible things happening to Jasmine raced through his mind as he searched. He kept looking while he called Hy.

"Jasmine's missing," he yelled before she had a chance to say hello.

"What? Impossible."

"It is possible, because she's not here, not anywhere."

"Calm down, Ian."

"Calm down? Calm down? How can I?"

"I'll be right over."

Hy flew out of the house and jumped into her truck. She didn't usually drive around the village. She walked or cycled, but this was obviously an emergency.

When she reached Ian's, he was a mess. His hair, what there was of it, was in complete disarray from dragging his fingers through it in despair.

She put a hand on his arm and propelled him from the kitchen while looking around the room to see if the bird was there.

"Let's go through the house."

"I've been through the house."

"Let's go again. You never know."

"I know. I know. She's not here."

"Then where could she be?"

***

"Thirty-two. Thirty-two. That's amazing." Ferguson smiled. Taking advantage of the fact that people didn't lock their doors in The Shores, he'd slipped into Ian's after he saw his truck speeding down the Island Way toward the causeway. He'd brought a cat cage with a few soda pop cans inside it. Jasmine, bored by Ian's absence, immediately took the bait. She hopped inside, and he banged the gate closed while she caterwauled, sounding like a dozen cats meowing in anger, pain, and various other emotions.

When he dumped the cage in the back seat of the car, she began to curse.

Ferguson almost drove off the road at one particular outburst of a series of "F" and "C" words, but he steadied himself and got Jasmine safely back to his place. He took her to his den in the barn. There he presented her with three cases of soda pop. Thirty-six. Enough to beat the world record.

She paid no attention at first to the pop cans, because she was transfixed by the fish, floating around in their marine world in the wall. She went beak to nose against several discus that came up to the glass, curious about the bird, thinking her another fish, a species they didn't know.

Ferguson rattled the cans and drew her attention to them.

Jasmine liked the game. That's why she put up with it. There was never any soda pop at home, never any beer cans, and she did like to pop them open. Even better if they fizzed and spewed liquid everywhere.

But this human was getting too intense, so Jasmine shut down. She tucked her head under her wing, and listened to him beg, ignoring him.

"C'mon, little one. Let's make it thirty-three. Huh? Huh?"

It might have helped if he'd remembered Jasmine's name.

***

Ian came bursting through the barn door. Seventy-five cats charged at him, their noses up against the pet screen barrier that kept them inside. The remaining four were unflappable – lying fast asleep in their comfy pillow beds.

"Ferguson." Ian yelled it out.

The door in the back of the barn creaked open.

"Thirty-two," said Ferguson, advancing toward Ian. "Thirty-two. Now we just have to get her speed up." He looked distressed. "It's taking her far too long." He looked at his watch. "Four minutes. The record is one."

Ian marched toward Ferguson down the side of the barn. Behind the screen, the cats followed along with him.

"Where is she?"

"Safe and sound. Trust me."

The two men stood face-to-face, chests thrust out in combat mode.

"Trust you? Why should I trust you? You've made off with my bird."

"She came willingly."

Ian knew that was a lie. He loved Jasmine, but he knew her. She didn't like most people.

"How'd you get her here?"

"In a cat cage."

Ian groaned. "I hope she gave you a hard time."

"Oh, no, she was an angel."

Another lie.

"Come. You'll see she's perfectly fine." Ferguson turned, and Ian followed, wanting to shove him, push him, smack him on the head, do something to relieve his anger. He knew better than to do anything until Jasmine was safely back with him.

Ferguson opened the door. Jasmine flapped her wings and flew straight for Ian, landing on his shoulder and nuzzling his neck. He stared at the massive aquarium. Fish and cats. Weird.

"Thirty-six! She's done thirty-six." Ferguson was staring in amazement at the three boxes of soda pop.

"Not in one minute." Ian nudged Jasmine with his chin, ruffled her neck feathers with a finger. Relieved she was back with him.

"Sadly, no. Time and practice will change that."

"No, they won't." Ian laid a possessive hand on Jasmine. "We have no interest in your world records. Your money-making schemes."

Ferguson looked genuinely shocked. He loved money, yes. But he was obsessed with breaking records for their own sake.

"This is not about making money. Bird tricks don't make money."

"Then why?"

"The honour. The fame. The game. Do you have any idea how lucky you are?"

"You're lucky that I don't ask Jamieson to charge you."

"Charge me with what?" Ferguson smirked. "Birdnapping?"

"Exactly that." Ian knew that Jamieson would not be happy to take on such a case. Before she came to The Shores, she'd had to solve a robbery of seaweed and another of stolen duck decoys. She wouldn't want to add birdnapping to that list.

"Birdnapping – and breaking and entering."

"Entering, perhaps, but surely not breaking. Your door was unlocked."

"You've been warned." Ian turned and marched out, the seventy-five cats that weren't sleeping accompanying him behind the screen to the front of the barn. He continued to clasp Jasmine on his shoulder. She was mimicking the different meows of all the cats beside them. Sounding sarcastic, as she always did when she meowed.

***

She was still doing her cat act when Ian stopped at Hy's house.

"You were right," he said. It was Hy who had suggested that Ferguson might have made off with Jasmine. He told her what Ferguson had been up to with the parrot.

"So his diabolical plan has been thwarted." She poured water into the kettle and turned it on.

"Yes, for now. But I'm worried. He seems so intense about it."

"You'll have to start locking your door. Or going everywhere with Jasmine."

"I guess. I should probably tell Jamieson about it."

"Maybe you should."

When they'd finished their tea, Ian drove home, but instead of stopping there, drove to the police house.

He remembered to knock on the door.

"Come in," Jamieson called.

She was staring at the ducky mugs. One, two, three on her kitchen counter. She had been looking for inspiration. A clue. Something. But the Ducky mugs weren't giving her anything. Ducky Hear No Evil. Ducky See No Evil. Ducky Speak No Evil. But had evil been done?

Ian told her about Ferguson making off with Jasmine.

Seaweed. Duck decoys. Ducky mugs. And birdnapping. It wasn't getting better for Jamieson. Sometimes she hoped for a nice clean murder. But murders were never clean.

"I'll charge him," she said.

"No, please, I don't want this to escalate. I'm afraid it will if you do that."

"But he's committed a crime. He should face charges. Otherwise, what am I here for?"

"Clearly, to keep the community stable. You've been doing a great job." His words rang hollow. They both knew it wasn't true. Her full-time presence in the village had not had an impact on the murder rate. It continued, steady as ever. And the number of deaths had increased. The only upside was that few were locals; most were from away.

"At the very least, I'll issue him a stern warning."

"Okay. That would be good. I'd appreciate that."

Jamieson left the police house right after Ian and drove to Ferguson's. She marched into the barn, disconcerted by sixty-eight cats following her and meowing. The other eleven were napping in their comfy pillow beds.

She rapped on the door of Ferguson's den.

He opened it and appeared surprised to see her. She was surprised to see the aquarium. Huge. Record-setting?

"Ian Simmons says you stole his bird."

Ferguson opened his arms, palms upward.

"There are no birds here." He smiled, indulgent. "Do you think there would be, with so many cats?"

She pointed at the tank. "And the fish? Are they safe?"

He shrugged. "As can be."

"I have no reason to disbelieve Ian."

"I'm afraid you both have the wrong end of the stick. I borrowed the bird." Ferguson still couldn't remember Jasmine's name.

"How can you borrow a bird?"

"For a test. A test that could make that bird and Ian Simmons famous."

"Guinness Book of World Records famous?"

Ian had told Jamieson all about Ferguson's plan for the parrot.

"Precisely. Who wouldn't want that?"

"Ian Simmons does not want that. So please leave him and his bird alone. Consider yourself lucky that I don't charge you. Simmons has asked me to hold off. But if anything like it happens again –"

"Nothing will, I assure you." His smile was phony. So was the depth of his voice, as he dropped it down a note to add a dash of what he thought was sincerity. "Nothing will."

Jamieson wasn't taken in. "It better not."

∗∗∗

But Ferguson didn't have control of the situation. Jasmine had got a taste of the cattery and of the fun of popping tabs on soda cans, and she took off again that evening when Ian left the door open for a moment.

Ian knew exactly where to find her and drove to Ferguson's in a fury of righteous indignation.

Ferguson shrugged.

"If you can't control your bird, what am I to do? By the way, she's at two minutes now."

Jasmine came home. Ian inspected her beak to be sure there was no damage, and, when he'd finished, she paraded a new assortment of meows for his entertainment. She mimicked each of seventy-two cats to perfection, hearing subtle differences humans didn't hear coming from the cats themselves, but did hear coming from Jasmine. The other seven were soundless cats, although Jasmine had managed to coax a hiss out of one of them.

Ian could hardly blame Ferguson for Jasmine's behaviour, only for having encouraged it in the first place. He certainly couldn't bother Jamieson with it. She had more important matters to deal with – the missing Abel.

∗∗∗

"Does Abel even exist?" Ian asked Hy, when he stopped by on the way home with Jasmine.

"What kind of question is that?"

125

"A legitimate one, I think. I've never seen him."

"How do you know?"

"What do you mean? I've either seen him or I haven't. I'm telling you I haven't."

"If you haven't seen him, how would you know? You wouldn't know what he looked like."

"That's convoluted."

"Still –"

"Okay, let's say I haven't…met…him. Have you?"

"I don't know."

"How's that?" Exasperated.

"I met a lot of people when I first came here. A lot of small, bowlegged guys with white hair…and balding. Was Abel one of them? Probably. I think he was more out and about back in those days. I've spent a lot of time with Gus, but I've never seen him in the house. Closest I've come is the ducky cup."

"Do you think Gus is imagining him?"

The thought had crossed Hy's mind. Had Abel died – long ago? Was he only missing in Gus's mind? Was she losing a grip on that razor-sharp mind? Was the sleepwalking episode a sign of it? Could it be Alzheimer's? She was in her mid-eighties, after all. She couldn't live – and thrive – forever. Although Hy wished she could – and would.

"That should be easy enough to find out." Ian stood up. "Check the records."

Chapter 19

It turned out not to be easy. The village church had burned down fifty years before, and the fire took a hundred and fifty years of records with it. Gus said she'd once had a copy of Abel's birth certificate that had been required for their marriage. It was a poor piece of evidence, created after the fact, in which the minister attested that Abel had been born in the village thirty-eight or forty years before, on a Sunday in midsummer. Gus couldn't find that paper now. So there was no record of Abel Mack's birth. There was no record of an Abel Mack having died in the last ten years in The Shores. Or the last twenty years. Those facts were certainly accurate. Had he died somewhere else? Abel had never been farther than Halifax, Gus said, adding: "…and he allus came back."

Even April couldn't call to mind when she'd last had a proper look at him. She just knew her baked goods kept disappearing through her back door as fast as Murdo was consuming them next to the front door. Most of the time she never saw anything clearly, partly because of poor sight, but mainly because of the blur of kids constantly circling around her. And because Abel was that way. There one minute, gone the next.

The rest of the villagers sang in harmony:

"Last time I saw Abel? Can't say really. The centenary year… mebbe."

"Don't know as I seen Abel in the last twenty years, mebbe longer. Not since he retired from fishin'."

Decade after decade Abel receded from sight.

Not seeing Abel didn't mean he wasn't there. It was status quo.

How it had become so, Hy couldn't figure out. Was no one curious?

***

Jamieson was. Very curious. There were only a few possibilities. One. Most likely. He was dead. If so, where? It had to be nearby, and they really had looked everywhere. Two. He'd been kidnapped. Highly unlikely. As she thought whenever that possibility came to mind, who'd want him? Three. He was hiding himself for some reason, some reason that Jamieson didn't know yet but was determined to find out. Some reason that maybe Gus could provide if she prodded.

***

"Did he act unusual in any way before he disappeared, was he thinking about something, was there something he maybe wanted to do?"

Gus looked smug. She'd recovered from the terrifying dream of a few nights before, putting it down to the little "lunch" she'd had before bed. Too much cheese. It helped that Jamieson was now taking Abel's disappearance seriously. Not dead. Abel was not dead. Just missing.

She knit the last few stitches on the needle, took the yarn in her mouth, and bit it off.

"He was talkin' about the fish."

"The fish?"

"The famous fish."

Jamieson turned at the sound. Hy had slipped into the room, and sat in the rocking chair by the window. With her, the scent of smoke had come into the room. It was on everybody.

Noticeable in Gus's kitchen because she kept it so clean.

"The big cod." Gus reached over and picked up her copy of *Time Was*. She flipped past the copyright and acknowledgement pages to the first photograph in the book. She passed it over to Jamieson.

It was that dramatic shot, taken by Elmer Cole, who'd missed his calling. He caught more with his camera than his fishing net. There was Abel, in a twenty-eight-foot dory powered by a one-cylinder engine, struggling to reel in a huge cod.

"It looks bigger than Abel."

"Reckon it was. Three hundred pounds, the fishermen figured. Maybe more. Abel, he was never more than a hundred and sixty."

"The one that got away," Hy grinned.

"No wonder." Jamieson passed the book back to Gus. "I didn't know cod got that big."

"No." Hy knew all about cod – and a lot of other things, trivia of all sorts – as a result of her work with clients, chief among them, the Department of Fisheries. She didn't need the money. For years her nest egg had been a secret, but now everyone knew she was heir to the perennially bestselling back-to-the-landers' bible, *A Life on the Land*, her mother's legacy.

Hy had written all about cod for the Department of Fisheries website. "They're usually about ten or twenty pounds, but in the deep waters of the Atlantic, some grow to a humungous size. Two hundred pounds. One weighed in at ninety-six kilos. You do the math. Bet that one ate a few lobsters in his time."

"Cod eat lobster?" Jamieson raised her eyebrows. Strange.

"Yup. Wild duck, too. They don't have to be big to do it either. Cod have some odd eating habits. They've opened them up and found wood, rope, pieces of clothing, old boots, jewellery, stones. Put that on your dinner table. And they're cannibals. It's a fish-eat-fish world. In some places more than half of them eat their own young."

"No wonder the industry died."

"I don't think eating each other was the problem."

"So, if Abel's cod was from the deep Atlantic, what was it

doing here?"

"Probably got blown this way, a freak. Brought in by a storm, a current, maybe slipped into the Gulf Stream somehow, although that might be warm for a cod."

Gus closed the book. "Abel never gave up on it. He wanted that fish bad. Bad. He never forgot."

"It wouldn't still be alive?" Abel, likely, wouldn't still be alive, either, Jamieson thought, a grim expression on her face. Hy could tell what she was thinking.

"Not that one. Maybe another. They can live fifteen to twenty years, but that's about it. One on record made it to twenty-seven."

"How could he possibly hope…twice in a lifetime…?"

"Why not?" Gus began putting a new set of stitches on her knitting needles. "He was good at finding 'em. Everyone'd follow Abel to the fishing grounds. He'd know where they were, the cod. He said he could hear them grunt."

"Grunt?" Jamieson looked mystified.

"That's how the male cod lets the female know he's ready." Hy grunted and grinned. "They call it the cod serenade. Lasts about fifteen minutes, then starts up again. Usually at night. It's not random grunting, there's a pattern to it, a melody of a kind."

"It wasn't just that, though." Gus slipped a needle into the wool, looped the yarn over and began a new row. "Not just the grunting. He could smell cod."

"Smell cod?" Hy and Jamieson spoke at the same time. Gus wondered why she was speaking of Abel in the past tense. *Well, that's just how she would have said it if he'd been sitting here in the room. That was past. The fishing. Twenty year or more.*

"I'll grant you, any fish can smell out of water, but in water?" Jamieson looked over at Hy for backup. "You can't smell fish in water."

Hy shrugged. "I don't know. I do know cod have a sense of smell. They can smell their prey. I don't know why they need to, since they eat practically everything. I do know about the grunting, and some kinky facts about their sex lives. Sometimes they engage in threesomes. That is, a single male will butt in, so to speak, on a mating couple and get his sperm in the mix. Then there's size. With cod, it matters. If a guy is smaller than a gal, no way he's going to get lucky. Our guy must have been very, very lucky. He probably had a deep voice, too, because the grunting gets deeper and deeper as the courtship heats up, and it's the deep grunting that attracts the female."

"You certainly know a lot about cod."

"It's the website work. I know everything you'd want to know about the sex lives of multiple species."

"C'mon." Jamieson had the hint of a smile. Her friendship with Hy was softening her.

Hy smiled. "Try me."

"Barnacle." Jamieson looked smug.

"Funny you should mention that. I happen to know that the barnacle has the largest sex organ of any animal, relative to its size."

"Not the whale?"

"Not the whale. The barnacle, stuck on a rock, or on a whale, for that matter, has to reach out, searching for a mate. There's no 'your place or mine?' They can both stay home. If he doesn't get lucky at the end of the night, he's bisexual, so he can f..."

Jamieson held up her hand, and indicated Gus with her eyes.

"...himself," Hy finished. She shook her head and smiled. "Cod only knows," she said on a sigh.

Had Abel gone on a quest for a big fish? What had happened to him on the way? Because Jamieson was sure something had happened. That Abel could not possibly be still alive. Not at his age, and not if he had taken to the open water.

***

The season was over, and Abel was taking a busman's holiday, some recreational fishing, hoping – as all fishermen do – to catch the big one.

He'd waited for the tide to cover the Big Bay sandbar and let his boat be carried by the current of water to the west of the bay, past the spit of land that boasted the tallest dunes on Red Island, massive heaps of soft golden sand dominating the shoreline, cutting off easy access.

Rod and reel. He was using rod and reel, a point of honour. Too easy to anchor a few lines to the back of the boat, or throw over a net and trawl. No. He wanted to really catch it. A big cod. A cod he had seen that summer. Seen and couldn't believe the size of.

The boat was bobbing on the water, and he leaned back and closed his eyes for a moment, the gentle rocking lulling him to sleep. It had been a long day; they were all long days, starting before dawn.

It was a bubbling sound that startled him awake. He sat up, looked down at the water, and saw the strangest thing.

The water was circling, around and around, the circle enlarging with each turnabout, soon grabbing at the boat and pulling it around, too. Around and around.

The water was bubbling, as if it were boiling.

Abel stood up, secured his rod, and leaned over and stuck a hand down into the water. He winced and pulled it out. Boiling. No, not boiling. Freezing. So cold it felt like heat, the point where the two extremes of temperature merged into one undifferentiated pain.

Cold. As cold as the deep Atlantic.

He stuck his hands in his armpits to warm them. His face screwed up in puzzlement. He knew these waters as well as he knew the land, the language of the sky, as well as he knew the cod.

In this newly strange place there were cod – that he knew, just from sniffing the air. He could smell them. There was the salt, of course, in the air and in the water. There was something mingling with the salt, something...metallic. He smelled it and tasted it on his lips.

And then he heard them – the cod. He heard them above the whistle of the wind and his own breathing.

The cods' grunts.

Unmistakable.

They were here – breeding.

The water was churning, the boat circling.

A tug on the line.

He grabbed the rod. He clung to it. Yanked it, and a giant cod leaped out of the water. A fish twice as big as he was.

He would never be able to bring it aboard. He couldn't - wouldn't - set it free.

It flipped around in the air, sending the boat rocking from one side to another, spinning, and then yanked the boat out of the circle, dragging it along, backwards, in a bid to escape, dragging it around the spit against the current, and all the way to Big Bay, where it dumped Abel's dory onto the sandbar and broke free, just after Elmer Cole snapped his shot.

The cod wove erratically, free of the tether, slapped its tail in the water, and, with one plunge, was gone.

***

There was that one photo only of Abel hanging onto the fish. It created a sensation in the village. The one that got away didn't belong to Abel alone. It belonged to everyone. The biggest cod they had ever seen. The local teacher at the time – a cousin of Abel's – tried and failed to get it into either the Guinness Book of World Records or the International Fish and Game Association's world records. There had been two stumbling blocks. The fish couldn't be weighed. And it hadn't been caught.

The Guinness people added that you couldn't tell in the photo that it even was a cod or that the photo wasn't faked. There were no supporting documents or witnesses. The villagers didn't see why any of that mattered.

"It was a damn big fish," Wally Fraser swore, out of hearing of his wife.

"Could of been a tuna," said Estelle Joudry.

Someone pointed out that tuna came bigger than that, much bigger, five hundred pounds and more.

"Believe it," carpenter Harold MacLean had said. "They

caught one in Nova Scotia not so long ago was more'n eleven hundred pounds."

Suddenly, their three-hundred-pound cod seemed puny.

"That's as may be, but tuna don't come into shore like that."

"Neither do cod," said Wally. "Not the big ones."

That's what the Guinness people didn't understand. Big cod had been found in the deep Atlantic but never in the benign waters of The Shores, warmed by the Gulf Stream.

"Abel never gave up on that fish," Gus said. "He tried his luck many times in that same place, but the conditions never were the same again. He always said something about the moon lining up with Ethan Cooke's chimbley."

The Shores fishermen fished cod the conventional way and caught plenty in the good years until the fishery was closed down. There was a time when only tourists could take cod, allowed ten pounds each on deep-sea fishing jaunts. They didn't usually want the fish, or not that much of it. They were in it for the experience. So the fishermen took home most of the catch. Not enough to sell, but enough to satisfy their own cravings for the tasty fish, worms and all.

"Would Abel have been allowed to keep a three-hundred-pounder after the moratorium?" Hy mused, then answered her own question. "Probably not."

Chapter 20

There was an unusual amount of activity on the west side of the massive dunes that sheltered Big Bay. They were difficult waters to manoeuvre because of the strong current that pulled vessels out to sea. Even large ones had to fight against it.

A fisheries vessel was motoring around a large pool of water, a swirling circle of exceptionally cold water created by an unexplained shift in the current. A shift that had redirected it, so that now it was pulling the cold waters of the deep Atlantic in. That's what had brought Seamus here, doing his private business on the public purse. He'd brought the old man with him.

He had them taking and comparing temperatures, assessing the size of the phenomenon, and dragging fishing nets, allowing them to get sucked down into the circling pool.

They had been trying to finish their work before the day began for the local fishermen, but they couldn't do everything in the dark. Even the dawn was dark, the sun's light filtered by the grey smoke from Quebec. When would it stop?

Cursing and coughing, two men hauled up an empty net, and, as they did so, there was a tug on the other net.

"Clear out! Clear out! Give us some room here." Seamus elbowed the two crewmen out of the way and grabbed the winch. Working it with difficulty, he pulled up the net, trembling with excitement.

Was this the prize?

There was a stunned silence when they saw what was in the net.

"Whew," someone whistled. "That's a two-hundred-pounder."

"Three-hundred-pounder, if you ask me."

It was more than Seamus could handle. The crew took over.

"I hope it's a girl," said one, hauling on the catch.

"Hard to tell." Seamus shook his head.

"With a three-hundred-pound cod you shouldn't have to squint."

But they all were. Squinting.

"Actually, impossible. Only if we cut it open," said Seamus. "Then where will we be?"

"Doing a tummy tuck on a cod."

"Can't you arouse her somehow?"

Seamus grinned. "You might, mate, but I wouldn't want to be on the receiving end of three hundred pounds of passionate codling. Especially if it was a he, not a she."

The men who'd been working the winch looked over at Seamus. Great excitement and high fives all around as they swung the net and poised it over a tank of sea water. Then the net lowered. The big fish didn't fit. The tank was too small. It was the biggest Seamus could fit on the boat, and that was after he'd stripped the vessel clean of everything but the bare essentials. There was only enough water in the tank to keep the fish alive until they got it back to Winterside. They wouldn't be taking it to Winterside.

"We'll have to throw him back," Seamus growled. So near and yet so far. For the first time, he knew what that meant.

He couldn't look. He turned his back on it as they swung the net down into the water and released the fish. It took a while, the fish was flipping around so much, but it found its way out and they hauled up the net, free of cod, with a couple of captive crabs in it.

Seamus, a bitter twist to his mouth, turned once the fish was gone, his back to the circle, the failure of his plan.

The Hat Man was staring, bewildered, at the empty tank across from him.

The fish had been here, hadn't it?
He couldn't remember.
One minute here; the next, gone.

***

The computer. Why hadn't anyone checked the computer? Hy picked up speed as she cycled along the Island Way, afraid that Jamieson might have the same thought and get to it before her. There were bound to be clues on it, something that would tell them where Abel was.

Her hands were shaking with excitement at what she might find out as she dashed up Gus's front stairs. She wrenched her wrist tugging on the metal screen door. It was locked. How unusual. Then she remembered. Gus had gone to Charlottetown overnight. That, too, was unusual. So was the occasion. It was Gus's seventieth eighth-grade reunion. All but one of the graduates were still alive. That made five. All grandmothers, Gus just barely, happily armed with photos of her latest accomplishment, Little Dottie, born since the women had last met. All the women, except Gus, were widowed.

Or was she? Gus had taken that doubt to Charlottetown, too.

***

"Do you have the fish?"

"What?"

"The fish. I thought you were getting a fish today."

"Any fisherman knows you can't predict if you're going to make a catch."

"You have the entire fisheries department at your disposal. All that, and you couldn't catch a fish?"

"We did catch one. Threw it back."

"Too small?"

"No, too big."

There was a long silence on the end of the line.

"Couldn't fit it in the tank."

More silence. *Too big?* "How big?"

"Three-hundred-pounder, easy."

"Can't you get a tank that will hold it?"

"That window is closing."

Ferguson didn't pick up on the anxiety in Seamus's voice – the fear of his boss's return. Imminent. And inconvenient.

"If we catch another, we have to find somewhere to put her."

Ferguson stood up and looked down over the fields to the pond.

"There's a lotta 'ifs'," Seamus persisted. "If we get another, if we can keep her alive, if we find somewhere to put her." *And if,* he thought privately, *he'd be able to transport a fish that big to Newfoundland.* Seamus had no idea how he was going to do that. His confidence that he could pull this off was sinking. He didn't feel like a hero right now.

Ferguson was shocked. *So close. They were so close.* "If…" he underlined the word with his tone. "…we get another, we'll find somewhere."

"Where?"

Ferguson had had it in mind all along. To get the fish here. Near him. The pond.

"The pond."

"The pond?"

"More or less the natural habitat. We can use it as a holding tank."

Seamus had to admit it was a possibility. It was a saltwater pond now, after last winter. Still – "Temperature can vary from one area to another. If the pond was right for cod, they'd be there already."

"I think it's our only option. The pond will be the ideal place," Ferguson insisted. "You can just drive the fish in there."

"You mean corral it?"

"Maybe. Get it on a line and chase it there. Or in a net and drag it there. I don't care how you do it, just get it there."

Seamus hung up, thinking The Hat Man might be useful. Move that cod out the old-fashioned way. It hadn't worked thirty years ago, but, who knows, it might today.

He might need the old man after all.

***

The piece of land that Letitia and Ferguson had bought cradled the pond, from its northernmost to southernmost tips. This half share didn't make it theirs. The pond, like the shore, belonged to the village. Not all the villagers were certain of that. Gladys Fraser assumed that if she owned that piece of property that hugged the pond, the pond would be hers, too. And why not? The person who owned the land on the other side of the pond was Jared MacPherson. When Ferguson found out the owner, Jared, was in jail, he went ahead and did what he wanted, without asking. Anyone.

***

So Gus was away for the day. Hy pondered it. That would give her a good long time to examine the computer and its files. Could she break into Gus's house? It didn't seem right, but she knew Gus wouldn't mind if she checked the computer.

That was the same as permission, wasn't it? And she wouldn't have to break in.

She knew where the spare key was. Under the pot that had been placed on the stoop for just that purpose. Every house had one. The back door led directly into the computer room, so she wouldn't have to tiptoe through the house like an intruder. Hy wheeled her bicycle around to the back, leaned it against the wall of the house, and skipped up the steps to the back door. She searched under the pot. Not there. Slid her fingers blindly everywhere. She touched something metal. It fell through a crack in the wooden decking into the dark underbelly of the house.

She peeked under the house and saw nothing. She wasn't going to crawl on her hands and knees in the dirt looking for it. Better wait until Gus got back.

**

The old man had discovered television. He'd only ever had two channels in his life, and he'd never seen a cartoon. Now, he couldn't get enough of them. It seemed, except at the odd moment, he'd forgotten all about the fish. Or maybe he thought he'd caught the fish. He'd been on the boat when they snagged the big one. He'd seen it come and go. He muttered a bit while watching *Finding Nemo,* but that was about it.

Most of the time, like now, he'd sit on the couch, devouring a bag of chips and the latest animated special. Seamus had just brought in fresh supplies. He didn't bother to put them away but just lined them up on the counter – chips, pizzas, Coke. The Hat Man would devour it all in no time. He was especially fascinated by the pizzas. Circle food. He would turn a pizza around, around and around, taking little bites of it.

The apartment looked like a dump. Fast-food cartons thrown on the floor, empty packaging on table and countertops.

Seamus knew they'd have to get out soon. He had no idea what he was going to do about the old man.

When he had no more use for him. That might be soon. He might never catch that fish.

He thought about driving him to some remote area and just letting him go. Like returning a beast to the wild. Like putting the elderly out on an ice floe.

There was no area more remote than where he'd come from in the first place, and Seamus didn't dare return him there.

It would be known. That was the thing. It would be known that Seamus had abducted him.

Was there a chance that it would not? Dare he take that chance?

He didn't want to kill him. He wasn't sure he could. Oh, it would be easy enough to smother him in his sleep. He'd thought about it. A lot.

***

Damn! Hy couldn't wait for Gus to return from Charlottetown, but she was going to have to. The brilliant idea simmered inside her, woven with a tight anxiety that Jamieson would think of it, too. But Jamieson wasn't as familiar with the Mack household as Hy was. She probably hadn't given the computer a thought, especially as it wasn't in the kitchen anymore.

Hy was wrong. The idea had occurred to Jamieson about the same time it came to her. She hadn't seen the computer in a while and didn't know if it was still there. Dot had used it when she was there. Had Abel begun to use it? Might there be something on it that would provide a clue to his whereabouts?

Jamieson and Hy were in the door together, moments after Gus returned that evening. She hadn't even had time to make a pot of tea, and here were the two of them descending on her, demanding to know where the computer was, who'd been using it…and all sorts. She waved them to the back room, continued making the tea, and left them to it. Whatever "it" was.

It wasn't much. Jamieson had let Hy hack into the computer – she couldn't have done it herself. And when they got in? Nothing. It had been wiped clean.

Like Abel's memory?

Chapter 21

Seamus was shaking. With anxiety and fear. When his boss got back, it wouldn't be long before she knew what he'd been up to – the trip in the fisheries boat, the helicopter jaunt, the purchase of the massive tank, and the use of personnel for his own purposes. The entire work of the department had come to a halt as he pursued his mad scheme. The bills were an unpleasant pile on his desk. Whenever he picked one up, there was another one underneath. He had to get Ferguson paying the bills, so he could pull out of his government job and realize his life's dream.

Bringing the cod fishery back to Newfoundland. Restoring the way of life of his father and grandfather, and generations of O'Malleys before them.

When he thought about it, he began to sweat – from both fear and pleasure. The cold sweat of fear that he wouldn't be able to pull it off. The warmth of the pleasure he felt rushing through his blood when he imagined himself, returning home, the conquering hero with a new kind of cod for a new life in Newfoundland.

He needed Ferguson, and what he thought was Ferguson's money, for that dream to come true.

It annoyed Seamus that Ferguson wanted to keep the cod in the pond when they got it. He would play along if he had to, to get money off him, but their phone conversation was not going well. Ferguson wanted a fish alive and in his pond. That would be difficult to deliver, as Seamus had already found out. So would getting a fish that size to Newfoundland. Could he strip it of its milt and ova, and then kill it?

"You don't need a live fish to establish a world record," he argued. "You just have to photograph and weigh the damn thing, and you're in. I might have to kill the cod after I harvest its ova and milt."

"Kill the fish." Ferguson frowned. It was true. The fish didn't need to be alive to achieve a world record. But he wanted that fish alive. Period. He didn't care what Seamus wanted. He'd just use him until the fish was reeled in.

"We can breed it in the pond. Find a mating pair." A desperate suggestion, and he knew it.

"You couldn't breed them for long in that pond."

"Why not?"

"Look at the size of it. Look at the size of the fish. Imagine if even a dozen codlings came to life. They'd be so overcrowded in the pond they'll kill each other, eat each other, die of disease, if they would even live and breed in warm water so close to the surface in the first place." *Another if.*

"I'll just keep one there." Ferguson had been doodling a drawing of a cod on a notepad. "I'll photograph it and weigh it, and leave it there."

"First we have to get it."

"How hard can that be? You've done it once… Now you know where they are, it's not as if a fish that size can hide."

"It's done pretty well the past thirty years."

Ferguson cracked his knuckles. "Things are different now." Silence. Ferguson took a deep breath.

"Let's just get the fish in that pond. I'll cover your costs." How he was going to get this past Letitia, he didn't know, but he smelled a record-breaking deal and was chasing it down, like a cod after a clam.

Seamus smiled, a sly smile.

This might turn out for him even better than he thought.

A big fish and a weighty partner. With money.

But Ferguson didn't have money. Not yet.

***

Ferguson surveyed The Shores pond, in the company of

143

a contractor.

"Fix the bridge. It was damaged last winter. The community will want it repaired."

His companion spat out a wad of chewing tobacco on the ground. Ferguson looked at it with distaste.

"Then build a frame and install this sluice gate." He stroked his engineering marvel, welded himself, from his own design. He'd inspected the outlet on the far side. There was nothing needed there. It had been plugged up by the storm that had changed the pond from fresh to salt. There was only a slight gap – too small for a big cod to get out.

A born Red Islander, the man knew his activity would attract attention. He also suspected the pond didn't belong to this man. "What if someone comes up and asks me what I'm doing?"

"Tell them you're with the Department of Fisheries…or Transportation…or something."

That's exactly what the man did when confronted by Jamieson on her daily rounds.

"What are you doing here?"

He'd put up yellow tape, to stop people from crossing the bridge.

"Fixin' the bridge," he said.

"Yes, it does need fixing. Who are you?"

"Department of Fisheries…or Transportation…or something." He spit a wad of tobacco close to her boot.

What was that supposed to mean? Was he supposed to have a license, something to show her? She really didn't know. Anyway, the bridge was getting fixed, that was the main thing.

***

Remembering. He was remembering. The fog cleared out of his brain and sent him spinning down into a memory.

A memory of the water circling.

A memory of the fish fighting.

A memory of the giant cod leaping into the air and dragging him out to sea. And then the near memory, the memory he almost never had. The fish hovering over the tank on the boat.

A memory that sent his heart beating, head pounding, arm shooting with pain.

He tried to get up, his feet touched down on open water, and he could find no solid footing. It felt real, the absence of a floor, of water, of something. The circles in the water became the room spinning around him, nothing firm anywhere.

He collapsed onto the floor, on the far side of the bed, beneath the windows. As he went down, he grabbed at the bedsheets and hauled them off. They fell on top of him.

***

It was an unusual repair job, everyone agreed, and a fast one. The man had it done in an afternoon. When he'd finished his work, they all walked down, one after another, to check it out. Wally Fraser waded into the pond shoulder deep to examine it and play with the new contraption under the bridge.

"It's a sluice gate. Opens and closes automatically." He pointed to a small black box in a plastic casing, with a red light pulsing. "Electronic. See, if I approach it, it opens up. Go through it, and it closes. Very clever."

"And you're very stupid," said his wife Gladys. "Get out of there, Wally, you'll catch your death. What do we need with a sluice gate?" she asked in her always-offended tone.

"Won't last long… I give it one storm…see what the tide makes of that…" and other such comments came from the assembled villagers.

"Good job on the bridge, though," said carpenter Harold MacLean. "That'll withstand a winter or two, though I hear the next is bound to be the worst in a decade." Harold was fond of predicting the weather, and people listened to him, though he was almost always wrong. When he nodded his head and said:

"There's talk of dirt comin'," they'd prepare for fine weather instead.

"A sluice gate?" That was the refrain around the village all afternoon and into the evening, diminishing curiosity as to the whereabouts of Abel Mack. "Why a sluice gate?"

The question wasn't answered, but they did solve part of the mystery. April Dewey had a cousin whose brother-in-law, Ken Campbell, was the guy who'd done the work. He said he'd done it for the cat fella, Brock Ferguson.

So then the refrain changed. It became: "Why'd he do that? What did he do it for? He paid for the bridge to be fixed and all."

The most popular phrase was "can't figure it out," accompanied by shaking heads.

***

"There's bound to be something we can do to find out the activities on that computer," Ian said, when Hy called him from Gus's on the phone with the long coiled cord that had been stretched so much it now reached from the dining room through the living room to the back room that used to be a porch. Hy and Jamieson were staring at the blank screen, hoping Ian would come up with something.

"I don't imagine Abel was canny enough to keep it all from us."

Ian frowned. Hy was right. Abel was not a techie. He was impressed that a guy in his nineties was using the technology at all.

"I'll be right over. See what I can do."

***

Ferguson had watched the villagers pointing, scratching their scalps, and shaking their heads over the work that he'd had done on the bridge. Too much attention being paid to the pond.

O'Malley wouldn't like it, he might bolt. He'd have to put a stop to it, create a diversion. He decided to do something for the village, to end their grumbling and bring them on side. A lobster dinner. The more he thought about it, the more he liked it. Yes, and he and Letitia would cook.

***

"A lobster dinner?" Gladys almost glowed. She would have if she'd ever spent any time outdoors, involved in healthy activity. "For the whole village?"

"Yes. For everyone." Ferguson's deep voice and creamy tones melted Gladys's hard heart.

"That would be wonderful. What should we do? I could make my famous badada salad." Gladys's potato salad was famous, because it had killed an old lady and made the rest of the villagers ill at a community dinner years before. Ferguson didn't know that.

"That would be great." He gave her one of his best smiles, eyes flashing.

Gladys smiled back. She never smiled. This would be her vindication. She'd never been asked to provide potato salad for the village since that unfortunate incident. At least, she reasoned, the dead woman had been Wally's cousin. Kept it in the family.

Letitia didn't object to spending a bundle on a community dinner. Not at first. Not until she knew the reason for it.

Madeline, in her innocence, let her know.

"Let the cat out of the bag," Gus chuckled when she heard.

"It's kind of you to be hosting this dinner," Madeline said when she next saw Letitia. "We usually have only one lobster dinner a year – after setting day – and we have to pay for that."

"We're happy to do it. It'll give us a chance to get to know the community better."

"And maybe they'll stop being mad about the sluice gate."

"The sluice gate...what?"

Madeline coloured. She could see she'd said something wrong. She wasn't sure what.

Letitia went barging out of the room, as fast as her asthma could carry her, and confronted Ferguson in his den.

She began to wheeze. He tried to keep a benign expression on his face, but he felt murderous. It revealed itself in the grip he now had on her shoulder.

The wheezing intensified.

"My...p...p...puffer..."

He was tempted, for a moment, to let her be, to let her die of breathlessness. Whether or not he would actually have gone through with that was not put to the test, because Madeline appeared with the puffer. She'd heard the wheezing from the cattery and went running to the kitchen and back to fetch the device. Now she was as breathless as Letitia.

How could anyone breathe in the smoky air of The Shores that summer?

***

Gus was enjoying her cup of tea in the kitchen, puzzling over an entirely different conundrum. She had, she thought, cut all the pieces for the quilt she was embarking on. She'd done it so many years ago, she couldn't swear to it, but it did have a piece of paper stuck in the plastic cover, and scrawled on it, the word "done."

There were some sails missing. Perhaps she'd counted wrong. Like Abel, they must be somewhere.

***

Letitia was shaking her fist at Ferguson and breathlessly attempting to shout at him.

"You should not have spent that money without my consent."

"Must I come begging and scraping to you for every loonie I spend?" It was demoralizing. It made a child of him. Especially as there was so much money.

"What's it for?" she demanded. "The sluice gate?"

The evidence was right there on Ferguson's computer screen. He'd sat down to admire the design. Not so much for the bridge, which was a pretty straightforward repair job, but for the sluice. Elegant, he thought. Just because something was practical didn't mean it couldn't have grace. Grace wed to function.

Ferguson angled the screen toward her. The engineering diagram meant nothing to her. She saw neither grace nor function.

"The bridge at the bottom of the pond, where the water comes in from the Gulf. It was badly in need of repair. I thought it would be a nice gesture to the community, to help smooth our way into the village."

Letitia's frown turned to a small smile.

"Yes, that is a nice gesture." There was a pause. Ferguson hoped it would silence her on the subject.

She was on the point of leaving, when she turned back.

"But the sluice. What's that for? The community? Does it need a sluice?"

"Not exactly."

"What does that mean? They either do or they don't."

"No, but I do."

"For what?"

"Nothing you should bother your head with, my dear." He stood up and reached a hand to her shoulder. He squeezed it lightly and lit up his eyes in that way he knew she loved and made her believe he loved her.

"It's a little experiment I'm trying. I need to have something to do with my time." He slid his arm around her shoulders and guided her out of the room.

"All in good time," he said. "I'll tell you all in good time. You'll like the idea, you'll see."

Letitia wasn't as much of a sucker for his charms as she led him to believe. That had worn off early in the marriage. But she needed to be loved. She felt so weak, so fragile, so unwanted that she welcomed any show of kindness, no matter how small. That's why the cats. She knew they loved her.

She let Ferguson lead her up to their bedroom for a "cuddle." It was all she could do anymore, in her state of health. It was all he could manage to do with her to keep the marriage alive and her money in his life.

He didn't know why he had let her gain the upper hand. She was so weak and vulnerable. But the money made her strong. She knew it, and he knew it. The money. How much stronger he would be if it were his.

Chapter 22

While Gus puzzled over her patches, Ian, Hy, and Jamieson were crowded into the tiny back room. Ian got on the iMac and began to fiddle around, clicking and scrolling, emitting the occasional "Hmmm." Every time he did it, Hy and Jamieson thought he might have found something. They'd lean forward over his shoulders and peer at an always-blank screen.

After a while, Hy became fed up and was about to slump down on the daybed along the inside wall with its faded white shingles. It had once been the outside wall of the built-in back porch. The day bed was piled high with patches, plastic bags full of folded material, thick rolls of cotton lining and baskets of thread. She began clearing herself a space when her hand struck something hard. She drew the hand up to her mouth and pressed on it to diffuse the pain. She looked down. A piece of black plastic or metal was sticking out from under a half-pieced quilt top. She reached down and grabbed it.

Her brow wrinkled. She turned the object over. Her face cleared. She addressed the backs of Jamieson and Ian.

"Look what I have here."

Ian and Jamieson spun around. As soon as he saw it, Ian grabbed at it. Hy pulled back playfully, keeping the treasure out of reach, teasing him. Jamieson looked bewildered.

Hy let Ian have the box.

"The back-up," he explained to Jamieson. "The files may

be on this."

"Or there may be nothing." Hy grinned as Ian shot her a hard look.

There was a lot more than nothing. There was what appeared to be everything. Files from Dot, Finn, and Abel.

Ian went straight for Abel's email. Jamieson turned her head away. She didn't want to be an accomplice to someone hacking an email account.

She might not have to worry about that. Ian wasn't having any luck.

***

When Seamus opened the apartment door, he was shocked to see no one in the room. No one in the bathroom either. Panicking, he looked under the sofa, under the bed. He even checked the side of the bed, but all he saw were sheets.

Then he heard a groan – coming from under the sheets. He flipped them up, and found the old man lifeless on the floor.

Lifeless? Dead? Please, God, no. He had wished it more than once. Thought about how he'd do it, even. It wasn't conscience stopping him. He had too much on his hands already. Now this.

Another groan. A good sign? His mind raced briefly with the idea of concealment if the old man died, but it would never work. He'd be in enough trouble already when what he'd been up to at fisheries was revealed. He couldn't conceal a dead man.

He pulled out his cellphone and called 911.

***

Having no luck in busting into Abel's email, Ian followed his tracks elsewhere on the computer. Abel could be seen more clearly here than in any other part of the house, his land, or the village. Here he was…ninety-two…and exploring…what exactly was he exploring, and would it help them find him?

"What is this?"

Ian had opened a file dedicated to the most unusual sea creatures in the world. It contained a stunning series of photographs of unimaginable creatures, like bizarre inhabitants of a future underwater world. If the site was to be believed, and it certainly looked authentic, these creatures existed here on earth…or, rather, in its waters.

The three gazed, transfixed, as a slideshow of the creatures filled the screen.

"The polychaete worm," Ian was reading, part skimming the article as all three gazed transfixed at the ugly creature – pink, reflecting rainbows off a shiny slippery skin. "A relentless predator, able to turn itself inside out to grab its prey."

"Yech." Hy shuddered. Jamieson struggled to maintain her composure. As a police officer, she'd run into a number of ugly sights, but nothing like this. Carnivorous coral, vampire squid from hell.

There was a long list of links… *Biggest Cod Ever Caught in Germany… Biggest Cod Ever Caught in England… Biggest Cod Ever Caught in Norway.*

A big hole in Abel's life. He might have caught the biggest cod ever in North America, in the world, but he hadn't. It had got away.

"Do you think Abel's left the island?" Ian was scanning the list of places big cod had been seen. Red Island wasn't one of them.

"Where would he go?" Hy was reading over Ian's shoulder. "How would he get there?"

"The same as anyone else…car, boat, train, and plane."

"Not plane," Gus interrupted, drawn to the back room in search of thread. "Abel never went on a plane and never planned to."

"Might he…maybe with Dot?" The idea came on Hy suddenly. It leapt from her mouth.

"You think Dot is part of this?" Jamieson's interest was piqued.

"I think we should consider it. They disappeared at the same time."

"She left afore. And she said goodbye."

"Not to Finn." Hy thought Finn might have seen through that goodbye. Asked questions.

"We'd have heard." Ian was still working the keyboard. "She'd have let us know something. She wouldn't leave us to worry over Abel, over something as stupid as a big fish."

"Now don't you let him hear you say that," Gus cautioned.

How could he hear? If the clues were any indication, he was miles from here.

"Anyway, you better get that machine back in the kitchen and give me back my aquarium and my Skype. I'll be wanting to hear from Dot whenever she gets where she's going. I can look at all the pretty fish while I wait."

Hy had tried to contact Dot, to tell her that her father was missing, but she'd had no luck. No answers to text messages. Voice mail full up and not recording any more. Jamieson had checked the airlines and car rentals. No one had a record of Dot. She might have paid with cash, thought Hy. She did know that if Dot wanted to reach her, she would. She hadn't. That silence might be a clue that she was with Abel, a possibility Hy hadn't considered until now.

When Ian had set up the computer in the kitchen, he tried to Skype. Dot was on the contact list. It wasn't a list. She was the only one on it. But she was offline.

"I know. Why didn't I think of it?" Ian clicked to Abel's email account and typed in the password, "Abel Mack."

The account opened. He shook his head. "As simple as that."

There were a few junk mails, accumulated since Abel's disappearance – and one from the Department of Fisheries. He opened it.

"Hi, Sir," it began.

"Hi, Sir?" Hy groaned. "Give me a break." She hated the "Hi" salutation anyway. Thought it ridiculous. But "Hi, Sir?" Even more so.

"The Department of Fisheries is interested in your experience with a large cod thirty years ago. Could you please inform us as to the location of your catch?"

Hy leaned in to look at it. Jamieson was tempted but still wasn't sure the role she should play, whether she should sanction hacking.

"I bet he didn't answer it," said Hy.

"He didn't." Ian made a check of Sent Mail. "He's never sent anything, or else he erased it all."

"The sender?" Hy asked.

"Seamus O'Malley."

Hy looked surprised. "Seamus O'Malley?"

"You know him?"

"A bit." There was a lot of Seamus O'Malley to know, she thought.

O'Malley was looking for the fish – through Abel Mack. It occurred to Hy that Ferguson had been looking for Abel, too, at the hall that day.

Were they all after the fish?

***

Seamus paced back and forth between the door of the apartment and the old man lying on the floor behind the bed. He considered pulling him out by the feet but didn't. If the man were dead or dying, whatever he did might be incriminating.

He felt helpless. The helplessness was chased away by panic when the sound of the ambulance siren pierced the air and came closer, more insistent with every second.

What should he say? What was this man doing here, unconscious or worse, in the government hospitality suite?

He took several long, deep breaths to calm himself. He couldn't possibly answer all these questions. Start with the most important, the most immediate.

Who was the man? What had happened to him? When had he found him? What had he eaten or had to drink?

The questions kept piling up. All this trouble, and he had no idea yet whether he was going to get his cod or not.

The alarm came screaming through the screen window. Still, The Hat Man did not budge. Deeply unconscious, he must be. Either that or dead.

***

Germaine always moaned after one of Estelle's "stick to your ribs" meals – in this case, macaroni and cheese, neither of which, as a heart patient, he should have been having. Estelle said she didn't "hold with that." The entire village had been brought up on macaroni. The good stuff. Not that stuff in a box the kids all wanted today.

So there they were, Germaine and Estelle, sitting as they did every night; he was moaning and occasionally burping and farting his appreciation of a fine meal. They were watching television, a local reality show. It was called *Who's Your Father?* It was the first question strangers asked when they met on Red Island. A first salvo. If you knew who someone's father was, you likely knew who they were, or someone who knew who they were, or someone they knew who knew their father – or maybe you actually knew them. Something like that.

The TV show brought together complete strangers, one an islander, the other a former islander or someone descended from an islander living away. The one who made the connection first was the winner and went on to challenge another stranger. In the final fifteen minutes of the show, if neither contestant had found the link between them, the game was thrown open to the audience, to phone in or tweet. The show catered to an aging population. They were more likely to call than to tweet.

"I know, I know, I know." Estelle bounced in her seat. Germaine paid her no attention. She always did that at this point in the show. She never knew but always claimed she had known, that it was "on the tip of her tongue." She'd pout at the contestant who, unfairly she felt, had stolen her victory by shouting out the right answer.

"I knew those Beirstos, father and son, cousins of my uncle's mother, well, her that was married to the other side of the fambly..." Estelle muttered as she stood up to turn off the television, when a moan came from Germaine that sounded like something more than appreciation of a fine meal. She looked over at him. His face was red, his hand on his heart. She leapt out of her chair and swooped down on him.

He was having palpitations.

Germaine had undergone a quadruple bypass a couple of years before.

Estelle knew paramedic Nathan Mack's phone number by heart. If she could stop her hands from shaking, she'd get through in no time.

***

It wasn't until he heard the creak of the elevator door and the pounding of the paramedics' feet coming up the stairs that Seamus realized his man could be identified. With hands trembling, he searched in the bright yellow jacket for a wallet. It wasn't hard to find. A wallet fat with bills. Thousand dollar bills. No longer minted, but still good currency.

How many thousands?

Pounding footsteps.

Trembling fingers, tearing at a bill. Just a few. In a wad that thick, they wouldn't be missed.

If the man could even remember he had them at all.

Seamus took some more.

Footsteps coming closer. He stuffed the bills in his pocket and fumbled through the rest of the wallet. No health card. No driver's license. No ID of any kind.

He slipped the wallet back in the jacket pocket as the knock came on the door.

On an impulse, he hid in the large antique wardrobe, just

managing to squeeze in. He didn't want this sticking to him. The walls of the wardrobe already were.

***

Jamieson had tried to track down O'Malley through the fisheries department with no luck.

"Not here," the receptionist told her, blowing up a big bubble with her gum and popping it in Jamieson's ear.

"Do you know when he will be there?"

"He's in and out." Pop. "In and out."

Jamieson didn't leave her name. She didn't want to scare him off.

***

The paramedics looked around for the person who had phoned, but there was nowhere much to look, except the bathroom. Puzzled and with no time to waste, they left with the old man on a stretcher.

Seamus stayed in the wardrobe longer than he needed to, afraid they might come back to make one last check, and also unsure how he was ever going to get himself out of this tight spot. When he finally did, most of him ached, his legs were like rubber, and he had to sit on the couch to recover.

Not for long. He realized he had to get on the move, get hold of the old man again or disappear himself. Along with all his hopes of catching the big fish. The image of his father, hanging at the end of that rope in the barn, galvanized him into a sort of action. He must find the old man again and go with him to catch the fish. Or convince Ferguson to do it his way.

Meantime, he could hide out at The Shores. He wouldn't be the first person who'd gone there to lie low from the law or a spouse or a bothersome relative.

Law enforcement barely existed there, he thought. Except in the form of Jane Jamieson, whom he didn't know.

It was all or nothing now. He'd be leaving his job and his tip of a house and be heading soon, hopefully, for home. The island. Not Red Island. The real island of Newfoundland.

Where he hoped to help cod make a big comeback.

Chapter 23

The three ducky mugs were still sitting on Jamieson's kitchen counter. She'd become tired of them staring at her, so she had turned their faces to the wall. Now she had three ducky bums greeting her whenever she went into the kitchen.

She had begun to use them. Was it right to use evidence? Were they evidence? Of what exactly? They were tricky to drink from. She had several episodes of what she called "missing the mandible," before she got the hang of it.

She was priding herself on the accomplishment, knocking back a big slug of coffee, when Finn came in the door without knocking, and, in an excess of familiarity he couldn't have explained, squeezed her waist from behind. Coffee came shooting out of her mouth, and, like a tsunami, reeled back on itself and surged down a reluctant throat. She began coughing and gasping, and Finn, thinking she was choking, began to perform the Heimlich manoeuvre.

Fists to the gut made Jamieson drop the ducky cup, and it crashed to pieces on the floor.

No longer a piece of evidence. Pieces of evidence?

Gasping, she fought to find her voice, prepared to be angry. But when she saw Finn's face, a mix of concern and apology, she burst out laughing. Looking at her, coffee wetting her chin and stains on her shirt, he started to laugh, too.

That's how Superintendent Constable found them. He stared at them and then at the ducky mugs on the counter.

Were things getting out of hand again at The Shores?

He had her report in his hand. A missing man. A death. Or two? It didn't look good. That's why he was here. He wanted to clear things up before his golf game this afternoon. Didn't want police matters affecting his stroke.

What he was seeing now didn't inspire him with confidence that it would work out that way.

***

"I'm ordering you to call off the search."

Jamieson immediately regretted having told Superintendent Constable her doubts. Doubts about Gus and her mental state. Abel and his. Her growing belief that he didn't exist at all, that he had died long ago, that the records had disappeared, just like Abel.

Jamieson had been thinking it was time to call off the search but had been reluctant to do it. She frowned at the complexity of community policing – it got you all tangled up with people, emotions, friendships. She'd never had friends before. Had she been better off without them? As a police officer, certainly yes.

She resented the order from her superior. It was random officiousness, as all his pronouncements were. Still she had to admit it would make it easier for her if she could blame it on him.

***

"What right does he have to call off the search?"

Jamieson could see the accusation in Hy's eyes. They said coward.

Jamieson had confided in Hy before she made it public.

"He's my superior officer."

Hy snorted. "Superior. Puh-leez."

Jamieson frowned. She couldn't be chummy with Hy on this point, even though she silently agreed with her.

"It's the villagers who are searching. He's not the boss of them."

"But he is my boss. And Murdo's boss."

Hy snorted again. Murdo did so little police work in the village, people had forgotten he was a Mountie. They never saw him in uniform…or on the beat, although he and April and the flock of little Deweys had been everywhere searching for Abel. April had even gone out, white cake in hand, trying to tempt Abel out of wherever it was that he was hidden. Like shaking a bag of treats to get the cat to come in from the cold. So far the only taker had been Murdo, slice after slice disappearing as they searched The Shores, until the cake was all gone, and they went home.

"He can't stop us from continuing the search."

"Noooo…" Jamieson drew out the word. "But I can't be part of it."

"I think you are, whether you like it or not. You're a villager now." Hy gave Jamieson a cheeky grin, and Jamieson nearly smiled back.

"Look, if you're going to continue the search, I'll give you what unofficial help I can. But here's what I think. I think we've searched everywhere. I also think Abel doesn't exist." Even so, she was following up Seamus's email to Abel. And wondering what business it was that Ferguson had with the old man. Was it all just a fish story?

"You mean he's dead?"

How to put it diplomatically? "Well, yes, but not recently."

The thought silenced Hy. Jamieson was suggesting that Gus was out of her mind. That wasn't true. It couldn't be true. She refused to believe it.

"You think the whole village has amnesia?"

That's exactly what Jamieson thought at times. The Shores was not just a village the world had forgotten, but also a village that couldn't remember itself.

"Doesn't that punch a hole in your argument?" Hy said smartly.

"I don't know. I think something's missing." She paused and rephrased it. "We're missing something."

"Abel," said Hy.

"No. Something more. Something that could take us to him."

"Not if we don't go looking. You'll see," Hy said, with a

confidence she didn't have. "I'll find him. This search has not been called off."

***

The ER nurse, Ed, and emergency doctor, Dr. Diamante, had seen it before. An old guy, dressed in his long johns and a bright yellow raincoat, brought in on a stretcher. Who dressed these old men, Ed always wondered. He himself had great fashion sense, even when it came to his scrubs.

Dr. Diamante – he of the big brown eyes, soft and warm as a cow's, arched by a single thick eyebrow that made him exotic – pronounced the old man "unconscious," and said he thought it might soon be "time to call the family."

Ed nodded. That's what Diamante always said. Until they could find out who this man was, and who the family was that should be called, the wise doctor gave his usual prescription. No drugs.

"Rest. Plenty of rest," he nodded, eyebrow diving in concern. "Then perhaps we will know who he is."

The man lying there was no longer unconscious, and, had they known that, he would still not have told them his name. He had no plans to get plenty of rest. His brain had come newly alive. He wanted to get out of town. He was clear on why. If not how.

He knew now that it had been a mistake to come here in the first place, although he was proud of having cycled himself all the way to Winterside. He'd forgotten that Seamus had driven him. There were still gaps in his memory.

The small figure in long johns peered out of the emergency room privacy curtains.

***

Nathan had driven Germaine and Estelle to the hospital. She was clinging to her husband as if he could save her from some horrible threat. He could. Just by living. Estelle couldn't imagine life without Germaine, even though he never did a thing for her, never lifted a hand around the house, never showed in any way that he cared for her.

She didn't need any of that. He was there. That's all she needed. For him to be there. She thought he made her less lonely. She didn't know that the empty feeling inside her came from him.

Estelle was going to stay with Germaine that night. Doctors had found nothing wrong with him but were keeping him overnight for observation. Estelle would be doing most of the observing, sitting in a hard hospital chair, doing the crossword, while he slept, as he always did. Soundly. Noisily. Grunting and snoring, peppered with sounds of deep satisfaction. Once they were settled, Nathan prepared to leave. He went to the bathroom and then stocked up on chocolate bars and soft drinks to keep him awake on the way back.

Dr. Diamante and Ed the nurse stood beside him, buying coffee from the machine.

"We should check on that old man again," said Ed. "Someone's bound to be looking for him."

Nathan whipped around. "An old man?"

"Yes, came in tonight. Nothing much wrong with him, except age," Ed said. "We don't know who he is."

"Maybe I know," said Nathan, eager. "Can you take me to him?"

When they got to the curtained-off area where the old man had been, the bed was empty. They began a fruitless search around the hospital, until they finally gave up. A couple of people thought they might have seen him, but couldn't be sure. They said he was there one minute, gone the next.

Nathan phoned Jamieson.

"Have we any idea...any idea at all...that it was him?" There was hope in Jamieson's tone.

"Only that he's an old man, suddenly appeared, suddenly disappeared, like Abel does."

"So he could be alive?" Jamieson brightened. There might yet be a good result.

"Could be. But where is he?"

"And what's he doing in Winterside?"

"I could prowl around the streets, if you'd like."

"I'd appreciate that, Nathan."

"No worries. Happy to do it."

Outside in the parking lot, the back door of Nathan's van opened and closed. Five minutes later, Nathan strode out of the hospital, hopped in the van and began a long, slow drive through the city with the man he was looking for in the back of his van.

***

A lobster supper. Ferguson smiled at his plan. It was the answer to a lot of things. Among them, the snickering and strange curiosity over the sluice gate. It would put a better face on things.

He boasted to Letitia at breakfast about how well it had been received.

"Good neighbourly relations," his voice striking a tone she always recognized as insincere.

But she agreed.

"I suppose it is a good way to get to know the neighbours."

"It'll build some good will. They weren't that happy about us bringing all these cats here. I think I turned that around rather nicely."

"Yes," she said, with a big sigh. "This might keep you out of mischief."

"Yes, dear." His tone was sugared with insincerity. It would sidetrack the cod hunt. It might also help expedite it. Goodwill could be a powerful tool.

Ferguson was stalled on the "cod initiative," as he had termed it. He needed a boat, equipment, and a fisherman who knew what he was doing. Seamus kept screwing up. Ferguson had become stuck on the idea that he needed Abel Mack. Probably because he couldn't have Abel Mack. Where was he? Ferguson had become fixated on the man as the one who could solve his problems. If he could be found. If he could get more money out of Letitia. Money. It would take more than Letitia would be willing to give for something she didn't believe in: the captivity of a wild creature.

***

Seamus had been parked outside the hospital, prepared to wait, if necessary, until morning to see if the Hat Man emerged. He didn't have to wait long. He saw the old man climb up into the back of a van and was about to go round him up when Nathan came out of the hospital and climbed into the driver's seat. Seamus decided to follow him. He wasn't prepared for the convoluted route, as Nathan drove up and down streets and lanes in search of the man who was in the back of his van. So intent had Nathan been on scouring the streets for a sign of Abel that he'd didn't notice the black PT Cruiser following him, like a Nazi in the night.

Winterside wasn't a big town, and the area around the hospital where a person could walk wasn't large. The town was bordered on two sides by water and two by highway. After an hour, Nathan had turned up nothing. Discouraged, he headed home, still completely unaware of his passenger.

Seamus in the black car behind him shot through the night, as Nathan picked up speed on the Island Way, headed for the only place it led to: The Shores.

***

The one advantage of being over ninety years old is it doesn't matter where you sleep, on an orthopedic mattress or the floor. When you wake up, everything hurts. Nathan's van had the advantage of being set up as an ambulance and therefore had two stretcher cots. Even so, the old man woke up on the floor, after finding it impossible to sleep on either cot. Everything hurt.

He peeked out the window of the van. His warm breath created fog on the glass, chilled by the overnight air. The sun was just coming up.

He'd slept for hours, before waking, confused about where he was.

The van was parked in Nathan's driveway. The old man eased open the back door and looked out. It took a few moments to register. Then he knew.

Home.

He was home.

Up and over the hill and down again.

Home.

But home wasn't where he was going. Not yet.

No one was up. He stretched a few times, and jumped out of the van with the vigour of a man half his age. He swung into the cab of the vehicle, not slamming the door, but easing it carefully to a close. It didn't quite catch, but he'd close it properly when he was on the road.

The keys were right where they should be. In the ignition. He popped into neutral and let the van roll back on the slight slope of the driveway, out onto the road, far from the house or any house. He turned on the motor and took off.

The sky grumbled behind him, bringing on a bank of big black clouds. The gulls had already disappeared from the shore, flocking inland to be out of the path of a storm threatening. It was the edge of a hurricane that might, or might not, hit Red Island. Hard to say. The cows weren't helping. They were doing what they do, defying local lore. Some were lying down. Some were standing up.

***

The information that there had been an old man checked in

at the hospital in Winterside gave Jamieson a new perspective – and possibly a new area for the search. They'd been looking around the neighbourhood, but what if Abel had not been in the neighbourhood at all?

It turned out that whether the search was on or off was immaterial. The villagers' interest in finding him had waned.

"What's the point?" said hardhearted Gladys Fraser, appearing more like a bulldog than usual. "He's probly dead anyway, and would we know him to see him?"

Jamieson and Hy considered Gladys and her attitude largely responsible for the dwindling number of volunteers on the search. They had gone over and over the same ground and come up with nothing. Fewer were showing up. Even the Macks – Ben, Annabelle, and Nathan – had stopped their search, sad but certain Abel would be found – dead. Meantime, there was a hay harvest to bring in, and theirs was an increasingly rare thing on Red Island – a real family farm. Everyone had to pitch in at the busy times. Finally, it was left to only Jamieson, Finn, Hy, and Ian. The Winterside police had come up with nothing after a quick sweep around the city. That didn't surprise Jamieson. Their concern for The Shores was nonexistent, their ability to find a missing villager equally absent, even if he had walked up and introduced himself.

It couldn't go on. Jamieson reluctantly announced she was bringing even the unofficial search to an end.

"Someone better tell Gus." Hy didn't want to be the one.

"Of course I will." Jamieson looked grim. "It's my duty."

"I'll come with you," said Hy, regretting her initial cowardice. She knew she should be there to support her friend. Both her friends. Jamieson and Gus.

Jamieson and Hy dragged their feet across the field to Gus's. Gus saw them coming through the big picture window that was like her village television channel. She guessed their news. Not good, she thought. Not the worst though, she decided, interpreting their gait with the knowledge accumulated through decades of observation through that window. "Through the looking glass," she thought of it.

She was ready when they came in.

After a few uncomfortable pleasantries, Jamieson cleared her throat. It was the smoke getting to her, she told herself.

"We're stopping the search."

Gus looked down at her knitting.

"Thought you'd have done that by now."

Jamieson and Hy exchanged a look.

"Maybe...if some evidence..." She shouldn't make promises she couldn't keep, hold out straws...

Gus just nodded. Neither Jamieson nor Hy could make out how she felt.

Jamieson turned to leave. When she reached the door, Gus spoke.

"Course, there's always the cove."

Jamieson spun around.

"The cove?"

Jamieson looked at Hy.

Hy shrugged and shook her head.

"Bloodsucker Cove. He kept a dory there." Gus continued plain, purl, plain, purl, not looking up. "'Spect there's nothing to it." Why hadn't she mentioned it before, thought of it before? Was she getting the old timers, too? Like Abel?

"Why didn't you mention it before?" Jamieson tried to keep the frustration out of her voice.

"Din't think of it. Forgot, I guess. No one's been there in a long time."

Someone had. Was, in fact, right now.

Chapter 24

He looked down from the cape.

His head bent forward, shoulders slumped in disappointment. No Dory. Or too many bloodsuckers. Jellyfish. He thought he could see the bump where the boat was, but he would never dig it out.

Bloodsucker Cove was a great place to hide a dory. Hide anything, in fact. No one went there because the waters were choking full of bloodsuckers, jellyfish long dead and rotting in the ocean and on the shore. The smell and sight of them was disgusting. They piled up on the shore in late July every year, year after year, until there were mountains of them. Winter would wash some away, but still they remained in the thousands. There probably was a dory in there somewhere, if you knew where to look. He hadn't been down in years, he remembered. He had expected to see his dory with its beautiful yellow-and-red striping. The dory he had almost caught that fish with. He turned, disheartened, and returned to Nathan's truck.

He'd go to Big Bay.

They were there.

They were waiting.

He had to get to them.

With a spring in his step, he climbed into the cab of the van and took off for the harbour.

Plenty of boats there.

***

Jamieson stood at the top of the cape, staring down in despair. Bloodsucker Cove was inaccessible. If she couldn't face going down there, neither could a ninety-year-old man, however remarkable he was. But there was something. Fresh vehicle tracks in the clay lane, beside her own. Footprints, too. New. Maybe this wasn't another wild goose chase. Perhaps she was finally on Abel's trail. Where was it leading her?

Before she was able to find out, she had other fish to fry.

***

Word had spread quickly through the village and guaranteed a big crowd for Ferguson's lobster supper. The villagers held their own community lobster feed every year. Gladys had to warn that the lobster would be "from away." From the south shore of Red Island, not the north. So, of course, they wouldn't be as good.

Several of the Women's Institute members had shown up to help prepare the supper.

"Leave it to us." Ferguson put a hand on Olive's shoulder and turned her away. She flushed red with pleasure at being touched by a man not her husband, and such a handsome one. With such a voice. He smiled, knowing the effect he, and especially his voice, had on women. Since he'd arrived, several of the local women had phoned him, just to hear him say "hello" in his basso profundo. Then they'd either hang up or claim they'd dialed a wrong number.

Letitia was used to it.

"Now come." Ferguson dropped his voice down even lower, sending a thrill through Olive of a kind she'd never experienced.

"You go set up the tables and let us take care of the dinner. Take it as our thank you for welcoming us into the community."

The W.I. ladies backed off, and Ferguson closed the kitchen door.

***

Everyone in the village turned out, including Gus, even though she didn't like lobster. No one missed Abel, because he had never attended community events, except, sometimes, on the sidelines.

Jamieson came, not for the social event, but so she could ask more questions about Abel and Bloodsucker Cove. Finn arrived at the same time and stayed at her side.

Jamieson had put Murdo on duty. Even so, he was at the hall with April Dewey and her brood, because, as he had pointed out to Jamieson, everyone in the village was in the hall, so if there was going to be trouble, that's where it was going to be.

He turned out to be right about that.

Ferguson had arrived at the hall before Letitia, saying he wanted to get things started. When she arrived, big pots were on the burners of the two stoves and steam was fogging the room.

"I see you've got them cooking."

"Yup. On the go."

She hugged him.

"You're so good to me."

She began to wheeze. To cough. To fight for breath. She pulled out her puffer. It didn't help. She went down on her knees, hand on her chest, gasping, then fell to the floor. When she fell, Letitia dropped her puffer, and, with one arm outstretched, groped for it.

Her chest felt as if someone were sitting on it. Her lungs gummed up in a cloud of thick mucus. Nothing she hadn't experienced before, but worse, worse this time. Her airway swelled and closed. She struggled for a breath, one breath, but it wouldn't come. She tried to speak, but couldn't make a sound. Her eyes appealed to Ferguson to help her. He stood there, looking at her, paralyzed by what was happening.

The kitchen was full of steam and the smell of the sea. The steam escaped through the cracks in the door and laid a film over the copper-coloured tin ceiling in the main hall. It became warm and the villagers began to disrobe – jackets and sweaters pulled off, some of the women rolling down their support hose into bulky lumps around their ankles.

Only Jamieson appeared unaffected. She'd trained herself not to show the heat, even wrapped in her police jacket, pants, and boots. It was one of the things that Finn admired about her. He himself was ready to pull off his T-shirt and expose his naked skin. It would never do.

"Mighty hot in here," someone said, finally.

It was, thought Jamieson. Too hot. She marched up the stairs to the kitchen and flung open the door.

A billow of steam hit her solidly in the face, burning, turning to water dripping down her skin. The vapour seeped around her and into the hall.

She could hardly see into the kitchen, so obscured was it by the clouds of steam coming from four big pots, boiling crustaceans to their deaths.

Coughing. Desperate coughing. Coughing, turned to choking.

"Help. Please help." It was Ferguson, somewhere on the other side of the room. On the floor?

Jamieson skirted the island counter and almost tripped over Letitia. She was rolling around on the floor, hand over her mouth in an instinctive but useless gesture. Ferguson was holding her head up and trying to still her.

The coughing continued. Harsh. Sharp. It was painful to hear.

"Get her out of here." Finn had followed Jamieson through the door. The steam was clearing; some of it had escaped through the open door. He strode over to where Letitia lay, Ferguson and Jamieson at her side.

She stopped coughing.

"Good," said Jamieson.

"Not good," said Finn. He knelt down beside Letitia, took her pulse.

"No pulse," he said, and motioning Jamieson and Ferguson out of the way, began CPR.

After ten minutes, he gave up.

"She's dead," he said, and looked at his watch. "Six forty-one p.m."

Jamieson slipped her notebook out of her pocket and wrote it down.

"Asthma?" she asked.

Finn nodded. "They'll have to confirm it in town, of course."

"Of course." Then she looked over at Ferguson.

"I'm sorry," she said. He had a curious look on his face. Not a smile, certainly. Not a frown. A grimace? She couldn't inter-pret it, she who was so good at reading body language. Body language, yes. Facial messages, not so much. Facial messages were too close to the emotions for Jamieson's comfort.

Finn snapped off all the elements on the two stoves. He stared into the pots.

"You may want these for evidence."

She looked up. Her eyes narrowed. Ferguson focused on Finn with intensity. She knew better than to ask Finn more right now. If he thought it was evidence – evidence of what? Why had he used that word?

"For now…" Finn opened and closed a few drawers until he found one with tablecloths in it. He drew out a large linen one.

"Finn, that's the best –"

"No better use for it then."

He unfolded it and laid it gently on the body of Letitia Fer-guson, her face more peaceful than it had been in years, with the racking coughing that had tortured her stopped. Forever.

"Best call Nathan," he said.

Many suppers at the hall had ended in disaster, and this one had, too. There had been the lobster rights activist who'd crashed the annual lobster supper, tossing pamphlets and slogans around; Gladys Fraser's poisonous potato salad that had killed a woman and sent the whole village to the bathroom; and the senior who'd died in the loo. Beans.

Now, a woman had died, and nobody got a feed of lobster.

The crowd dispersed, with some mumbles and grumbles about there being no free lunch...or supper.

Jamieson asked Finn to stay behind with her and prepared to seal the kitchen area with yellow police tape.

The body must be moved first. Where was Nathan?

As if the thought had summoned him up, he came through the door and shrugged, his mouth a grim line.

"The van is gone."

"Gone?"

"Gone."

It sounded as if Abel were missing all over again. *Gone. Gone? Gone.*

"Left it in my driveway as usual after coming back from Winterside."

"When did it disappear?"

Nathan shrugged again. "Didn't know until you called, and there it...wasn't," he ended, weakly.

"All day, and you didn't notice?"

"I was up all night. I slept in and then Lili and I –" Lili was Nathan's yogi girlfriend and the village flower farmer.

Jamieson held up a hand.

"Enough information," she said. "For now. We'll deal with the van later, but right now we'll have to call Winterside." Jamieson slipped out her cellphone and clicked on the contact.

Nathan's paramedic van – stolen? So now she was missing an old man and a van. Jamieson thought of the fresh tracks at the cove. Were they related?

For a moment, she didn't know what to do first. Go after the elusive Abel – assuming he had taken the van – or deal with the death on her doorstep?

Just a death? She'd learned to consider all possibilities. Was there any chance it might be murder?

No. No chance. She'd seen the woman die herself. Black and white. The way she liked it. None of those greys. The smoky sky. The disappearance of Abel. The stolen van.

***

The old man knew places beyond Big Bay that were even more secret than Bloodsucker Cove. He'd driven Nathan's van to one of these hidden spots off the road, the only road. A lonely road. The Island Way, where, beyond Big Bay, it circled around on itself and headed back to civilization, through The Shores and then straight on to Winterside. Made lonelier now by the sudden silence that descended. A silence so profound it seemed like a roar. The gulls had moved inland. They knew what was coming. So did Abel. He hoped to get out on the water before it arrived.

***

Seamus had waited most of the previous night and following day in a glade at the edge of Nathan's property, where the van was clearly visible. He didn't dare take his eyes off it and let the old man escape again. He wasn't sure what he was going to do with him, but, whatever it was, it wasn't going to happen in Nathan's driveway. It would have to be a more secluded spot.

He'd missed his chance when Abel turned off onto Bloodsucker Cove. Seamus was driving without lights on and had no idea there was a lane there. Abel just veered off the main road without signalling. Seamus went squealing by. The road narrowed to not much more than one lane, with deep ditches on either side as it crossed over marshland.

He finally found a place to pull off the road. When he did, the van shot past him, and Seamus continued following at a careful distance, lights out. The van slipped into a secluded place off the road, and Seamus parked close by, hidden from the road and from his quarry by a stand of evergreens. He'd been drinking coffee and knocking back caffeinated candies to stay awake, but, in spite of his best efforts, he fell asleep.

It didn't matter, not then, because Abel had fallen asleep, too.

Chapter 25

Jamieson was shocked the next morning to find out that Letitia's body had been cremated, and she was to be buried that day in The Shores Pioneer Cemetery. Ferguson had moved fast, but within legal limits. He had Dr. Dunn issue the death certificate and the body released before most of the villagers had finished a disappointing supper at home, robbed of the promised lobster feast.

It took a few hours to burn her remains at the crematorium in Winterside. A few hours to cool the ashes down. Popped into a cardboard box, the cheapest conveyance for "cremains" available, Letitia returned to The Shores in the back of Ferguson's car. The local gravedigger had shovelled out a hole three feet deep in the Pioneer Cemetery, Letitia's final resting place acquired with a generous donation to the local Anglican church.

***

The sky was black and oppressive over The Shores. The smoke from Quebec mingled with the dark calm of the storm coming, the mood set perfectly for the funeral of a woman few of them had known. The cemetery was on a sweep of land high above the capes and the ocean, where the wind whispered on a calm day; on wild ones it "blew a gale" that flattened the tall grasses. It was never neutral, always moody in some way. Today, silence circled the place where the bones of the earliest European islanders lay. The unseeing dead had a better view than the living – of the village and fields below, the ocean curving in and out, defining Montgomery Shore, Vanishing Point, and Mack's Shore. On a clear day a person could see all the way to Big Bay. That day was not today, with its thick ridge of black clouds rumbling over the land and water.

There was no church at the graveyard. The bodies had been buried there before a church was built. When it was, it was located inside the village, and the dead were left to shift for themselves on that wildly beautiful swath of land.

The entrance was a black wrought-iron gate – a gate in the middle of nowhere. Visitors didn't have to go through it to get to the graves. They could, and usually did, enter on either side of it. But it defined the place, as did the big granite rock that marked the graves no longer seen, hidden by time, the last resting place of the pioneers. Pioneers with their familiar names. Mack. Toombs. Fraser. Joudry. Dewey. Everyone had someone here.

The grass was cut the way Red Islanders liked it – short as a crewcut and maintained that way through the growing season. Around the outside of the clifftop cemetery, the wild grass grew, waving in the wind, moving to its command, blowing life through this place of death.

What a waste, thought Ferguson. It was a property he longed to possess. He wouldn't mind the crumbling bones beneath him, but he might mind being so close to Letitia's remains. It was too bad Letitia was dead, but now he'd have the money, to use as he wished. No more asking. Except, of course, there'd be a temporary freeze on all her assets. That would be a spanner in the works. Still, people would know he was good for the money.

In an exhibition of undue haste, Ferguson had requested the lawyer's presence immediately after the burial, so that they could get right down to business.

All the villagers showed up for the send-off. They loved a funeral, and they loved their Pioneer Cemetery. It was a major tourist stop on the Island Way. That comforted them – knowing that people would always be coming to visit, even if they were strangers from away. They'd be buried next to their neighbours and visited by folk from around the world. They wouldn't be lonely in death.

Connoisseurs of funerals, the villagers had been expecting something more traditional than Ferguson provided. The minister was of uncertain faith. There was no praying, no Twenty-Third Psalm, no "*In my Father's house there are many dwelling places*," and no kind words about the dead woman. They watched, mystified, when Ferguson took off as soon as he could, leaving strangers to stand by Letitia's grave, ears assaulted by the bagpipe playing of Millie Fraser, Gladys's granddaughter. She was as bad at the pipes as she was at singing and step dancing. Gladys, critical of everything, had a big blind spot about her granddaughter's talents and had provided her services for the funeral, unbidden and unknown to Ferguson. She beamed as the girl tortured the pipes, their sound like seagulls screeching. She thought Millie was doing Letitia a great favour. She didn't see the irony in having bagpipes, an instrument that required healthy lungs and a large breathing capacity, played at the funeral of a woman who had spent years unable to catch a breath. And had died because she could not.

Gus surveyed the graveyard, looked down at the open grave, tossed a handful of earth onto the cardboard box. "She don't know anyone here," she said to no one in particular. She shook her head, unable to imagine being buried in a place she didn't come from, without her neighbours close by. The graves were ready and waiting for her and her kin, with their names and birthdates carved in stone, lacking only that final date.

The Macks had a massive monument, detailing the deaths of generations. Ben and Annabelle's names and birthdates were there, too, waiting with a dash. Annabelle found it creepy, but Gus found it comforting. What disturbed her was the possibility that Abel might not make it here, to lie beside her through all eternity.

Would Abel ever find his grave, Gus wondered, as she stood considering the monument. Was he dead, with nothing to be found, none of him to bury? What did you do when someone was "missing and presumed dead"? Did you dig a hole and fill it back up? Would he have anywhere to go after, if he didn't start from the right place, this grave here, waiting for him? And when did you presume? Seven years, that's what she'd heard. She didn't expect she'd live another seven years. What would he do if he came back, and she wasn't there?

She shuffled away with her troubling thoughts. She hadn't lost her faith that Abel would be found and found alive. But he might have lost himself.

He might be found and not know who he was, who she was.

Chapter 26

"What did you mean…evidence?" Jamieson and Finn were back in the hall, still closed, the villagers grumbling that the Friday night crokinole evening might be cancelled.

"Evidence of what killed her," said Finn.

"You said asthma."

"That's what it was, I'm certain. Asthma. But, when I looked in those pots, it made me think."

"What?"

"She may have been murdered."

"But I saw it. She obviously had asthma…or was choking on a piece of food."

"No, I cleared out her tubes when I did the CPR. Nothing there. I bet she had The Lung."

"The Lung. What's that?"

"Crab asthma."

"Crab asthma?"

"Like regular asthma, only it affects people who work in fish plants, mostly women, because that's who works there. They become allergic to the crabs. The asthma is carried on the steam, you might say. Like any asthma, it can kill a vulnerable person."

"What makes it crab asthma?"

"The steam from cooking crabs carries proteins that can cause asthma."

"But it was a lobster dinner. Can lobster do it?"

"No. But you're wrong. That's crab in those pots. Change of menu."

Jamieson flushed. She hadn't looked in the pots. She ducked under the yellow police tape and motioned him to follow. She marched into the kitchen and lifted a lid off one of the pots. Then the next. Then another. And the final one. Crabs in all of them.

The scent of eight-dozen crabs sitting overnight in lukewarm water was overpowering.

"Phew. That could kill anyone," said Finn.

"This is what you meant when you said evidence."

"Yup."

"What should I do with them?"

"You can't keep them. Unless you want to freeze some, but it's not like they contain a poison or anything. Why don't you photograph them and then get Murdo to come and clean up?"

Jamieson thought that was a great idea. The ladies had been ordered out of the hall and wouldn't appreciate being ordered back in to clean up. Get Murdo to do some work for a change, while she went over to ask Ferguson a few questions. But first, she had to field a call from the Superintendent.

***

"You've dropped the ball, Jamieson."

Jamieson could hear that she was on speakerphone, that hollow sound. There was another sound, too, periodically, as she spoke to Superintendent Constable. A "whack," followed sometimes by a curse.

The Superintendent was practising his golf swing. It wasn't going well. The reason: his irritation and impatience at having to deal with police matters when he was due on the links in less than an hour. He was especially anxious to get there, as he was going to be playing his favourite partner, the only one he could beat.

"You've got to keep your eye on the ball. On the ball," he

repeated, lining his club up for another swing. He swung. Missed.

"Around here, you need eyes in the back of your head."

A moment's pause as the Superintendent took what turned out to be an extremely satisfactory swing.

"That's as may be, but you can't have people dying on your watch all the time. This woman now. You said natural causes?"

"Apparently."

"Apparently? Apparently? What kind of answer is that?"

"Apparently –" she dared to be cheeky – "not a good one." It was the sort of thing, she thought, that Hy would say. Was she rubbing off on her? Probably. The entire village had been rubbing off on her.

He grunted.

Like a cod in heat, she thought. More Hy.

"So what were the causes?" Swing. Whack.

"Our forensic man…" she thought that sounded more professional than "Finn." And Finn *was* a fully certified forensic scientist. "Our forensic man says…"

"Damn!"

"No…"

"Damn!" A sound like an impact of some kind. A golf club and a wall?

"…says it could be crab asthma."

"Oh, yes. Stands to reason."

Jamieson didn't think it stood to reason at all. She had expected the superintendent to be surprised, curious, disbelieving. Anything but matter-of-fact.

She didn't know he'd spent his early years as a Mountie in Newfoundland. He'd seen crab asthma kill. Many times. Fish-plant workers. Mostly women.

"Then why was she here?" He rapped out a series of questions, anxious to return to his golf practice. "Who brought her here, now? In the current conditions? Why was she cooking crabs?"

It was maybe the smartest thing the superintendent had ever said or thought. The most useful words he'd spoken in his long, lacklustre career.

The light went on for Jamieson. What *had* brought Letitia here – and why?

"I don't know."

"Find out." He rang off, leaving Jamieson thinking. Maybe this was not a death from natural causes. Murder? Again?

How did you prove someone – Ferguson? – had killed someone with crab asthma?

***

The lawyer didn't stay long, and it was soon all over the village. The lawyer was married to one of the Dunn girls, the medical and mortician family.

"He's practically left out of the will." Estelle Joudry had considered the information too important to relay by phone, and had trotted down to communicate it to Gus in person.

"He's got enough to live on very comfortably, but most of the money..." She paused for dramatic effect, "...most of the money goes to the cats."

Gus's eyes and mouth opened wide.

"Imagine," she said. Maybe the man had known what he was doing leaving his wife in that lonely grave.

Hy burst through the door. "Did you hear...?"

Gus and Estelle nodded their heads.

"Gladys might be wanting to adopt those cats herself now."

"Now that they're rich."

Privately, Hy was thinking that Letitia might have left her money to the cats to protect them from Ferguson.

"I bet you don't know this." Hy grinned with anticipation at the gossip she was about to impart.

"She's left the house and the barn and caring for the cats to Billy and Madeline. With an income."

"Moira will be wanting them cats now." Estelle's smile was mean.

"This calls for a fresh pot of tea." Gus hoisted herself out of her chair and padded to the pantry.

***

"So you heard about the will?" Finn had dropped by the police house as soon as he found out about it.

"No. I imagine Ferguson's a very rich man now."

"Not at all."

"No?" Jamieson looked surprised.

"Left it to her cats – and Billy and Madeline."

Jamieson had made a pot of coffee. She poured some into the two ducky mugs. She'd begun using them all the time. Partly because, like Hy wearing the Tilley hat, she hoped it would lead her to Abel.

She gave Finn a mug and they both sat down.

"Nothing for him?"

"It's something, but just a trust fund, keeps him on a leash. Two million. In trust. For life."

"That's a lot, and not a lot, at the same time. How did he react?"

"Shoved the lawyer out of the house. Dropped the F-bomb four times. Looked grim. Spoke to no one. Certainly not the media. Lester Joudry and his pals were waiting outside the house along with some villagers."

"And you."

"And me. The paparazzi hardly even got a decent shot. He was lowering his head and covering his face like a criminal." He paused. Grinned. "Maybe he's practising."

"Two million…in trust…is a pretty good price to put on a wife."

"Sixteen million is better. That's how much she had."

"You think someone might kill for the prospect of sixteen million, but not if they knew it would be just two…in trust."

"The question is, what did he know? Maybe he thought the whole sixteen would be his."

"True. She must have made that will very recently, to include

Madeline and Billy."

"Consider it now. If Ferguson did murder Letitia, it's going to be hard to pin down a conviction. The money helps. But we need more. The fact is, if he'd known he wasn't going to get all the money, that could have been a disincentive."

"A reason to keep her alive."

They both sipped their coffee, silent for a moment.

"I think this suggests we revisit the case." Finn hesitated when he said it. He knew Jamieson didn't like people giving her advice. But she liked Finn. More than liked Finn. Now that Dot was out of the way...

"But she could have died of ordinary asthma, right? Simply that."

"Absolutely. If she had it badly enough, this smoky environment won't have been good for her, and the steam might have tripped off an attack."

"So what are you saying?"

"I'm not sure what I'm saying."

"You are saying natural causes? Or not natural causes?"

"I'm not sure."

"So what was she doing, cooking crabs?"

"Good question."

"Could we prove it medically?"

He didn't answer. Of course they couldn't, with Letitia reduced to ashes and in her grave.

"We can only say it was asthma, not definitively that it was caused by crabs."

"So we'd need a motive. A strong motive."

"Money's all we've got," said Finn.

"And a modus? The change in menu?"

"So we need to find out how, why, who made the change."

"Exactly."

It had been too good to be true. A whole year at The Shores without a murder.

Chapter 27

Ferguson was at his most charming when he opened the door to Jamieson's knock. He hardly looked like a man bereaved, she thought, as he ushered her in with a sweep of his arm.

"And to what do I owe the pleasure?" he inquired as he led her down the long hall into the parlour, still very much a parlour in this old house, with the wrought-iron coal fireplace surround gleaming black beauty under a marble mantel.

"Please." Ferguson motioned to a dainty needlework-covered chair beside the fireplace. She declined. For one thing, it looked too small. For another, she didn't want to make him – or herself – too comfortable by sitting down. Standing up helped her keep her edge.

Because she was standing, he remained standing, too. Two can play at that game, he thought. Had he sat down, he would have had to look up at her to respond. This way, though Jamieson was tall, he still had a few inches the advantage.

Jamieson cut right to it.

"Your wife was ill."

"Apparently so."

"Are you saying you didn't know?"

"Letitia was…of delicate health, it's true."

"Did you know about the smoke before you came?"

"Of course not. What exactly are you insinuating?"

"Nothing – yet. I'm just asking questions, as I'm bound to do as a law enforcement officer when there has been a death."

Ferguson gave up his advantage and slumped down on a

French provincial loveseat, a dainty piece that exaggerated his size. He buried his face in his hands.

Jamieson was familiar with the gesture. People did that when they didn't want you to see their face. When they wanted you to think they were grief-stricken. Easier than producing crocodile tears, and more convincing.

Uninterested in taking part in a charade, Jamieson got right to it.

"Did you know your wife had crab asthma? Did you kill her by substituting crab for lobster?"

***

Ian and Hy had retreated to their most useful tool in cracking crime: Ian's computer. They googled Brock Ferguson.

"Woohoo," said Hy and stabbed a finger at a link halfway down the screen.

"Minister leaves community in disgrace," Ian read.

Hy picked it up.

"Anglican priest Brock Ferguson, 41, has been removed from his parish for improper relations with parishioners whom he was counselling."

"A priest!"

"Minister."

"Yes, but Anglican. That makes him a priest."

"What does it matter? Still a holy man."

Ian clicked to the newspaper article. "Not that holy."

"Wow." Hy read along with him.

Three women have come forward, claiming Reverend Ferguson made sexual advances when they were meeting with him to discuss personal problems. Their marriages were the problem. That's what Ferguson told them, encouraging them to leave their husbands and insinuating that he would be happy to take up where their men had left off. In all cases, that was the beginning of a series of sexual overtures. The women had two things in common: they were Anglicans, and they were wealthy.

Ian returned to the Google page. There were six more postings about the scandal.

"No charges were ever laid."

"What?"

"It looks like the women ran scared after they'd opened up to the media. None would press charges against a minister. I bet there was some kind of deal between the powers-that-be in the church and police. Who's to say? It's a small place. Smaller than here, and look what people get away with here."

Murder, thought Hy. Jamieson or no Jamieson.

"There's nothing more. He apparently left the church and the area…until he turned up in the village of Seven Houses. He lived in the eighth. That was over six years ago."

"Before he met and married Letitia."

"After she won the lottery. The first time."

"Wait until Jamieson sees this. She is so going to charge his ass."

"Whoa."

"Why 'whoa'?"

"Just because he was a scumbag priest doesn't make him guilty of murdering his wife."

"Oh c'mon, Ian, you know as well as I do."

"I'm not sure I do. I haven't figured out how you think asthma can be murder."

"Because it's not in the method, Ian, it's in the intent."

Ian shrugged his shoulders.

"If a charge of murder came every time a person thought of killing someone, we'd all be in jail."

"Intent is not thought, it's plan. In this case, I think there was a plan."

***

"Preposterous." Ferguson's face puffed up with the word, his deep voice lending it weight, authority.

Jamieson wasn't convinced. *Preposterous? What an unusual word. Who said preposterous anymore?* She wrote it down, as something to think about after the interview. Jamieson was trained in reading body language, and part of that language was language itself – the words people chose to express their innocence, or, unconsciously, their guilt. There were movements, too, that went with the choice of words. Like Ferguson's puffed-up face, the way he straightened his back, thrust out his chest.

The only problem with reading this kind of language was interpreting it correctly.

That word "preposterous," that straightening up might mean he was guilty of something, or merely that he felt guilty about something – or he might simply be insulted.

She said nothing but waited, creating a silence into which he might pour words that would be of value to her. She was not wrong. People hated silences and usually jumped in to fill the dead air.

"Preposterous." He repeated the word, putting extra stress on the second syllable to lend weight to it. "Ludicrous."

Another word to note. Jamieson scribbled it down. Her action wasn't lost on Ferguson. He hadn't said anything else, except these two words. Why was she writing them down?

"Simply ludicrous," he said, to see what she would do.

Nothing. She'd already written down that word.

"I'm only asking."

"It's preposterous." That word again. "She died of asthma. You were there. There was no weapon."

No weapon that she knew of, she had to agree. Finn had been there, too. Letitia couldn't breathe, couldn't be made to breathe; she was choking from her old ailment. That's what Finn said, and there was no reason not to believe him. He was a forensic scientist after all, a luxury and a real treasure in a backwater like The Shores. Even he couldn't confirm that Letitia had died of crab asthma.

Then why was she pursuing this? Why wasn't it adding up for her?

"As I said, I was just asking."

"On what grounds are you asking? Why on earth would you think that I might have killed my wife, however I might have done it? The conclusion was natural causes. Naturally. That's what it was."

"The money's not natural. It's extraordinary. That bothers me." Jamieson played with his "why on earth" in her mind. Was he protesting too much?

"Where there's a death and a whack of money, you see how it gives rise to suspicion. That's why we're having this little talk. To clear the air."

Would the air ever be clear, she wondered. Not just about Letitia, but that smoke from Quebec, smudging life in The Shores.

"Letitia's money was my money. I hardly needed to kill her for it. You have no proof of any kind. Quite the opposite, I'd say."

Jamieson was circling the word "preposterous" on her note pad. "You didn't get all the money."

"No," he darted a look at the cat enclosure. "No, I didn't."

"You see, that brings us back to my problem with this."

Chapter 28

Finn had waited outside for Jamieson, and they stopped by Ian's on the way back to the police house. Hy and Ian told them about Ferguson's seedy past.

"So you've been nosing around Letitia's death?" Jamieson looked annoyed.

"Yes, we have. I guess that's obvious." Ian gestured toward the computer screen, on which a headline screamed: *Minister "Knows" Church Ladies.*

"Sex always brings a certain something to a murder," said Finn. Jamieson shot him a sharp look.

"Murder?" Hy jumped in. "Letitia? Are you thinking of it as a murder?"

"There have been no charges laid." Jamieson's lips tightened. She didn't want to have this conversation.

"Except in your mind?" Hy saw right through her.

"If it is a murder, it's going to be a difficult one to prove." Finn said. Jamieson looked a warning at him.

"How do you figure?" Ian.

"She may have had a serious kind of asthma. We're checking medical records. In the meantime, we're trying to determine how much Ferguson may have influenced her in coming to this deathly place and engaging in the fatal cook-off."

"Money the motive?" asked Hy.

It was clear, as they looked at each other, that they all believed it was. His history with women and money wasn't pretty.

***

"Abel may be in good shape, but there's no way he could

be much beyond shouting distance of The Shores." Hy was hunkered down in front of Ian's wood stove. He'd stuffed it with paper, kindling, and a couple of small logs after Jamieson and Finn had left. The evening was cool with a fall feel to it, and Ian was in the process of adding his own smoke to the village atmosphere.

Jamieson had tried to stop people from using their wood stoves and running their furnaces, idling their cars and farm equipment, but it had made no difference. Why, the villagers thought, should they make room for smoke from away that was doing nothing for them, not keeping them warm, not driving them to town like their own fumes. Red Island fumes. Smoke made in The Shores. Not healthy either, but at least they were used to it.

"You think he's close by somewhere?'

Hy nodded.

"What makes you think that?"

"How far could a ninety-year-old man get and us not know about it? A man lost in a place where everybody knows everybody's business, where they are, where they've been, and where they're going to."

They didn't know about the sighting of an old man in Winterside. Jamieson had asked Nathan not to tell, because there was no real proof that it was Abel.

Ian put a match to the kindling and sat back to watch the fire roar.

"True." He tossed the match into the flames and shut the glass door.

"He uses cash only, never credit." Jamieson wasn't prepared for that. She thought she might follow a credit trail to find him."

"There'd be a limit to how much cash he had at home. Surely. He couldn't get far for long."

"That's what Jamieson said. She asked Gus. Gus didn't know."

"He must have a bank account. Hasn't Jamieson followed that up?"

"She found no trace. He may have kept all his money under

the mattress."

"Did anyone look?"

Hy grinned.

"We did. Me, Finn, Jamieson. Gus showed us."

A spark of interest in his eyes. For what she was saying, and for the flames playing on her copper hair.

"What?"

"Guess," she said teasing, the warmth of the fire melting her into a playful mood. He reached over and twisted a tendril of her hair around his finger.

"Three blind mice."

"No, several hundred one-dollar bills. Gus said he was waiting for them to make a comeback."

Ian whistled. "That was all of his money?"

"No. Gus said there should be more. She didn't know if he put it somewhere else or took it with him."

She nodded. The tendril of hair slipped from his grasp. He moved his hand away.

"How much?"

"All his life savings. Thousands?" She shrugged. "Tens of thousands?"

Ian whistled again. "What about Gus?"

"What about Gus?

"What about her money? Her pension…"

"Oh, she uses a bank, but she won't have anything to do with automatic deposit. She wants the money in her hand."

"The money? They send her cash?"

"No, dummy, they send her a cheque, and she takes it to the bank. She says Abel never liked banks, and she doesn't suppose he ever used them."

"This gets better and better. A ninety-year-old man wandering around with tens of thousands…"

"Maybe hundreds of thousands," Hy broke in, teasing.

"In thousand-dollar bills, is that the next thing you're going to tell me?"

"Could be. The mint doesn't make them anymore, but Abel's

money would come from way back when they did, so there'd be a lot of thousand-dollar bills, is my guess. Gus says Abel worried about it when they stopped making them, worried they'd go the way of the one-dollar bill, and he'd be out of his life savings. I gather he got reassurance on that."

"Or he put his money somewhere no one, not even Gus, can find it."

"When you think about it, how hard could it be to find a ninety-year-old man who's buying things with thousand-dollar bills?"

But it was proving difficult. Impossible. They slipped into silence, contemplating, one more time, the disappearance of Abel Mack.

Hy stared, mesmerized, at the flickering flames. The warmth was wafting across the room, and, oddly, that first burst of heat made her shiver. It always did. Ian was accustomed to it. It was one of those small habits that endeared her to him. He waited for it every time he lit the fire. That, and the flickering light catching her red-gold curls. Charming.

He slid closer to her, as they both stared into the flames, nursing brandies as they had so many times before. In the past few years, added to that picture was most often a mystery or murder. Murder, usually. But Abel hadn't been murdered, had he?

And Letitia?

Ian slipped an arm around Hy's shoulder. She seemed not to notice. At least, she didn't react. She kept on thinking aloud. "I wonder if Jamieson has followed the cash."

"Forget about Jamieson." Ian bent down to kiss her.

Before long, they had both fallen asleep on the floor in front of the fire.

***

Toward dawn – a dawn that couldn't really be seen or appreciated because of the smoke in the air – Hy woke up. She was an early riser, and especially when she fell asleep on Ian's floor. One too many brandies.

She extricated herself from Ian's arm underneath her neck and the other arm thrown across her body. He grunted, but didn't wake. He began a light snore to confirm it.

Had anything happened?

She didn't think so. She was fully clothed.

The kiss. Yes, there had been a kiss. One or two. Three maybe. She passed her fingers through her hair, and that reminded her that he had, too. Passed his fingers through her hair. There was something about it that she liked. She smiled a small smile as she hauled herself up onto her feet. Then she frowned. There was something about it that she didn't like.

They were friends. Close friends, but there had to be a limit. Limits. There must be limits. That worrisome thought kept her awake when she got home and tried to catch more sleep. She couldn't. The puzzle of Abel's disappearance kept playing on her mind.

Three hours passed as she tossed and turned on her bed. How ridiculous that she was able to fall asleep – pass out? – on a wooden floor, but couldn't in her own good bed.

***

He hadn't come out of the van all night or all morning.

What was he doing?

Every bit of Seamus was aching from having spent the night and the last several hours in his Cruiser. His right foot and left hand kept falling asleep, his bum was numb, and the boredom caused a physical ache, a twisting in his stomach.

He had to keep his eye on the old man. He couldn't let him go around talking about the fish and the kidnapping. There was still a chance The Hat Man might lead him to the fish, the fish Seamus was sure the old man hoped to catch. He wanted to be there when that happened. It would be easy enough to relieve him of it.

He eased himself out of his vehicle, crept over to the van, and noted with satisfaction that, while the lock was rusted out, there were two handles, one on each rear door. They could be linked together to trap the old man in the back of the makeshift ambulance that had no access to the front, a peculiar arrangement the previous owner had welded into place for some unknown reason. It suited Seamus perfectly, and would buy him time to figure out what he was going to do next.

He scrambled back to his own vehicle, pulled some strong rope out of the trunk, returned, and looped it through the rear-door handles of the van, knotting it securely.

He was shaking with fear, fear of what he was doing now, fear of what he had done already, fear of exposure at fisheries. He had a couple of days, maybe, and then his actions would begin to be known, and they'd be after him, asking questions he didn't want to answer. He turned the car on, and with it the radio. He was in time to hear the news:

"A woman who won the lottery three times has died of asthma at the community hall in The Shores. She's left almost all of a 16 million dollar fortune to her cats. That's 79 happy pussies…"

Definitely not the CBC.

What did it mean? Did it mean Ferguson had no money – or was it all in trust to the cats? Seamus had to find out. He drove off without looking back at the van, where he believed his captive was secured inside. But he'd closed the barn doors after the horse got out, and he didn't know it.

Abel's face stared out from the driver's-side window.

***

Ian had woken that morning on the floor, sore and disgruntled to find Hy gone. As he got up, a stabbing pain ripped through his back. He couldn't straighten up. He shuffled across the room, each movement causing excruciating pain. He gave up when he got as far as the couch. He sat down. Stinging pain. He lay down. Deep throbbing pain. Fortunately, his phone was on the coffee table right beside the couch. He reached for it. His back sliced in half. It was lucky he only needed one movement to call Hy. She was number one on his speed dial.

Hy searched for the phone, diving around her kitchen, trying to get it before it went to voice mail. Just made it.

"Hy? Ian."

As if he had to identify himself.

"Oh, hi." She sounded uncomfortable. Ian found that painful, but not as painful as his back.

"Hy, I can't move. I've wrecked my back."

"Ouch. Sorry to hear that. Can you walk?"

"Not really."

It wasn't good. Ian had suffered back trouble before and been sidelined for weeks.

"What can I do?"

"I'm not sure, yet. I could kill for a coffee, and Jasmine will be wanting her food."

"Okay, okay. I'll be up in a bit."

Well, Ian thought as he put down the phone, nothing was going to come out of last night.

***

Finn and Jamieson found Ferguson sobbing over the sink in the kitchen.

Ferguson turned when he heard them enter – without a knock. She didn't usually walk right in on people. It was a strategy. Jamieson had found out a lot of things when taking people by surprise. But it was she who was surprised.

Was Ferguson grieving the loss of his wife? It certainly looked like it. A face already reddened by emotion became redder with embarrassment, his eyes flooded with tears. As he turned from the sink to face them, teardrops fell on the glass kitchen table.

Ferguson put an arm up to his face, excused himself, and headed for the bathroom, his nose trumpeting down the hall as he scattered Kleenex in his wake.

Finn fumbled in his breast pocket and pulled out a small plastic box.

"What's that?"

"Always keep these on hand," said Finn, slipping out a few glass squares. "For whenever I smell –"

"A rat?"

"Yes." He screwed up his face. "And onion."

She watched as he expertly slipped the tears from the table onto the glass slides, secured them, and slid them back into the box. He held the box upright in one hand so as not to disturb the contents.

"Just wondering what your plans are now," Jamieson said when Ferguson returned to the kitchen. She wanted to keep him in her sights.

"I don't expect to stay here." There was disgust in his intonation and on his face. It transformed to sorrow, as he added: "Not without Letitia."

"Don't be going anywhere without letting me know." She turned to leave. Turned back.

"By the way," she said. "Did you ever find Abel Mack?"

"No." Ferguson looked at her with a sly expression. If she was trying to provoke him, he could play the same game. "Did you?"

She didn't answer. She had no evidence of any kind linking Ferguson with Abel – a possible killing, a kidnapping? She just wanted Ferguson on notice that she was keeping tabs on him for more than one reason.

"That performance was entirely for our benefit," Finn said as they got into the police car.

"I agree, but can you prove it?"

Finn held up the little plastic box. "In here," he said. "Alligator tears...or onion tears."

"You said you smelled onion."

"You didn't?"

"I don't have a great sense of smell."

"I'll say. He must have pressed a honking big onion to his face when he saw us coming up the drive. He had a clear view from the kitchen."

"Can you actually prove he was faking it – with those?" She gestured to the box.

"You'll be the judge."

***

Seamus offered his condolences on Letitia's death. Ferguson was surprised that he knew. The whole island knew. Any death was a community event. This one was especially newsworthy because of the money and the cats. Ferguson had received condolences from a lot of people he didn't know. Some sounded substantially more sincere than Seamus. His social duty done, Seamus slipped his cellphone from his pocket, glancing, as people do, to see if anything more important than the person he was with had come up.

"How did she die?" Seamus asked, phone in hand, scrolling his emails as he sat down. Ferguson could tell there was no sincerity behind the question, but he answered it, his voice flat.

"Asthma. Of course, people will say I killed her."

"What?" Seamus looked up from his phone and down again. His fingers played quickly over the screen.

"I said…" Ferguson paused. "Of course people will say I killed her." Ferguson was irritated – by the idea and by Seamus, fiddling around with his cellphone.

"Did you?"

"Do you think I'm a fool? Risk losing all that money?"

Ferguson looked around his den. Not his den for much longer. He was going to have to leave and go…where? What about his aquarium? His fish? *The* fish?

"If you've come for money, I can't give you any. I have to look out for myself now. I've paid to have the pond ready to receive that fish if you get it. Soon. It won't be mine for long. So get it...now."

"Can't do that. Nope." Seamus shook his head. "No can do, *amigo*."

Amigo? The guy was nuts, talking like this.

"No *dinero*. No fish."

"The well has run dry." Ferguson shrugged.

"What well? Were we talking about a well? I thought we were talking about a pond. Money. Moola."

That crazy talk again. Why had he ever got mixed up with this idiot?

"There is no money."

Seamus stood up and looked around the room. His gaze swept, unseeing, over the fish jockeying for attention in the aquarium. He strolled over to the window and surveyed the long swath of field, diving down to the shore, to the pond, with its bridge and sluice gate.

"That looks a lot like money to me." Seamus turned and smiled. "None to spare?"

"No, *señor*." Ferguson spat out the last word, laced with sarcasm.

"It's all yours now, isn't it? Don't have to go begging to Mummy."

"She left it all to her cats. I thought everyone knew that."

That's what they'd said on the news, but Seamus didn't believe it. He couldn't afford to believe it. He was sure there was something in the bank somewhere, and that it was time to rob it.

His thumbs tapped on the cellphone.

His insurance plan.

Chapter 29

"They were not tears of sadness. He was faking it."

"There were certainly lots of them."

"That doesn't make them genuine."

"How do you know they weren't?"

"Apart from the smell of onion, take a look."

Finn had unpacked a travelling case of forensics. A favourite occupation was putting stuff under the microscope.

He slipped one of the slides from his own collection and, after adjusting the focus, invited Jamieson to look.

Jamieson peered through the microscope. A dense, intricate pattern showed on the slide.

"That's a tear?" She continued to look through the microscope.

"Yup. Dried. It's crystallized salt that forms into different patterns." He reached over and slid another image onto the microscope plate.

"Wow." She studied the geometric crystalline effect. "That's beautiful."

"That's a tear of sadness," said Finn. He pulled the slide out and put the original one in. "That's a tear created by smoke, or an onion, or dust, or wind."

"How do you tell the difference?"

"From their different formations. Like snowflakes and fingermarks, no two tears are alike."

"So how do you tell the happy from the sad?"

"Some say you have to know the source to begin with. You know it's a tear of sadness so that's how the image is labelled. Or you already know there were tears of happiness and so on, but I've been puzzling over this for a while, and I believe I see patterns that tell me what kind of tear it is even if I don't know to begin with. No one tear is the same, but there are patterns. See here…"

Finn produced a series of images for Jamieson to look at, and slowly she began to recognize the patterns he was pointing out to her.

"You get the hang of it after a bit," said Finn, leaning over to put a slide in place, lightly brushing up against Jamieson. It sent a shiver through her.

"There are only three different kinds, so the pattern begins to emerge. Here's a basal tear, the kind you use to lubricate your eyes." He put in a fresh slide, adjusted the lens, and pushed it toward her, grazing her fingertips. Not a shiver this time. Pleasure.

"The second kind…reflex tears…your reaction to wind, dust, onions, tear gas, smoke."

"And the third…" Another slide, another light touch, this one intended, bringing her closer to the microscope. "Psychic tears…joy and sorrow, the emotions. They come from the same place but look different. Here's joy." He placed another slide under the microscope, then exchanged it, saying: "And here's sorrow. The emotional tears contain protein-based hormones."

Jamieson looked up. "They are different. Why?"

"The circumstances, how much you cry, the microscope settings, and other factors affect how the tear looks close up. It's far from an exact science."

He put one of Ferguson's tears under the microscope. "He may say he was crying over Letitia's death, but he wasn't. That's a reflex tear, not sadness."

"So he was insincere. That doesn't mean he's a murderer."

"No. But it helps stack the cards."

"This is impressive." Jamieson switched two of the slides again. And again. Peered. Admired. Then straightened. "As you say, not an exact science."

"Far from it."

"Like body language. People may fake it, but it can still be telling." Jamieson considered herself an expert in the art.

What about now? Here with Finn. There was no question

his body movements had been tactile. The tricky part was interpreting. Finn might have been touching her, tentatively, to put her at her ease. Or he might mean something more. Which?

It mattered to Jamieson.

"This may be farfetched," said Finn, "but water imprinted with love and gratitude develops highly complex beauty. Water imbued with negativity loses its incredible patterning and looks disordered."

"Do you have any slides of that?"

Finn smiled. "I'm sorry, no. If I do get hold of any, I'll invite you up to see them." He winked. "And my etchings."

Her porcelain skin flushed pink. Involuntary body language. How could she be so obvious? He was probably just teasing. What about Dot?

What about Dot? Gone. Like Abel. With Abel?

When Jamieson was leaving, Finn placed a hand on her arm, squeezed, and gave her a peck on her forehead. Jamieson fought the feeling it aroused in her, shoved it down. She was unwilling to let it out into the light, lest the light shine through and dissolve it. Could feelings be visibly captured in some scientific way and put under a microscope? She hoped not.

Finn was holding something inside, too, his feelings for Dot, torn by this new complication. But Dot had left and not said goodbye, well able to take care of herself. Jamieson was, too, but she was hiding under a tough front. He wanted her to let her defenses down. Would she?

He expected it would have made her furious that he was having romantic thoughts about her. There was a good chance it would have made her steer clear of him.

In the end, she had no choice. They would be forced to collaborate.

***

Seamus placed the cellphone on Ferguson's desk.

Ferguson was puzzled.

"I think you can find some money for me. Listen."

Seamus lifted his finger to his lips for silence and turned the device on.

Ferguson's deep, sonorous voice boomed out of the tiny recorder in the iPhone. Seamus worked the recording app at lightning speed.

"Of course people will say I killed her."

Ferguson shrugged his shoulders. He couldn't imagine what the idiot was up to.

"Oops," said Seamus. "Hit the wrong pad there. Afraid I may have lost a word or two." He turned the device on again and gave Ferguson a sly smile.

"Of course... I killed her." Then once again. "Of course... I killed her."

"Turn that off!" Ferguson's voice drowned out his own taped voice.

Seamus looked up, thumbs poised. He raised an eyebrow. Ferguson's face was flushed with anger.

"You tampered with that. You know I said: 'Of course, people will think I killed her.' Not: 'Of course I killed her.'"

"Got that now," said Seamus. He'd been recording Ferguson again. He replayed it.

"Of course I killed her."

Seamus smiled at Ferguson. "The unedited confession." He slipped the phone into his pocket. "I could play more of our conversation, but I find that's the most interesting part. Don't you?" His eyebrows rose. He smiled. The best use he'd ever made of a phone camera.

"Of course I killed her."

Both men were startled by Ferguson's voice emanating from the rafters of the barn.

Jasmine flew out, circled the space and was out the barn doors before Ferguson could shut them, taking with her his voice.

"Of course I killed her." Followed by a trail of meows, borrowed from the captive cats.

Jasmine had come for a visit and was going home with a whole new repertoire.

Ferguson's eyes followed her, and then fixed on Seamus, who smiled smugly and savoured his own next words.

"Now let's talk money. Moola. *Dinero.*"

Ferguson was eyeing the distance between his hands and Seamus's throat, separated by the barrier of the desk between them.

But he wasn't a murderer.

Certainly not that kind of murderer.

For now, he'd talk money, even though he didn't have it. Then he'd think about a mass execution of the cats. See who the money would go to then.

And the parrot. He had to shut her up. Whether it was true or not, her repetition of it all over the village – in his voice – would taint him with the murder of his wife.

The truth was, he was sorry about Letitia. Very, very sorry.

***

"Could you feed Jasmine for me?" Ian asked when Hy arrived.

"Jasmine? Where is she?" Hy quickly scanned the room, for all the parrot's usual perches. "I'm surprised she's not on your shoulder."

"It was too painful," Ian grimaced. "It was painful shrugging her off as well."

"Has she gone off in a snit?"

"Could you look around?"

Hy combed the house and couldn't find Jasmine anywhere.

"Do you think she's at the cattery?"

"I hope not, but she could be."

Hy's cellphone rang. They both jumped. Ian yelped with pain. Hy looked at the screen. Finn.

"Where have you been all night?" Finn's tone was teasing, but he had been slightly concerned. With Abel's disappearance, who knew what might be going on?

"I was home." She had been. For a few hours.

"So you say."

"Stuff it, Finn. Ian's done his back in."

"How'd that happen?"

"I don't know. He leaned over to pick up a pencil." Sarcasm edged her voice. He heard it but ignored it, teasing her.

"Really?"

"I told you, I don't know. Could you come up and stay with him for a while?"

"Happy to. Do I get his room?" There was no other suitable room in Ian's house. Finn knew that.

"I think it's safe to say yes. This lad's not going to be climbing stairs for a while."

Finn could "charm the birds out of the trees." That's what his grandmother used to say about Ray, father of Hy and Finn. "He could charm the birds out of the trees." Said in a way that made it a reprehensible ability.

Whatever it was, Finn had inherited it, and it turned out to be handy, because by the time he got to Ian's, Hy and Ian had decided that Jasmine must have got loose and was at the cattery again.

They found her there – outside, in a tree, of all places. Jasmine didn't normally do trees, but standing beneath her was Ferguson, watching intently, waiting for the bird to make a move so he could grab her.

Hy tried to coax her down with treats, but it didn't work.

She turned to Ferguson. "Could you please leave? I think you're upsetting her."

"Ordering me about on my own property?"

"Is it?" It was, she knew, in half-ownership with Billy and Madeline. It was unlikely Ferguson would put up with that for long.

He frowned and turned back to the house.

Still Jasmine would not come down.

Finn tried. Finn was a different matter.

With a whimper, an unbirdlike whimper, a human whimper, and a sigh, Jasmine fluttered down when he called her and landed, claws digging into his shoulder so that he winced. He smoothed down her ruffled feathers, and she began to groom – herself, Finn, herself again, picking away at imaginary fleas in her feathers and his hair. It was something she loved to do, but never could with Ian, he had so little hair.

They left, Ferguson glowering at them through the front-door window.

***

The evening was cooling. Ian dragged a shirt over his T-shirt, grimacing as he did so, every movement a discomfort. Jasmine flew off her perch and landed on his shoulder. Even that hurt. He was about to scratch her head when she said it.

"I killed her. Of course."

It was the unmistakable voice of Brock Ferguson, coming out of Jasmine's beak.

Ian was thinking about what prompt he could use to get her to say it again, but he didn't have to. Jasmine was on one of her repetitive jags. She'd caught Ian's full attention, and had no plans to let it go.

"People… I killed her. Of course."

That deep voice. Cream and whisky.

Ian hardly noticed the pain shooting across his lower back as he leaned forward to grab his cellphone. Number two on his speed dial. Jamieson.

***

The rope hung like a limp sneer, mocking Seamus.

My God! Had The Hat Man got away? Got away? From him. From his kidnapper. Seamus slowed to a halt, reluctant to face the possibility. Probability. He squeezed out of the car, huffed over to the van, and yanked the doors open. Wide open.

Inside?

Inside it was dark. He peered in, placed a hesitant foot up onto the back step.

And was shoved inside. So fast, so sudden was it that he couldn't push back. He tipped forward, his weight taking him down, wedging him between the two cots.

The doors slammed shut behind him. He couldn't move. He was stuck where he was, his face jammed inches from the floor, breathing in the rusty metal smell, his clothing smeared with rust-red clay.

He could hear the ropes being wrapped around the handles of the door.

"Help! Let me out!" The sound was muffled. The old man was paying him no attention. When the rope was secured, he patted the van a couple of times and made a nimble retreat to Seamus's car. Keys in. As they should be. He started it, but couldn't pull out at first. It was stuck in the clay.

Forward. Reverse. Forward. Reverse. The sound of the car punctuated by Seamus's weakening cries for help.

The car came free, and the old man, with a smug smile on his face, pulled a 180 and headed into the night.

Chapter 30

It came as a shadow in the night. Hy couldn't sleep and had been puzzling over the disappearance of Abel and Dot, still inaccessible on her cell or email. She kept going over it. Ferguson coming to the hall on the hunt for Abel, and Seamus O'Malley phoning her about him. There was that email, asking where Abel had found the cod. Were they all after the big fish? She spent some time googling, copied the links, and fired off an email to Ian.

She was waiting for an answer when a shadow crossed her side window, the one that looked out on the field that rolled down to the shore. It had passed under her outdoor light and flickered an image she couldn't quite capture. It went by again, some minutes later, as if it had rounded the house, intent on casting the shadow again.

And a third time.

Hy grabbed her jacket, stuck her feet in her desert boots, and grabbed a flashlight but didn't turn it on.

The shadow slipped on up ahead of her, into the field of timothy.

She followed. Could it be Abel?

Why would she expect to see Abel now, now that he was missing, when she'd never seen him in all that time she'd spent in his house? All those years she had been his wife's close friend. Twenty years and more, and she had never seen him.

But she was beginning to share Gus's faith that Abel was alive, that his was the shadow she was following, that, as Gus had suggested, he was after the big fish. That's what she had told Ian in the email, told him to check out the links to see if he agreed that O'Malley and Ferguson might be on the trail, too, for their own reasons.

She shivered in the cold autumnal night, the cool bringing with it a clear sky so full of stars and satellites it made her dizzy and delighted to look up at them. She shouldn't be distracted. She had to follow the shadow. But there was no movement ahead of her now. She stood, frozen, until she could no longer feel her limbs, aching to stretch them, to fight the pins and needles numbing her legs, from the small prickles in her toes to the shaking of her thighs.

Finally, there was rustling in the tall grass, but no one to be seen, even on a night like tonight, when the smoke was blown away and the village was bathed in starlight, light and sound travelling easily through the crisp air. She heard the rustles, and she saw the tips of the grass moving as the creature – human or otherwise – made its way across a fallow field.

Hy followed, keeping her distance and her own rustling to a minimum, but, if she fell back, her prey slowed, too, as if waiting, inviting her along.

As the moon began to rise almost perfectly aligned with Ethan Cooke's chimney, she thought that she caught a glimpse of a Tilley hat, but black clouds threatening a storm soon shrouded the night again, and she saw nothing more.

She followed blindly, she was not sure whom or what.

Inevitably, she lost her way. She'd lost the rustling sound to the whipping of the wind; the night was dark as pitch. She had lost the road, too, and found herself stumbling on rough terrain, not entirely sure where she was headed, with no stars visible to guide her.

She ended up going in circles, the circles widening and confusing her sense of direction.

Circles. Circles were part of it. Explained in the links, the places where the big fish gathered, mated, bred. She'd seen the circles. Here on Red Island. Not mentioned in any of the links.

She could hear the ocean near but had no idea she was on the edge of a cape until she stepped off it and went tumbling down, sliding to the bottom, scraping her hands as she tried to grasp onto the sandstone. She fell sideways onto the sand and lay there several minutes, trying to figure out what to do next. Where to go.

Wait until morning. It wouldn't be long now.

***

When he got to Big Bay, the old man concealed Seamus's car behind a derelict building, home to a colony of feral cats. He was tempted to take the *Annaben*, his brother and sister-in-law's boat, or one of the other lobster boats. He couldn't take another fisherman's boat. No, that wasn't done, unless the fella said you could. He wanted a smaller vessel anyway.

He looked into Ben's fishing shack. There was just what he needed.

A triumph. A triumph of remembering. He knew why he was here, what it was he wanted. Fishing tackle and an inflatable boat. It took him several trips to get it all to the water's edge. His strength and focus increased with each step.

He inflated the rubber dinghy, powered by a small and ancient one-cylinder motor. It took only five minutes until the oars were snapped in place.

Then he waited out the tide.

***

Morning came as black as night. Hy wasn't sure when night had turned to day. She'd been wandering for several hours. It must have been well past daybreak when she found a sheltered spot, soft sand scooped into a hole in the cape. She had snuggled down, promising herself she was only taking a short break.

She woke several hours later, shocked that she'd fallen asleep. Hours lost. She jumped up and stumbled along the shore, crawled up the cape, and back on the road to Big Bay.

Dark storm clouds scudded across the water from the west and thick smoke billowed in from the north. It was one of Harold MacLean's "dirty days," as he proclaimed them with a trace of affection in his expression, nostalgia for storms past, so many he'd weathered.

Hy had found her way, uncertainly, along the shoreline to Big Bay.

***

The small boat was bobbing on the water off Big Bay, hidden behind the swell of the incoming tide over the sandbar that sheltered the entrance to the harbour.

The woman on the wharf wearing a Tilley hat had been certain he would come, as sure as the moon rose up on the chimney line of Ethan Cooke's hovel.

She waited, snakes of impatience squirming in her stomach.

Let the hunt begin, she was thinking, as she unlooped the *Annaben* from its moorings. She hoped Ben and Annabelle would forgive her for stealing their boat, but she had to follow him, to make sure he was okay. She had to make sure he didn't see her, unless she had to rescue him. He wouldn't forgive her watching over him. That's what she called it. He would call it intruding.

At least he was back in her sights.

He would be easy to follow.

The rubber dinghy was nearly out of sight, rounding the capes with the massive dunes reaching up to the sky, the nine-foot boat churning out into the open sea. She pulled the rope free and started up the vessel.

Just as she did, a deep boom thundered down the coast, black clouds chasing the sound.

They were in for some weather.

For a few moments, she stared anxiously after the inflatable, but it kept propelling around the cape, distancing itself from her.

He would not be giving up.

Neither would she.

The storm, when it came, would last all night. It would come, like the sea, in waves.

***

The *Annaben* wasn't there. There was a gap in the lineup of boats at the harbour. Between *Tide's In* and *The Caper.* Hy was sure Abel must have taken it. He'd be after the fish, no doubt.

It was Abel she'd been following until she got lost. Now he must have taken to the water, but she couldn't see a thing. The black storm clouds had dropped down low on the horizon, shrouding everything.

She listened carefully – she heard the low thrum of a boat's motor, mingling with the thunder rolling up the coast. It must be the *Annaben*. It must be Abel.

The *Annaben* was the only boat Hy had ever captained. Years before, after she had overcome her trauma-induced fear of water, she went out with Ben and Annabelle frequently to "learn the ropes." Eventually took the helm and found she had a knack for it. It was not a skill she had ever expected to need.

She strode down the line of boats, a physical urgency propelling her from one to another, rejecting one after another. Whose could she take? Who would be forgiving?

None of them.

She spotted Will Fairweather's *Cape Islander*, both the name and the type of boat. The perfect boat in a storm, designed for big, long, ocean swells. Its flat bottom would pound over the waves. Fairweather was a summer resident, and it was more boat than he needed. He certainly didn't need it now. He'd left The Shores soon after the smoke began billowing from Quebec.

He'd asked Hy to email him when things cleared up. He'd never expected it would last so long. Hy knew where he kept the key. He'd taken her for a spin once. He rather fancied her, and he was used to women falling for, if not his personality, his money.

But Hy had money of her own. And he had no personality.

With luck, he'd never know she'd taken it out.

***

"Hy is missing? How do you know?"

Finn shrugged. "We pass like ships in the night, but when you live in the same house as someone, you know if they've been there or not. I see no sign that she's been home since last night. No sign of her, but her bicycle and truck are both there."

Jamieson frowned.

"When did you last see her?"

"We rescued Jasmine yesterday from the cattery."

"That's still going on?"

"I don't think Jasmine will be going back. She got a good scare from Ferguson."

"Why?"

"Not sure why. Thought he liked her. Anyway, she'll stay home now, I think. Unlike Hy."

"She's been gone less than twenty-four hours. Not exactly enough time to call out search and rescue."

"I know. But doesn't Hy have friends in high places?" He winked.

The thought of Hy being missing made Jamieson feel strangely lonely.

Gone only a day, but missing. What if she were really missing? Jamieson felt hollow. Without Hy, she was on her own. She felt it, reluctantly admitting to herself that what she called Hy's "interference" was actually helpful to her. So she was glad to have Finn tag along, arguing all the way as Hy would have.

Jamieson and Finn were looking for Nathan's van, driving up

and down lanes and farm roads, all the way to the end of the Island Way and back, and no luck.

Where the cruiser couldn't go, they walked. The wind had shifted again with the impending storm, and they breathed in the smell of another place, Quebec, other troubles. People had lost their homes, others were waiting, packed and ready to leave if they had to, to lose their homes to the fires that were engulfing that province.

It made their worries seem small. Yes, a man missing, but an old man who'd had a long and fulfilling life. And a woman missing, Hy, but there was no reason to believe, not yet, that anything had happened to her. If it had –

"She's been in scrapes before and got out of them."

"What?"

Finn's voice startled her. Jamieson hadn't realized she'd spoken out loud. "I was thinking about Hy. Where she might be. What has happened."

"I'm thinking about her, too. Thinking. But not worrying."

"No?"

Finn pressed his lips together, his brow wrinkled. "Not yet."

She didn't believe him. Those were worry lines on his forehead.

They were. Hy had disappeared, along with Abel. What was going on?

***

"I killed her. Of course."

"My God." Finn's eyes opened wide. Jamieson said nothing. Jasmine spoke again:

"People... I killed her. Of course."

"That is Brock Ferguson, no doubt." Jamieson sat down, silenced by shock. She believed Ferguson had killed his wife, but she had no proof. Could this be proof? "Where did this come from?"

Ian shrugged his shoulders. Winced. It hurt. What didn't?

Jamieson and Finn had been on their way to the police house. They were almost at Ian's when Jamieson got his urgent message.

"Could it have been television?"

Ian shook his head. "You hear it. That voice is as distinctive as a fingerprint. Anyone would know who it was."

The voice, it's true, was unmistakable. But how could she possibly use...

"...the testimony of a parrot." She completed the thought out loud.

"It's not testimony."

No, it was not testimony. It was a confession. An admission of guilt. Not coming from the man. Coming from the bird.

"What am I going to do with it?" Jamieson's eyes appealed to Finn, then to Ian. They were silenced by the rarity of the situation. Jamieson, asking their advice? Finn was more used to it because of his forensic role in some of her investigations. Still – what she had sought from him had been facts, not advice on how to conduct an investigation.

"We better use it, however we do, soon. Jasmine goes on these jags. This may be the only thing she'll say for days or weeks, then she'll bury it and never say it again." Ian stroked Jasmine's tail feathers, something she particularly liked.

"Days...or weeks?" Jamieson looked over at Ian.

"Best to say days. At most, days. She likes to get attention, so if she's getting it, she'll keep it up."

"I killed her, Jasmine?" Finn coaxed. "Did you say I killed her?"

Jasmine was stubbornly silent.

"She doesn't respond to coaxing. If she knows you want it, she won't give it to you. Best to ignore her for a bit, and she'll do it again."

She did – over and over again, much to the trio's satisfaction. Jasmine, star of her own show, the bird at the centre of...what? A criminal investigation? A murder?

"I killed her. Of course."

"It's a keeper alright." Ian smiled.

"How do we use it?"

Asking their advice again. And using "we."

"Can you confront him with the bird?" Finn smiled, and, suddenly, they were all laughing. It was a serious matter, but it seemed so ridiculous.

"I could ask him to the police house. Jasmine could be there."

"Better bring him here. Jasmine won't go without me." Ian ruffled her feathers. She bit him and flapped away, landing on Finn's shoulder.

So much for parrot loyalty. Ian held out a finger, and wiggled it, a silent signal that always brought her to him, because it was always followed by a treat.

"She went to the barn without you."

"That was different."

"Of course."

"Of course. I killed her." Jasmine flew off Finn's shoulder and around the room. "Killed her. Killed her. Killed her."

"Oh, yes, she likes this one." Ian held out a hand for Jasmine to return to him. Still, she didn't. "She's improvising."

Jasmine perched back on Finn's shoulder. "Did my 'of course' trigger that?"

"Of course. Of course... Of course." Jasmine was flying around the room again.

"How much does she improvise? Turn the words around?"

Ian shook his head. "Not that much. She takes them to pieces, divides them into parts, but she doesn't create new meaning." He paused for a moment. "Not usually."

Jamieson sighed. She was that close to a conviction, and her best witness was a bird, a bird that liked to play with words that could convict.

Of course.

She didn't speak out loud when the idea came to her, for fear of triggering another frenzy from Jasmine. She'd need documentation.

"Lester."

Ian and Finn looked at her, confused.

"Lester," she repeated. "He can document it." Lester was

here because his father Germaine was in hospital. He was a videographer who'd been making a killing the past several years from…well…killings at The Shores.

"Of course." Ian regretted the words as soon as they were out of his mouth.

"Of course, of course, of course," Jasmine spiralled the words up to the ceiling.

Chapter 31

The waves formed in long funnels, rushing at the shore, smacking into the boat, spilling water over its sides.

Dot huddled in the cabin, tossed on the black waves, the water threatening to engulf the boat. Why had she come here? Why had he come – rocking on the waves instead of the comfort of his rocking chair? She knew why. She knew Abel. She was her father's daughter and as stubborn as he.

That's why she was out here on the water, and he was, too, but nowhere to be seen now. So good at eluding others. He had brought her up to it, playing hide and seek with her. She was never as good as he. She couldn't stay hidden for long, but he could disappear for a day or more, even when she'd go to the harbour to catch him as he came in from a day's fishing. He became so good at it that he'd begun to recede further and further into the background of their lives.

A wave loomed over the deck, and smashed down onto it, rocking the boat up on its side and almost over. Dot was thrown to one side of the cabin. She clutched the steering wheel. It was not an attempt to gain control of the craft. That, she knew, was impossible. She would just have to ride it out.

***

"Perhaps you could explain why you've asked me here."

"Of…" Jamieson almost said "course," but she didn't want to trigger Jasmine too soon. Not that anyone had any control of the bird. She'd mouth off at any moment if she felt like it. All it might take was the sound of Ferguson's voice, no matter what it was that he said. Jamieson knew that, but she wanted some control over the meeting. She looked at the parrot, occupied with chewing at her feathers. In the bookshelf next to her, Lester had concealed a camera, which was trained on Jamieson and Ferguson. It wasn't procedure and might overturn a conviction if she got one, but, under the circumstances, it seemed the only thing to do.

"It's about your wife's death."

"Of course."

That did it.

Jasmine squawked, and flew up from her perch. She circled the room, and continued squawking.

The squawk transformed into the unmistakable, booming voice of Brock Ferguson.

"I killed her. Of course. I killed…killed…killed her."

Ferguson flushed beet red, to the tips of his ears.

He opened his mouth to speak but was unable to, emitting only a few choked sounds that Jasmine immediately took up and mixed with her running repertoire.

Ferguson was staring daggers at the bird. Jasmine continued her flight around the room, apparently oblivious to him but well aware of the attention her words were getting.

"Killed…killed…killed…course…course…course." She began to wind down and perched on the back of the sofa, biting at her feathers.

Ferguson looked as if he wanted to grab the parrot and choke her.

"Do you have anything to say?"

If Jamieson was hoping for a confession – and she was – she wasn't going to get it. Ferguson's mouth had dropped open, but he appeared to have nothing to say.

"Or perhaps it's all been said?" She pressed the point.

Finally, Ferguson found his voice.

"This is ludicrous," he directed a sharp look at Jasmine. "Are you going to believe a bird?"

"Believe a bird, about what? I haven't said a thing, made any accusation, but you've heard what the bird had to say – in your voice."

"Yes, stole my voice and used it for a ludicrous purpose. This means nothing. The bird could have been trained to say that."

He obviously didn't know Jasmine. "Training" was one word not in her vocabulary.

"Okay. How about this? Did you kill your wife?"

A faint "killed...killed...killed..." in Ferguson's definitely masculine voice came from the bird on the sofa plucking her feathers. Then Jasmine changed her tune.

"Killed." In her Mick Jagger voice.

"Killed." Britney Spears.

Oh no, thought Jamieson. Jasmine was beginning to improvise. Ferguson hadn't answered.

"I asked you – did you kill your wife?"

"No, I did not. She died, as you know, of natural causes."

"You see, the thing is, I don't know that."

"That's your problem, not mine."

"I have every intention of making it yours."

"Not with that bird, you won't." He stabbed a finger at Jasmine.

"I'll ask you one more time." She changed the question slightly. "Did you intend to kill your wife?"

Jasmine looked up from her feather plucking.

"Of course," she said, in Ferguson's booming voice.

Ferguson sighed deeply. "What I did say, in a private conversation, is that people are saying, of course I killed my wife."

"People," Jasmine grabbed on to the rest of the phrase she'd been missing. "People are saying, of course I killed my wife."

Jamieson deflated. She felt embarrassed at having followed a wild parrot chase.

"You'll excuse me," she said to Ferguson. "Nonetheless, I must ask that you not leave the area until, and unless, I give you permission."

"Perhaps. But I may be speaking to your superior officer."

"Officer killed my wife. Officer killed my wife." With those words, in Ferguson's deep baritone, Jasmine erased any credibility she might have had.

*∗∗

Still, they had it all recorded. Jamieson, Finn, and Ian reviewed the whole thing on Ian's computer. It was uncanny, the two of them – the man and the bird – sounding exactly alike.

"I wonder what the voice graphs would look like." Jamieson advanced to the start again and ran it again.

"They'd be remarkably similar." Ian had studied the field precisely because of Jasmine and knew something about it.

"Similar, but not exact. A voiceprint is even more unique than a fingerprint. They say fingerprints are an exact way to tell a person's identity, but they're not, actually. Mistakes have been made."

"I don't know what to do with this, now that we have it. Now that Jasmine has changed her tune…"

Ian had thought the "we" – she'd said it a few times – included him in a way that Jamieson never had before. He frowned. Now he realized the "we" meant Finn, not him.

*∗∗

Hy's heart was pounding, her hands gripping the wheel of the *Cape Islander,* bouncing on the swells churned up by the force of the wind. She was soaked through and shivering, cursing herself for having come out in this storm. But she'd had to. Curiosity drove her. She knew she was on the trail of Abel. She had followed the shadow to Big Bay, or nearly, and she had seen the hat. The boat was taking her to him, aboard the

Annaben, wearing his Tilley hat.

***

Dot came to, great black clouds billowing over her. She was amazed to be alive, surprised she'd fallen asleep in the storm. Then she felt the lump on the back of her head. When she moved it, her head pounded with pain. She'd been knocked out. Unconscious. Abel's hat had saved her. She had stuffed it with things she didn't want to lose – her cellphone, her watch, and the sterling silver necklace of a whale that Finn had given her. She'd wrapped it all up securely in a waterproof plastic pack and stuck it in the hat then secured it to her head. It was still on. Without that padding, the blow might have been fatal. She eased herself up and stood, finding her balance.

She spotted another lobster boat. There was someone on the deck, waving.

Dot squinted. Was it? It couldn't be…

"Hy!" Her voice was lost in the wind.

"Hy!" she called again and began to wave her hands above her head, piercing pain knifing through her with every movement.

The engine had conked out. She ducked into the cabin to restart the boat. It wouldn't engage. Again and again she flicked the ignition, until she must surely have flooded the engine.

The other boat had full power. It was heading toward her. The closer it came, the clearer it became to her.

Hy. It was Hy.

Thank God.

***

It had taken Seamus hours to pull himself out from between the two cots in the back of Nathan's van. He had collapsed onto one of them, his face an unhealthy red, sweat dripping down his forehead and blurring his vision. He was too fat to fit on the cot or stay lying on it for long. Half of him was over the edge.

He had begun to panic and had jumped up, bashed his head on the roof, and slammed his fists into the sides of the van until his knuckles were bruised and bloody. He had yelled and kicked at the doors, but they didn't give. Not an inch. Tied securely. As he had tied them securely when he closed the old man in. Or thought he had.

He sat down and started to cry.

***

A huge wave curled up and attacked the deck, like a giant tongue licking at its surface. The tip of the tongue scooped Dot up and shoved her over the gunwales and into the ocean, the Tilley hat still on her head. The water swirled around and drew her under. Hy had pulled alongside the *Annaben* just as Dot went over.

Dot.

Tall, slender, female. Dot wearing the Tilley hat.

Hy raced to the side of the *Cape Islander* in time to see Dot go down.

"Dot! Dot!"

Hy leaped from one boat to the other, taking no time to secure Fairweather's boat. She didn't even think of it.

She raced across the deck of the *Annaben* and leaned over the side.

Dot surfaced, her eyes closed. She appeared unconscious. So swift had the wave been in grabbing her up and casting her off that Hy hadn't seen her head smash up against the side of the boat on her way into the water.

Dot could swim, Hy knew, but not if she were unconscious. Hy could swim, too, but her skill hadn't been tested in years. She was frozen, her blood spiked with adrenalin, her breathing ragged and shot with fear. She watched as Dot's body spun, was sucked down and thrown back up. Hy's hands clung to the gunwale. She peeled them off, searched quickly for a rope. Grabbed it. Tied it around her waist. Looked desperately for somewhere to secure the other end. She tied the rope to the steering wheel.

A mistake.

Hy summoned her courage and climbed onto the railing. She closed her eyes so she wouldn't have to look when she flung herself into the water.

She didn't have to. Look. Or fling herself overboard. Before she could, a wave slapped her from behind and sent her flying into the churning water. She swallowed a mouthful of salt water as she went under and struggled back up to the surface, choking.

She began treading water but knew she couldn't hold out for long in the surging sea, sapping her strength and chilling her to the bone. She spun around and saw Dot surface again. With her eyes closed, she looked like a corpse.

Maybe she was.

Several strong strokes propelled Hy to Dot, to Dot's body, tossed by the water, floating like a jellyfish, with no motion of her own.

Hy was determined to bring her out.

Dead or alive.

Chapter 32

Ian tried for the umpteenth time to call Hy on her cellphone, but there was no answer, just the voice mail. It was full – full of his messages to her. He hadn't been able to leave any since yesterday.

Finn was up on the widow's walk at Ian's place, the same concerns plaguing him, his worry both for his sister and Dot. Finn could see Big Bay from here. He saw no one in the harbour, along the shore, nor the capes, no one in the village, all chased indoors by the vicious storm. Here he was, getting drenched, and where was Hy? Abel? Safe? Somehow he doubted it.

There was no point in standing, soaking in the rain. He must at least attempt to find them. He turned and sped down the narrow staircase, almost tripping in his haste. He didn't stop to let Ian know what he was up to, but he didn't have to. Ian guessed when Finn streaked through the kitchen, grabbed Ian's keys off the table, held them up for permission, and slammed the door behind him. One more thing to make Ian feel impotent, stuck here on this couch, with only a parrot as a minder.

Lights flashed on and off in his rear-view mirror as Finn backed out of the driveway in Ian's truck. A vehicle was blocking him in.

Jamieson. She'd come back to have another look at the video, or so she told herself. She'd really come back for Finn.

He stuck his head out the window. She stuck her head out of hers.

"Where are you going?" she called out above the rain, rivulets of water running down her face.

"Looking for Hy."

"Why?" Jamieson frowned. Had Hy actually disappeared?

Finn yanked his door open and strode over to Jamieson's

cruiser.

"I'm worried," he said. "She's been gone too long. I don't believe Hy would leave without a word, unless something was up."

"Probably not." Jamieson had been thinking that herself. "Jump in. We'll go looking."

"We should take Ian's vehicle," he said. "It's got four-wheel drive."

"Okay. Good idea."

Not so good, as it turned out.

***

Hy battled the swell and grabbed Dot's lifeless body. She knew she had to get out of the water fast. It was cold; they were at risk of hypothermia. Hy knew all about that. This was the third time in her life she'd faced it, the third time there had been extreme danger for her in the water. Third time lucky? She'd been lucky the first and second times. Could that kind of luck hold?

She tugged at Dot's body. She couldn't move both herself and Dot through the turbulence. They were two separate bodies; she would have a better chance if they became one.

She entwined herself around Dot and kicked one leg to swim forward, one arm tugging on the rope around her waist to get them back to the boat.

It was slow and frustrating. She regretted that she'd attached the rope at the other end to the steering wheel. It gave it play; the wheel moved back and forth at the will of the waves and Hy's tugging.

She didn't know how long it took her. She would have said an hour, but it was minutes only. It could only have been minutes, she knew, otherwise they would both be dead. She had that consolation to keep her going: they were not dead, not she, nor Dot. Dot's eyes were closed, and she wasn't moving on her own, but Hy put a hand around her wrist and could feel her steady, slow pulse.

Now for the tricky part. Gripping onto Dot with one arm, Hy began to undo the rope from her own waist. If she freed herself from the rope and attached it to Dot to secure her, Hy could climb up the outside of the boat, get on deck, and then pull Dot up after her.

If she could take the weight. If the rocking of the boat didn't pitch her back into the water, where they'd both be lost.

Panic struck her – squeezing the air out of her lungs and refusing to let any in. Her mouth open, gasping for air, water gushing into it. Choking. Her heart racing, pounding with the swell of the sea.

Lost. They were lost. There was no hope.

The rope slipped from her waist, slipped from her hands. They were adrift. Hy clung to Dot. Dot was her life raft. And she was Dot's.

***

Finn had set him up so that Ian was able to work on his computer from the couch, with his wireless keyboard and the big screen in front of him. It was his window on the world for now. He had texted Jamieson, asking her to keep him informed, and she had said she would.

He opened his email.

Damn! How had he missed it? An email from Hy. Yesterday night. It was buried in a thread of postings, and it had become hidden, not noticed.

She had gone looking. For Abel. For the fish.

She'd left a link she said explained it all.

Feeding the World in the Future. That was the website. Dozens of links covered everything from the giant vegetables of Findhorn to ocean areas where giant sea creatures were forming, in strange new pockets that seemed to nurture them in inexplicable ways. Continuous breeding seasons. Long lifespans. Not just cod, but other species. A lobster had been found – as big as a boat.

Hy believed one of those breeding places of oceanic giants was here, on Red Island. She was convinced that Abel had stumbled on it thirty years before, and now it had reappeared, fully formed, possibly teeming with giant cod that might save the Atlantic fishery. How many giant cod would it take to do that?

Clearly, they would have to be farmed, spawned in vitro, caged as they grew in the cold Atlantic waters they favoured, in giant fish farms. The appearance of these big fish along this coast could be critical to a revival of the industry. That was why the fellow at fisheries, Seamus O'Malley, had asked Hy about Abel, looking for the only man on Red Island who'd encountered one of these giant specimens. O'Malley wanted to be in on the ocean floor.

It's in the circles, Hy's email had said. *The circles beyond Big Bay.*

It all came together, like pieces of a puzzle in a snug fit. Abel was after the big fish. He wanted one. So, it seemed, did O'Malley. And Ferguson. Yes, Ferguson, too. He'd announced at the hall, in front of the entire village, that he was looking for Abel. None of Abel's neighbours had seen him for years, so what else could have led Ferguson to him than the photograph and the fish? That episode had been forgotten in the continuing absence of Abel, the distraction of the cattery coming to the village, and the tragedy at the lobster supper. It had been lost, for Ian, in his worries over Jasmine. It wasn't hard to figure out why Ferguson wanted the fish. It could only have been to satisfy his record-setting mania.

Beyond Big Bay. That's where the circles were.

That's where he'd be. Abel. That's where she'd be. Hy.

Did Finn and Jamieson know what he knew now? The search for the big fish, by unscrupulous people like O'Malley and Ferguson, might have put Abel in danger. Maybe Hy, as well.

Jamieson and Finn were mobile. He wasn't. They could do something. He couldn't. Life was unfair.

He grabbed his cell from the table, the movement so fast it sent a stab of pain across his back. Ignoring it, he speed-dialed Jamieson.

No answer. Voice mail full.

Finn.

No answer. Voice mail full.

Damn.

Ian hated texting, especially anything of length, but he had to let Finn and Jamieson know what was going on. He began the laborious task, full of misspellings and poor punctuation.

***

A massive wave loomed over them.

This is it, she thought. Hy closed her eyes and clung hard to Dot, just managing to keep both their heads above water. She wasn't sure why – because that wave was about to well and truly drown them.

The impact ripped Dot from her grasp and sent Hy spinning, spinning underwater, her eyes still closed, no idea where she was headed, where Dot was, if the boat was being tossed in her direction, too, and might kill her before the killer wave did.

But this wave turned out to be a saviour.

***

The storm had driven the inflatable back to Big Bay, where it got caught on the sandbar now that the tide was low. The big waves chased up by the storm shoved it farther across the sand with each surge. He was getting nowhere near the fish, near the prize, but Abel hadn't reached the age of ninety without good luck dogging him all his life. As it was about to do.

***

Hy was deposited with a thump on shore. Dot was thrown clear of the rocks beside her.

The seas and the sky went calm. The rain stopped. The wind died down. The calm in the midst of the storm. The storm pausing to gather its strength and launch another attack.

In the relative calm, the *Annaben* slid up onto the shore, nesting by a fall of sandstone tumbling down from the cape. *The Cape Islander* was nowhere to be seen.

Hy wanted to close her eyes and sleep. Sleep. She could get a blanket from the boat. No, she didn't need it. She was warm. Nice and warm.

The warmth began to build. Hot now.

Hypothermia. Her old enemy. She had to fight it.

She dragged herself onto all fours and crawled toward the boat.

No! Dot. She must take care of Dot first. Fight the heat. Fight the cold. She couldn't tell one from the other, burned with it, shivered right to her core.

She struggled to where Dot lay with her face planted in the sand and tried to roll her over. Her muscles felt like they were tearing apart with the effort. Dot was a lump, an unmoving, unyielding lump.

A dead weight.

Or simply – dead?

***

Finn headed for Big Bay. If Hy were chasing Abel and Abel were chasing the fish, then it made sense to go where the boats and the water were.

The harbour was deserted. No activity except the rain pelting down on the wharf. Rain so thick it formed a curtain beyond which they could not see. Could not see the small human huddled in the watercraft shifting on the sandbar.

They paid no attention to the lone car, a black PT Cruiser, parked behind a shed of some kind. It could be anyone's.

Finn and Jamieson got out and walked down the pier.

Finn pointed.

"The *Annaben*. It's gone."

They looked at the gap where the *Annaben* should have been. There was another space, too, at the end of the line of boats, but neither Finn nor Jamieson was aware that it was Fairweather's berth, that there was another boat on the water that night.

"Do you think that Hy has gone out in the boat?"

"I'm sure she has," he said.

"We better call the coast guard." Jamieson pulled out her cellphone and activated her contact list. But she couldn't use it. The bar across the top read *No service*. It flickered on and off – a quick single bar of reception, teasing but not functioning. She turned to Finn. "Can we follow?"

"Maybe," he said, a scheme forming in his mind. "Maybe we can take one of these other boats."

"No."

"What do you mean, no?"

"No. We can't do that. It would be stealing."

They made their way back to the truck, rain at first easing then pouring down on them. In the cab, Finn's phone was flashing. He'd left the truck idling and the cell plugged in to power it up. Now the sound of his ringtone – a couple of bars from The Proclaimers' *Letter from America* – filled the air with its heartrending message, and Finn answered.

"Ian," he mouthed at Jamieson. "Yes… Big Bay…no…they're not here… Where?… Text?… Link?… Okay."

Finn checked his messages, the service band flickering on his phone, too. He scanned Ian's message.

The service cut out.

"Damn," he said, shaking the phone as if that would fix it.

Jamieson observed him, questioning. He stuck the phone in his pocket. At least it was charged.

"So, you don't want to borrow a boat?"

Jamieson frowned. Is that what Ian was suggesting, too?

"You're not going to like the alternative any better."

Chapter 33

Hy stared up at the massive dunes behind them. They were stuck here.

She'd never get Dot out.

The whole thing had been a complete failure.

She'd tried to roll Dot over, torso and head, but her arm flopped back and brought the rest of her with it. It was like grappling with jelly, but she kept at it.

Finally she managed. As she rolled Dot onto her side, a flood of water came out of her mouth, out of her lungs. She coughed. She gasped. She was breathing, but she didn't wake.

Hy had no idea what to do.

***

"They'll have gone to the circle of cods," said Finn, pressing hard on the accelerator, the speed indicator hitting forty kilometres per hour above the limit. With a Mountie in the car. "I gather it's kind of like a pool, with conditions of its own."

"A pool? There's a whole ocean out there. Who needs a pool?" Jamieson was being irritating on purpose. She didn't want to tell Finn to slow down. She should, she knew, but the truth was she wanted him to go even faster.

"The giant cods apparently do."

Jamieson smirked. "Is this some kind of seafaring myth?"

"No. Ian says they exist and a few people are interested in them. Hy emailed Ian before she took off."

"What else did she say?"

"It's what Abel's after. A giant cod. Some guy at fisheries is involved...a Seamus O'Malley, and, get this, Hy thinks Brock

Ferguson wants a piece of the pie."

"I'm still asking why?"

"Hy seems to think they're all nuts, a bunch of kooks."

Jamieson smiled a small smile.

If it came to kooks, she wouldn't rule out Hy or Abel, or practically anyone in the village.

Jamieson did remember Gus talking about the big cod, but she hadn't thought much of it. Her mind still played with the possibility that Abel didn't exist. As for giant cod…

***

As Jamieson and Finn drove away from Big Bay, the inflatable boat came free of the sandbar, and the waves began to toss it out to sea. A dark shape loomed in front of the tiny rubber boat.

The *Cape Islander* was pounding on the waves, its wide, flat bottom keeping it stable. It moved relentlessly forward toward the tiny craft, bumping on the waves. It kept coming closer, seeming to eat up the sea and the space between itself and Abel's rubber boat.

***

The pile of sandstone next to the *Annaben* allowed Hy to climb with ease onto the boat. She went into the cabin and down to the hold. There was Annabelle and Ben's double bed, the unusual feature that had convinced them to buy the boat. There were their duvet and wool blanket, and Hy grabbed them both. She wrapped herself in the blanket.

A Thermos was lying on its side on the floor of the cabin. She recognized it as Dot's. She opened it. Steaming hot tea. She sipped it, and the liquid seeped into her and warmed her.

She was still at risk of hypothermia, but Dot must be, too – if she were still alive.

That thought galvanized Hy. Securing the Thermos, she stumbled across the deck, threw the blanket and duvet onto the sand, and climbed out.

Dot lay on her back. Hy approached her and turned her face sideways, set the Thermos down, and covered her with the blanket. Then she touched her, lightly, on the face.

No response.

She put her hand in front of Dot's nose.

She couldn't feel a breath.

She unscrewed the cap of the Thermos, poured a tiny bit into it, and held it to Dot's mouth.

The tea dribbled down onto the sand.

A terrible fear gripped Hy.

Was Dot dead?

And the other question still dogged her.

Where was Abel?

***

The old man had never seen waves this high in these waters. The waves would shove the big craft toward him and then bat it back. Forward. Back. Forward. It spun around as a huge wave launched his boat into the air. He was flying in the little rubber boat. Flying. Arching. And then propelling down to what he imagined would be a bouncy landing on water.

But that's not what happened.

***

Finn pulled over to the side of the road. He turned off the ignition and opened his door.

"Now we walk," he said.

"Walk?" Jamieson questioned, as she, too, got out of the vehicle.

"Yup. Only way in, unless you've got a boat." He hauled a

rucksack out of the cab and shoved it at Jamieson.

"Here. Put this on."

Before she could object, he pulled out another for himself.

"Emergency gear. Ian's well supplied." He slammed the truck door shut and aimed his flashlight at the terrain ahead, the tall dunes that encircled the coast beyond Big Bay Harbour.

"We're walking through those?"

The dunes loomed up ahead and seemed to roll on forever – to the horizon and beyond.

"It's not as bad as it looks." Finn knew them well. He'd been here before, exploring the strange environmental oddities that seemed to have collected around this region of Red Island. Not like anywhere else. Certainly not like the rest of the island.

***

Hy had dragged Dot under an overhang in the cape, drilled out by the waves to form a shallow cave, high enough to sit in. Normally it would not be a safe place – the sandstone so unstable, it could collapse on their heads at any time, especially in a storm. The cave offered little real shelter. But she had to get Dot warm and dry. There was some driftwood in the back, and a lobster trap, in pieces. Hy broke up the wood and laid a fire.

A match.

On the boat? She dashed back, climbed aboard, and found a box of matches in the galley. She also found some flares. She shoved them under her jacket.

Dot was still not moving. Breathing? Hy put her hand in front of Dot's mouth. Did something stir? She bent over and concentrated. She might be imagining it, but she thought she had felt something. As long as there was breath, even a thin thread of breath…

Hy put a match to the fire, and it burst into flame. It wouldn't last long. She began to itemize the things aboard the *Annaben* that might be burned. Wood cabinet doors, railings, the bed frame – all beautifully crafted, a shame to destroy them. It was a matter of life and death. Surely Ben and Annabelle would forgive her for stripping the boat of its beautiful wood fittings.

Hy set off the flares, doubting they would be seen. But they were.

***

"You're sure we should be doing this?" Jamieson and Finn had begun the trudge to the dunes, looming up ahead of them.

"Pretty sure. Sure enough to try."

As if on cue, a flare went up. Then another.

"That's her. That's bound to be Hy. Come on."

They picked up the pace.

Thank God, thought Jamieson.

***

Brock Ferguson's unmistakable voice boomed through Ian's house. There was the clump of feet crossing the kitchen floor.

"Simmons. You here? Alone?"

No. Not alone. Jasmine was there, snoozing. She'd woken up at the sound of Ferguson's voice.

"I killed her. Of course. I killed her." An exact mimic of his booming voice, sounding sleepy.

"Ah. Not alone, I see. Good. Good."

It didn't sound good to Ian. Nor to Jasmine.

Ferguson strolled across the room, as if it were a casual visit, but Ian could see the malicious intent in his eyes and the tightness of his body. Ferguson's eyes darted sideways, aimed at Jasmine and not looking where he was going. He tripped over the footstool beside the couch – the one that held Ian's pain pills and jug of water.

The empty glass and full jug went flying across the carpet.

"Don't worry about it," Ian spoke on automatic pilot, as if this were a social visit. He knew it was not a social visit, far from it, but Ferguson kept up the pretense that it was.

He sat on the arm of the teak chair. It fell off, and he landed on the floor. Ian grinned. Ferguson dusted himself off and stood up, thrown off for a moment.

"So, you have injured your back?" The information had been all over the village the moment Dr. Dunn had left his patient's house.

"Yes. Afraid so."

"How bad is it?"

"Pretty bad."

"Can you walk?"

"No... I...uh...what does it matter to you?" Ian was alert. This man might be a killer. At the least, he had killed his wife by neglect. His presence here was unnerving.

"Just inquiring, as a neighbour. What about...when you need to relieve yourself?"

Hardly a neighbourly question, Ian thought.

"I have ways," he said.

"I see." Ferguson inclined his head. "So you really cannot walk at all?"

Ian didn't answer. He saw now that Ferguson had backed him into a corner, that he had been trying to establish if Ian could move. He couldn't. Even if he were to say he could, the lie would be uncovered. He could not walk. He could barely blink his eyes without a severe pain in his neck.

He could tell that Ferguson knew from the look in his eyes. The eyes that now shifted from him back to Jasmine.

"No one else here? Just us three?"

For a moment, all three froze.

***

Warmed by the fire, Hy tried to shove the *Annaben* back into

240

the water. Impossible, but anything was worth trying. It seemed the only way of escape. She couldn't haul Dot across the dunes. The times she'd crossed them with only the weight of a backpack had been a challenge.

She couldn't do it. And she wouldn't leave Dot and head out herself to bring back help. That had crossed her mind. It entered and left in the same moment. Impossible. Unless she wanted them both to die.

Hy gave a last, desperate push at the boat and collapsed down onto the rocks, tears of frustration spilling from her eyes.

She picked herself up and, shaking off the self-pity, grasped onto a slim line of hope.

Someone must find them in the morning. They weren't invisible here. The *Annaben* was gone. That would be noticed.

Surely.

***

"I can't do this anymore." Jamieson crouched down in the sand, hands on her back, stretching. "How much farther?"

"A half-hour, maybe."

"Too long. Too long since those flares went off. They could be anywhere – on shore or at sea."

"Still not too late to go back to Plan A."

"Refresh my memory. What's plan A?"

"Take a boat. It's calmer now. It wouldn't be dangerous. We'd get to them faster."

To Finn's surprise, Jamieson caved.

"Okay. But we do it my way. You go get the boat, and I'll continue through the dunes."

Finn was about to object, but she lifted a hand to silence him.

"I can turn a blind eye to what you do, but I can't actually take one of those boats myself. Even if I didn't get called on the carpet, the fishermen would never let me live it down."

"Couldn't you commandeer it?"

"Requisition it? Maybe...but let's do it my way." The way she said it made it clear that was exactly what they were going to do.

"Will you be okay?" Concern crossed his face.

"I'm a triathlete. I can make it over those silly dunes in less than half an hour, trust me. You'd just slow me down."

"A few minutes ago, you were giving up, saying you couldn't do this anymore."

"I meant I couldn't do it the way we were doing it. Waste of resources. Better to have a two-pronged attack – at land and at sea."

"Okay, that makes sense."

"We'll keep in touch by cell."

"You think so?"

For a moment Jamieson had forgotten there was no reception.

"Keep trying. If you get service, we may still be able to call in the coast guard. We may get lucky."

"That'd be a nice change."

***

She couldn't believe what she was seeing.

Hy had decided to spare the boat and search for more, dry driftwood. She'd walked far along the shore.

Propped up against a big chunk of sandstone was...

A toboggan.

She picked up her pace, pitched forward a couple of times and scraped her hands on the shells and stones. She didn't feel it. She didn't feel a thing right now – except the joy of an escape.

A possible escape.

As soon as she was close enough, Hy grabbed the toboggan. She checked it out. It was firm, unbroken.

What was it doing here?

Strange things got washed out to sea, and back in again. It might have come from the kids who brought their sleds out here to ride the big dunes, summer and winter. She didn't know, and she didn't care. She could put Dot on this and drag her to safety.

As a plan, it had holes, but she chose to ignore them. To ignore the fact that Dot, while slim, would be a heavy load. That Hy herself was played out physically by what she'd been through.

It was all she could do. She couldn't let Dot die.

Chapter 34

Ferguson began to move, to glide across the floor, seamlessly, toward the object of his desire.

Jasmine. He was going to kill the bird.

As soon as he could get his hands on her, he would throttle her. Break her neck. End it. End any threat. That the threat should be a bird was laughable. He should feed her to the cats.

Ian could see where Ferguson was headed and what his plan was. With a great deal of pain, he had turned his head in her direction and tried to signal her.

Signal her to do what?

She wasn't budging. She was frozen in place on the back of the chair at his desk. Ian knew her not-going-anywhere posture.

Not now, Jasmine, he willed. Don't be stubborn now. He wanted to shout it, sure that she would understand, but he couldn't. He must keep silent. He felt impotent, unable to help her, the bird he had once rescued, given a second chance at life.

Ferguson got closer. Neither Ian nor Jasmine moved. He, because he couldn't. Not even to save her. And she? Resigned to her fate?

It appeared so. She didn't move, she didn't flinch as Ferguson's big hairy hand reached out to grasp her.

***

Jamieson waited a few minutes until Finn was out of sight. She reached forward and undid her boots, pulled off her socks, and wiggled her toes. She stood up, stretched, and, head down, meditated for some minutes. Her lips moved, but no sound came from them. Then she tilted her head back up and rotated her shoulders and neck several times.

And took off.

She wasn't, as she'd planned to be, out of sight of Finn. He had scaled one dune and turned around to see if he could catch a glimpse of her.

A glimpse was all he could get as she streaked across the dunes.

A barefoot speed runner. A skill she'd exhibited only once before in The Shores, and not to Finn. It remained part of the mystery that was Jamieson.

He watched, but she didn't reappear.

She was long gone.

Of course. Triathlete. And something about being a barefooted runner like the ones in Africa. One of Jamieson's secrets. Her many secrets, beginning to reveal themselves, the more time she spent in the village, the more she allowed The Shores to penetrate her outer defenses. It would be Finn who peeled away the last layer.

***

It was harder than Hy had imagined it would be, pulling the toboggan. Nearly impossible. She had managed to roll Dot onto it, relieved to find she was breathing, that her breath was stronger, that she even co-operated a little when Hy pushed her over. The toboggan wasn't long enough, and Dot's legs stretched beyond the end and dug into the sand when Hy tried to pull it forward. She had harnessed herself to the sled, and, still tied to it, she slipped down onto the sand.

***

Time stood still. Ferguson's hairy hand was poised to grab Jasmine. Jasmine, frozen with fear, was glued to the back of

Ian's computer chair. Ian, nearly unable to move, was stretching his neck beyond its pain threshold, keeping his beloved bird in his sight.

The three of them might have been there always. Their entire focus was on the moment.

"Aaaawk."

With impeccable timing, Jasmine took off from the chair and, screeching in fluent bird, swooped at Ferguson's face and aimed her beak at his eyes. She dove at him as he fell back and stumbled over the footstool next to Ian.

Experiencing excruciating pain, Ian had ducked his head as Jasmine swooped by. He had no reason to fear her, but a bird flying wild in a room is an unnerving and scary thing.

Jasmine kept moving. Not for a moment was she going to give Ferguson a chance to get near her. She had him down on the floor now, and she swooped within an inch of him, too fast and too unpredictable for him to grab her. She flew around and around the room, until both Ian and Ferguson were dizzy with watching her.

Ferguson was having trouble getting up off the floor. Counted down by a bird? Ridiculous.

He regained his feet. Jasmine swooped low over him.

"Aaaaawk," she screamed in his ear as she darted by. The piercing sound left his ears ringing, his balance uncertain.

Jasmine took a victory flyby, but her triumph was premature.

Ferguson had grabbed the poker from in front of the wood stove.

Jasmine had perched a safe distance on top of an antique lamp made of solid iron.

Ferguson leapt forward and brought the poker slashing down. It hit the lampstand, and the force of the collision sent tremors through his hand and arm.

"Bloody bird. I'm going to kill you!" Ferguson's face was engorged with rage, skin stretched to bursting and face an unhealthy red.

"Killed her. Of course," Jasmine screeched back and began to laugh the hyena laugh she hadn't used in a couple of years – not since Moira Toombs showed up at Ian's with a tight new perm.

That fired up Ferguson even more, and he began flailing about with the poker, knocking pictures askew on the wall, almost smashing Ian's computer, and Ian himself.

Jasmine's bird brain had been working on a new strategy, instead of just flying about randomly. That had been effective, but now she began to fly, back and forth, across the picture window. She was too fast for Ferguson, who smashed away with the poker, constantly missing her, but coming close to the glass. Finally, the timing was perfect.

Jasmine stalled for just a moment. The poker slashed through the air. She budged. The poker smashed through the glass. The glass shattered, and tiny bits flew across the room, some like Christmas tree needles to places from which they wouldn't emerge for years.

Ferguson had dropped the poker and ducked.

Ian slipped down under his blanket for a moment but emerged to see Jasmine fly out the window through a bird-sized hole at the point of impact, the glass around it shattered but not broken.

Ian felt a huge relief as he watched her get away.

He hoped she wouldn't come back until Ferguson was gone.

He didn't know she'd left to get reinforcements.

***

"Jamieson!"

Was she seeing things? Hy thought it might be a mirage. She'd never seen anyone move that fast. Except Jamieson. When she got closer, the bare feet confirmed it, before the facial features fell into shape.

"Jamieson!" Hy had slipped out of the harness and she was running, arms outstretched, as if –

As if she would hug Jamieson? Had she ever? No. Never. And it wasn't going to happen now.

Jamieson slowed at the sight of Hy. Hy ran toward her. Jamieson came to a full stop and stared.

"McAllister. You're looking pretty rough."

Hy grinned. She really did want to hug Jamieson. She wondered if anybody ever had, other than a lover. She wondered if there had been many of those. Surely one. Jamieson couldn't be a virgin. Could she?

"You're looking pretty fast." Hy cocked her head in a query, a query that wasn't answered. She wasn't surprised. Jamieson had been close-mouthed about her fleet- footedness the last time she had demonstrated it, when swift movement had been necessary to rescue the village children from a collapsing wind turbine.

"Wish I'd been faster. You look like you could've used some help a while ago."

Jamieson surveyed the debris – the *Annaben* beached, the shelter in the cape, the embers of the fire, Dot bundled aboard the toboggan.

"What's been going on?" Jamieson walked over and knelt beside Dot.

"We were aboard the *Annaben*."

"We?" Jamieson's eyebrows raised and looked down at Dot.

"Dot and I."

Jamieson flicked her eyes at Hy.

"With permission?"

Hy didn't answer right away.

"Not exactly."

"Not exactly, or not at all?"

Hy said nothing. Jamieson knew what that meant. She sighed. She'd given up threatening to charge Hy. The threats over the years had all been valid, but empty.

"And there's Fairweather's *Cape Islander*," Hy mumbled.

"You took that?"

Hy said nothing.

"Two boats. Two boats? Where is the second?" Jamieson looked around but saw only one.

Hy shrugged. "I had to abandon ship to save Dot."

"I assume you'll make reparations."

"Of course," said Hy. She had the money to buy several lobster boats and more.

Jamieson had been examining Dot. Now, seemingly satisfied, she secured the blanket around her. "She's breathing, but she's unconscious. Little we can do but get her medical care as soon as possible."

"And how do we do that?" Hy looked behind her at the dunes, and then back at the water.

All the while thinking: was Abel out there?

***

Propelled by a giant wave, the rubber boat had flown above the water, smacked down on the deck of the *Cape Islander* and slid into the shelter in the middle of the boat. The simple structure protected the old man from the wind and some of the rain. He tried to start it up, but the boat was out of gas and was moving at the will of the waves. Moving, like the giant cod, in circles. Around one after another of the tiny islands that dotted the gulf at the entrance to Big Bay.

Abel worked the wheel for a while but couldn't fight the rough seas.

The *Cape Islander* was like a creature set free on the water, riding the wind and the waves. He sat back to enjoy the ride.

***

Ferguson was staring out the hole in the window, through which Jasmine had disappeared. Ian was trying to prop himself up to do the same thing, when they both heard it. The unmistakable whining siren of an ambulance.

The whole village heard it. It was one of the sounds on which their world turned. With each new bar of sound, a light went on in the village. The first to hear it, the first to turn on the lights.

Lights went on in sequence at the Joudrys', Macks', and April Dewey's, illuminating the Shore Lane. The Toombs's lights beside the Hall went on. Throughout the village, all the way to Nathan the paramedic's house, the ambulance siren could be heard. Nathan flipped his lights on and raced outside in his boxers, his skinny legs shining white in the light, so he could find out what was going on

It wasn't his glued-together van that was making the noise. It wasn't there. He'd forgotten it had been stolen. He wondered if Jamieson had made any progress finding it.

No, it wasn't Nathan's van. It was Jasmine. Summoning help, with one of her favourite sounds, one common in The Shores, a village heavy on the elderly. The ambulance siren. She blared it over and over again, and people looking out their windows were confused about where it was coming from, and, more importantly, going. The phones were ringing all over the village as Olive and Gladys and Rose Rose, the minister's wife, tried to figure out where the ambulance was headed.

Jasmine was now exhorting Ben Mack out of bed to come to Ian's help. He was the biggest and most able villager she knew. So far he and Annabelle had managed to sleep right through her siren imitation, perhaps because Ben snored so loudly.

But Jasmine's imitation of an old girlfriend of Ian's pierced Ben's night. An imitation of that woman having an orgasm.

It woke Ben up. And Annabelle. They looked at each other in surprise. They heard the ambulance siren. So close. Gus. She always came to their minds when they heard that siren. It was not for her.

This sound was at their window. There was a beak tapping on it.

Jasmine.

Ben eased himself out of bed and opened the window.

They could see the lights at Ian's from here. They could see the lights all over the village. It wasn't a real ambulance. It was the bird.

"Something must be up." Ben was pulling on his jeans while Jasmine watched from her perch on the bedpost.

"Shall I come?" Annabelle had volunteered, but she really didn't want to get out of bed and go into the stormy night. If it were something Ben couldn't handle, she couldn't help.

Jasmine hopped onto Ben's shoulder after he put on his old fisherman's sweater. It smelled deliciously of fish to Jasmine. Ben pecked Annabelle on the cheek, while Jasmine nuzzled into his beard. She'd always had a soft spot for Ben, and it wasn't just because he smelled of fish. She loved burrowing into his beard and hair and pecking around to see what she could find in there. She did find stuff. Snacks.

Ben jumped in his truck and headed up the Shore Lane. Ahead on Shipwreck Hill, an SUV pulled out of Ian's driveway.

***

Finn hadn't expected this. Not this. How would he ever get back to the harbour now?

He climbed out of the vehicle that had refused to budge out of this thick fudge of clay it was stuck in. He'd been stupid enough to take a shortcut, a rough clay road that would have saved him about five minutes on his way to Big Bay Harbour.

He'd lost those five minutes – and more.

The truck's wheels were stuck deep into the clay, and nothing, it seemed, would move them.

He climbed back into the vehicle to try again. He couldn't understand it. This was a four-wheel drive, only two years old, but it didn't seem to be working.

There was a reason for that.

Ian never used the four-wheel drive. Over time, the shifter had seized up.

People wondered why Ian had such a heavy-duty vehicle. He wouldn't carry wood or heavy, bulky items or waste of any kind because these would damage the vehicle's looks. As for the four-wheel drive, it was practical and necessary in such an out-of-the-way place as The Shores, but Ian never went out in the kind of weather, or on the kinds of roads, for which four-wheel drive was required.

Finn didn't know Ian had never used the drive. All he knew was it wasn't working. He'd have to walk. That would take fifteen minutes at least, all for trying to save five. And he'd lost another ten messing around here.

He began the trudge, his feet sinking into sneaker-sucking clay.

He pulled out his cellphone.

Still no service.

Chapter 35

"The place looks great, Ian." Ben surveyed the damage caused by the fight between man and bird. Pictures hanging crookedly on the wall, lamps knocked over, shattered window glass.

"You been in a bad mood, or what?"

"Yeah, but I'm feeling better now you're here."

Jasmine jumped off Ben's shoulder and landed on Ian's head. Ian winced.

"So, been up to anything lately?"

Ian grinned at Ben's dry humour.

"Ferguson."

"Ferguson did this?" Ben surveyed the room again.

"Ferguson and Jasmine. Bird vs. Man. Bird won."

Ben whistled, held out his hand to Jasmine. She flew over and buried her head in his beard.

"Let me patch up that window for you. Lucky it's summer. Then, mebbe you'd like to come stay with us overnight."

"Ben, nice offer, but I can't move."

"Too right. Well then I'll doss down here ta keep you company."

"Ben, it's not necessary."

"Looks to me like it might be. Let me get a fire going and patch up the window. Like a tea?"

"I'd kill for one. Uh oh."

"What?"

Off Jasmine went, on the "killed of course" theme.

***

Jamieson pulled out her cellphone. It was flickering between *no service* and one unsteady bar of reception. In between moments of fleeting service and no service, she punched out a brief text to Finn.

"Found them. Dunes shore. Alert coast guard."

She repeated the text several times, hoping at least one would get through, that when Finn reached Big Bay there would be cellphone service, in spite of the poor reception earlier. The storm had been coming in waves – an assault of wind and rain followed by calm. A calm that might allow cellphone reception.

She was punching at her phone, angry that she hadn't handled this better, that she hadn't turned around and gone back to the village and alerted the coast guard immediately when she saw that the *Annaben* was gone. She should not have tried to play heroine and endangered them all. Had she been showing off for Finn?

She stuck the phone in her pocket, checked Dot's pulse again. At least she had one.

"What were you two up to?" she demanded of Hy.

"I was following Dot. I thought I was following Abel, but I guess she was."

"Abel? Not Abel? Not really?" Disbelief in Jamieson's voice and expression.

"Yes, really. I know you don't think he exists, but that's ridiculous. Dot's his daughter."

"Like father, like daughter then? She nearly disappeared, too."

"Yes, because she's been following him."

"How do you know?"

"I don't know. Not for sure. But I'd bet on it. It's about the big fish, I'm sure it is."

"He's gone after the big fish?"

"Yes. They think there's a pool of them off this stretch of coast here, and Abel wants to get one."

"They?"

"Abel, Dot, Seamus, Ferguson."

"Seamus...?"

"The fisheries guy who sent Abel the email. I don't think his business is strictly official."

Jameson nodded. "And Ferguson?"

Hy grinned. "Ferguson's probably after a Guinness record. They want the fish, and I think they hoped Abel would lead them to it."

"Willingly?"

Hy shrugged. "Not sure. Anyway, he came here of his own free will. Like I said, I think we followed him here."

"And –?"

"We lost him."

Jamieson sighed.

Dot moaned.

***

Finn was back at Big Bay Harbour. He was staring at the line of boats docked on the pier. Wondering which one he'd take. Which one he dared to take. Which one he'd be able to start. Boats were different from cars. Fishermen didn't leave their keys in the ignition. A boat was worth a lot more than a car. It was a man's livelihood.

He pulled out his cellphone, and the service indicator showed some low reception.

He clicked. The service indicator cut out.

No service.

***

By the time Ian had told Ben the whole story about Ferguson, it was the early hours of the morning. He and Ben had tried several times to reach Jamieson to fill her in, but there was no response. Not at the police house. Not on her cellphone.

They'd phoned Finn as well. No answer. His voice mail was full.

They even tried Murdo, but his phone was on the kitchen table, and he was snuggled upstairs in bed with April.

What had started with one old man missing had turned into a list of missing people.

Abel.

Hy.

Jamieson.

Finn.

Four people missing. They ought to do something. But what? It wasn't as if Ian could do much at all.

***

"Finn's bound to be at Big Bay by now." Jamieson was standing close to the water's edge, looking out into the dark.

"I could make us some tea," Hy volunteered.

Jamieson turned. Her expression brightened.

"I'd kill for some tea." It made her think of Jasmine. She could almost hear the parrot picking up on the word "killed," and saying "of course."

Hy prepared tea in the galley of the *Annaben*.

Although it was a serious situation, she felt like Robinson Crusoe, energized by the thought of taking supplies from the beached boat and carving out comfort in the wild.

She came out with a pot and three cups. She nodded over at Dot.

"I'm hoping to get some down her throat."

Jamieson helped Hy position Dot. She held her upright as Hy gently slipped the cup between her lips and tilted it. Some of the liquid spilled out.

Hy tilted the cup some more. This time there was no liquid

dripping out. Dot swallowed a tiny bit of tea. Then a tiny bit more.

Slowly, her eyes opened.

"Thank God," said Hy.

"Where's Abel?" asked Dot.

***

The *Cape Islander* had visited every one of the islands that dotted Big Bay. Now she appeared to be returning home. Home, toward the sandbar that guarded the entrance to the harbour. When she hit it, her prow rose high in the air and the little inflatable boat came sliding off the back and into the water again.

Abel tipped his hat to her, and fired up his engine, remembering that he had a mission.

The fish. But would the fish be out in this weather?

***

The fish was circling, disturbed by the storm. The waves were upsetting its pattern. Around and around, all three hundred pounds of it circled, until it was caught in a current it couldn't fight and drawn out into the opening of Big Bay harbour.

It smelled the man.

It smelled a fight in the offing.

The old man smelled something, too. He smelled cod. Peering out over the water he saw a circle, big and boiling, the thrusts of a mammoth fish churning up the already choppy waters. He smiled, and prepared his fishing line.

***

Finn's cellphone had been taunting him with its service, no

service signals.

Finally, he got a steady signal and was able to get his text messages. There were a few of them, but they all said basically the same thing. Jamieson had found Dot and Hy, and she wanted him to call the coast guard. Of course that made sense. Now it did, anyway. They'd been forced to try to execute a maverick rescue, because they had no cellphone reception. Now he did.

He'd better move quickly before he lost it.

He couldn't move quickly, though. His hands were shaking and fingers kept missing their tiny targets. He made three unsuccessful attempts before he clicked on the three numbers in the right sequence.

911. Emergency.

His impatience grew as the phone rang five times before a woman answered.

He blurted out the details, and she appeared to take them in, until he gave the location. The Shores didn't register in the consciousness of most islanders. Some didn't know it existed. This woman might be one of them.

"The...where?" She sounded confused when he said "The Shores." There were shores all around Red Island, weren't there? That's why there was a coast guard.

"Big Bay Harbour," he spat out, despairing of explaining any more to her. They'd just have to come here, and he would direct them to Jamieson.

He did manage to convince her that it was an emergency.

He disconnected, satisfied that the woman was going to initiate an immediate response. She had assured him a helicopter would be on its way in moments. Not quite the cavalry, but Red Island's version of it.

He felt a strand of guilt. He didn't know who he was worried about more. His sister, Hy? Dot, the woman he'd spent the past year with? Or Jamieson, intruding on that affection, executing a powerful pull on his emotions?

Finn realized that once the helicopter came, he was going to have to get home on his own steam. The truck. Stuck. Who was going to rescue him?

There was a glimmer of light on the horizon that shone an outline around a small vessel. He squinted to see more. There didn't appear to be anyone in it.

It disappeared as quickly as it had appeared. The vision was there one moment, gone the next. So fast, Finn wasn't sure what he'd seen, if anything.

There was nothing on the horizon now except the metallic glint of the sun rising.

A sliver, shrouded in black cloud.

Chapter 36

The coast guard took Jamieson, Hy, and Dot to Winterside.

The three women had implored the pilot to circle around and search for Abel.

"He might be out there and in danger," Hy insisted.

"Might be…isn't is," said the pilot in a pile up of verbs that was nearly incomprehensible.

"Unless this cop orders me, I ain't going out over that water, even though the storm's settled down. Who knows but it might not kick up again. That's what they say it's gonna do. We're going over land. My orders concern that lady there, not some gent who isn't where he oughta be." He jerked his head at Dot behind him, who appeared to once again have lost consciousness.

Jamieson said nothing. She wasn't going to risk four lives for one elusive individual.

They landed in an airfield on the old army base, where an ambulance met them and took them to the Red Island Royal Hospital Emergency. Dot was admitted immediately, and Dr. Diamante wanted to keep Hy in as well for observation, but she refused. They couldn't give up the search for Abel when they were so close. As she was leaving the hospital she tripped and fell to the floor. She couldn't get up right away. Couldn't get up at all.

Dr. Diamante was there, placing a hand on her elbow to gently lift her up, his caterpillar eyebrow on the move as it arched in concern.

"Deezee?" he asked.

She shook her head and nearly fell again, despite his support. *What had he said?* The word spun in her mind. Finally, she got it.

"Yes, dizzy," she said, frustrated that she would not be able to return to The Shores with Jamieson.

***

Finn had no success in getting Ian's truck out of the rut. He pulled out his flashlight to examine it more closely, and the light sparked off something metallic behind a grove of trees.

He walked over, aiming the light at what turned out to be the snout of Nathan's paramedic van.

Found. At least something had been found. He pulled open the driver's door. Keys in the ignition.

Finn started up the vehicle.

In the back, Seamus shot up, woken by the roar of the engine. He'd been exhausted by the effort of pounding at the van and shouting until his throat was raw. As the van began to move over the lumpy ground, he was paralyzed. He didn't know whether to make himself known or not. He didn't know who was driving.

Was it the old man? Someone else? If so, he'd have to make up a story about what he was doing here. It was a story he'd have to make up sooner or later, because even if he kept quiet in the back of the van, someone would be bound to open it sometime. Or he might die in there, starving and dehydrated.

Finn had no idea of his passenger in the back. His eyes and interest were focused straight ahead, and when he arrived at Ian's, he opened the driver door, hopped out, and headed straight for the house.

Seamus froze when he heard the driver get out, until he heard the footsteps moving away from the van. Going where? He had no idea where he was.

Finn stuck his head in the door of the house and Jasmine came flapping down on him. She sat on his head and smacked kisses on his cheek.

She was hungry.

Finn was focused on the room, reduced to a shambles by the fight between man and bird. His eyes fixed on Ian, on the couch.

"So…big party?"

"Ferguson."

"Ferguson did this?" Finn moved into the room, kicking some shards of glass off the carpet.

"With help from Jasmine."

"They had a disagreement?"

"You might say. He tried to kill her."

"What?" Finn dropped down into the chair with the broken arm. "Why?"

"Killed her," said Jasmine in that deep voice, right into Finn's ear.

"Of course," said Finn.

"Of course I killed her," Jasmine chorused. "Of course, of course, of course." She began to snore, imitating the sound drifting from upstairs, where Ben had fallen asleep. He'd stayed to help but hadn't done much.

"What're you driving?" Ian was looking with curiosity at his driveway, visible through his shattered front window.

"I couldn't drive it back. Had to leave it near Big Bay. Stuck in mud. Four-wheel drive wouldn't work."

Ian flushed. He liked his equipment – computer and otherwise – to be in good nick.

"So what's that?" There was a sneer in Ian's tone, as he jutted his chin forward and regretted it, wincing with pain.

Finn walked over to the window, crunching glass beneath his feet.

"Nathan's van. Found it near your vehicle. Abandoned, I guess, by whoever stole it."

"Did you check in the back?"

Finn hadn't thought of that. "Not sure I should. Crime scene."

"Already polluted. You drove it. Fingermarks all over the steering wheel."

"Still…"

"What if Abel's in there?"

"You'd have thought he'd make himself heard."

"Not if he didn't know who was driving, which he didn't." Ian paused. "Not if he's dead, either."

Finn went outside. He walked to the back of the van, banging on the side as he went.

"Anyone in there?"

No response.

When he saw the back door handles roped shut, he decided it was time to phone Jamieson.

No answer. Voice mail full.

***

"I always thought there was something creepy about that guy." Ben had come down from upstairs and was making coffee. Ian found it an odd thing for Ben to say. He was such an easygoing man.

"In what way?"

"There was all that toing and froing over the lobster dinner."

"What do you mean?"

"First he wanted lobster, then it was crab. It's not like I had stock of my own. It's not our season. So there I was like a fool ordering a ton of lobster and changing it to crab."

Ian's brow wrinkled.

"I thought the lobster wasn't available. That's what everyone said."

"Yeah, I heard him say it, too. But there was plenty of lobster. He just changed his mind."

"I wonder what that was all about."

Ben shrugged. "Beats me." He scratched his head, ran his hands through his beard.

"Mind if I clean up?"

Ian's face brightened, then dimmed, as Ben headed for the bathroom.

He'd thought Ben meant clean up the house.

***

They had been put in beds beside each other in a curtained area of the emergency room. Hy had dozed off but woke up when she heard a stirring in the next bed. She looked over. Dot was awake. She pressed the buzzer to alert the nursing station, and Ed trundled down the hall, lighting up when he saw Dot sitting up in bed.

"Now take it easy. I'll get the doctor to come and have a look at you."

Dr. Diamante and his fascinating eyebrow arrived, and he checked Dot over.

"Rest," he said. "Plenty of rest."

That's not what happened when he left.

"Out with it," said Hy. "What on earth has been going on?"

"Before I left, I knew what he was up to. It was all over his browser history on the Internet."

"Yes, we saw that. On the backup."

"He wiped the computer clean, but I already had a backup just in case. I left it where I did, hoping it would be found, if something happened to me."

"He was after the fish."

"Yes. I knew it a few days before, so I left ahead of him. Left Dottie with cousins in Halifax and came back to stalk him, make sure he didn't get into any trouble."

"How did you stalk him?"

"You mean…?"

"Get around. How did you get around?"

"I took my jeep to Halifax. I threw a bike from home in there just in case. Left the jeep in Winterside, and since then it's been cycle and walk – as you know. You followed me."

"Why didn't you stop him?"

Dot laughed. "You obviously don't know Abel."

"That's true." Hy grinned.

"I couldn't stop him, for two reasons. One, I couldn't stop him, literally. I'd have had to hold him down. And two, I couldn't break his heart. He's over ninety. It was the one thing he wanted in the world, to chase down that fish."

"Cod only knows why."

"The thing is, I screwed up at the start. He took off before I expected. I tracked him to the fisheries building. That's where I scooped the hat."

"The hat, but not him."

"No. He went…or was taken… I don't know where. I lost the trail, what there was of it. So I came back to The Shores, out to Big Bay, on the off chance he'd land there. I have no idea why he went to Winterside – or was taken there."

"I followed the hat. Only it was you in the hat. I thought it was Abel. Did you mean for me to follow you?"

"I was thinking about letting you know, asking your help. I circled your house a bunch of times that night thinking about it then decided to strike out on my own. I didn't even know where Abel was."

"But he was at Big Bay."

"Yes. I thought I'd found him, but I lost him again."

A look of despair clouded Dot's face.

"How could he possibly have survived on that little inflatable boat?"

"David and Goliath?"

***

Time reeled back thirty years, as Abel tried to land the giant cod. It looked like the same fish; it had the same telltale smudge on the stripe down one side. It had the same fighting instincts.

265

Abel was thirty years older than he had been, but he was still a fighter as well.

***

Finn was standing in the shelter of Ian's front porch, staring at the van, wondering what – or who – might be inside. Now that Ian had raised his suspicions about the possible cargo, he wanted to keep the van in sight. He continued to try connecting with Jamieson. He continued to have no luck.

Jamieson was on her way back to The Shores. She'd hauled Murdo out of April's comfy kitchen with the wood range fired up, into a steady stream of new rain, the aftermath of the storm. Murdo had fetched the cruiser from Ian's driveway some time before Finn got there. He'd "manned up" and driven it into Winterside to fetch Jamieson. Murdo hated driving in the rain, his sight was so poor. It was a secret Jamieson kept for him, or he'd have been put on a desk job. Then, he might actually have had to work.

On the drive back, she had taken over the wheel. When Finn finally got through and told her about Ferguson's assault on Ian's parrot and house, she pressed hard on the accelerator and squealed around the tricky curve coming off the causeway.

"I'm on my way," she told Finn.

When he told her about Nathan's van and Ian's suggestion that Abel might be dead inside, she wanted to be in three places at once.

"I'll be right there. Don't touch anything."

"I haven't. Well, I drove the van, but – the back doors are roped shut."

Jamieson didn't like the sound of that.

Finn didn't like the sound that came from inside the van.

A thump.

Followed by a groan.

"Someone's groaning in there."

Could it be Abel? Dying?

"I'm on my way."

Jamieson put the accelerator to the floor and screeched along the Island Way. Murdo couldn't see a thing, even though his eyes were wide open.

***

Visibility was poor. The sky was grey. The sea was grey. The rain was coming down in a sheet of grey. There was one dot of white on the water.

A gull?

Not likely. The gulls had gone inland for shelter before the storm. They hadn't come back yet.

The white dot was on the water. Bobbing.

Bobbing.

Suddenly the blob stopped bobbing and began streaking across the water, heading from Big Bay to Mack's Shore.

Something being dragged –

Dragged –

By a fish.

A huge fish.

Abel had hooked the big cod. But the battle wasn't over. For two cunning old men of the sea, this was only the beginning. They had exchanged moments of being in charge – Abel yanking back on the line, the cod stalling, then pulling forward. Until it was all forward, all cod power, heading for the run. The run and the pond; safe haven in the storm.

The sluice gate yawned wide open in welcome.

Chapter 37

"And who the hell are you?"

Jamieson and Finn had loosed the rope and swung open the doors of the van.

Seamus was scrunched up inside, stuffed like a sausage too big for its casing.

A woman and a thin man. Could he outfox them? Make a bold leap forward, punch through them and run. Run? Who was he kidding? He hadn't run since he was five years old.

He knew the jig was up when Murdo loomed behind the other two.

"Seamus O'Malley," he squeaked.

The email man. No wonder she hadn't been able to find him.

"Did you steal this van?" Jamieson entered the name on her phone. It came up immediately. The fisheries department had notified police to detain O'Malley for questioning if they found him. Something about misuse of resources and funds.

She looked up from the phone.

"Well, did you?"

"No. Yes. I borrowed it."

"It seems you've borrowed some other things, too." She'd have to question him – about that and about Abel. "I'm taking you into custody."

How was she going to do that?

She nodded at Finn, and he understood right away. They each slammed a door of the van, and Finn tied the rope.

Seamus screamed, in terror of being locked inside again. He'd always had a touch of claustrophobia, but this experience had made it worse.

"Water. Water," he called out pitifully.

Jamieson nodded at Finn, and he went into the house to get it.

Murdo inspected the cab and took down details, including license plate number, registration, and year and make of the vehicle – an automatic routine he had not lost the habit of, though he hadn't threaded a stitch of police work in at least a year. He'd never even cleared the crabs from the hall. April had done it for him.

Jamieson made a call for reinforcements – cruiser and cops. She ordered Murdo to wait for them – outside.

Inside, Finn forgot all about the water when Ian and Ben told him about Ferguson's seafood switch. Finn cocked his head for a moment, thinking, and said:

"Of course."

Finn's words, fortunately, didn't trigger Jasmine. She had been in a subdued state since Ferguson came after her.

"He *did* kill her."

Jamieson came in the door.

"Who killed who?"

"Ferguson killed Letitia. By changing the lobster to a crab dinner purposely – he was exploiting her crab asthma. Intentionally. If you need intent to pin him down, you've got it."

"Back up. What's this all about?"

"Ben says Ferguson switched from lobster to crab on purpose. Ferguson said the lobster wasn't available, but Ben says it was. He switched it for crab, purposely."

"I don't get it." Ian was missing something.

"The Lung," Jamieson said by way of explanation.

Ian still looked puzzled.

"She likely had crab asthma," Finn explained. "He probably called it a lobster dinner in the first place but planned for crab all along. The crab steam, but not lobster, releases a protein that's toxic. It can kill you if you've got The Lung. An asthmatic allergy to crabs. I'm betting that Ferguson changed the food on the menu with the intention of killing her."

"And succeeded."

"He's got a lot more to answer for then than this." Jamieson looked around the room. There was still glass everywhere and cardboard taped to the big front window.

***

When Ben came out of the bathroom, he confirmed to Jamieson that Ferguson had purposely made the menu change, that he was never out of lobster, as Ferguson claimed, but that Ferguson had made the switch on purpose.

"If you don't mind, seein' as you're all here, I'll head back home. Don't think we'll be out fishin' today, though." He looked out on the dark sky, the dark clouds, the dark water – and the dark expressions on Finn and Jamieson's faces.

The *Annaben.*

"About that," Jamieson put a hand on Ben's shoulder. *Hard as a rock.*

"There's been a small problem…"

Small problem? What, was she an idiot? Embarrassed by her own inability to communicate, she steered Ben away from the interested faces of Ian and Finn. Ian, because he didn't know what she was talking about. Finn, because he did and wanted to know how she'd break the news.

"Hy took it out on the water last night."

Ben looked startled, eyebrows rising.

"Rough weather last night."

"Yes. The thing is, it's beached."

"Beached?" His eyebrows rose higher. "Where?"

She told him.

He went tearing out of the house.

He came tearing back in.

"That's Nathan's van in the driveway." He was pointing, and his eyebrows were on permanent rise.

"Yes, we know, Ben." She wasn't sure what else to say.

"Shall I take it back to him?"

"Not yet." She thought of Seamus O'Malley inside. She'd have to deal with him later. Right now she had bigger fish to fry. Murder trumped missing.

"We need it for the investigation."

"Stolen vehicle."

"Yes, well that, too."

Ben left, scratching his head, wondering what Nathan's van had to with an investigation other than the fact that it had been stolen. He patted the vehicle on his way by – and was surprised by the high whine that came from inside.

***

Jamieson could hardly believe it. Detachment had actually sent the reinforcements she requested.

The officers, Tommy Fyshe and Brad Martin, were the same novice summer replacements, who'd seen – and lost sight of – Abel when he'd cycled out of The Shores days ago. They didn't know there was anyone out here. They didn't really know where they were.

Jamieson came to greet them and told them their man was in the van.

"Take him into custody and charge him with…with…they'll know in town."

They wouldn't know all of it yet. She didn't know either. Besides misuse of funds, of stealing a van, he would face charges of kidnapping.

If they found out that's what he'd done.

The two officers opened up the van, and Seamus, at the ready, burst out. Three hundred pounds of human is hard to restrain, but they managed. Mostly because Tommy put a hand on his gun. Rested it there. That, he had been taught, would quiet down all but the worst of offenders.

It worked on Seamus. He let his shoulders drop down and lifted both hands in a gesture of surrender. Martin patted him down – and removed from his pocket a wad of thousand-dollar bills. The cops eyed their suspect with interest.

Then the Mountie did another thing he'd been taught, and for which he had a particular talent.

He handcuffed Seamus. With amazing speed. Tommy was legendary for that ability in police training. It would remain his claim to fame in the force until he retired – given, not a gold watch, but a pair of silver cufflinks shaped like handcuffs.

Brad and Tommy shoved Seamus into the back of the cruiser and returned to the welcome familiarity of town. Seamus found himself in a claustrophobic but uncluttered jail cell.

***

Now Jamieson had only two places she needed to be. Looking for Abel. And looking for Ferguson. She weighed her options. Abel had continued to be elusive. She had no idea where he was. Out on the water – or in it. Not just gone, but long gone. Two boats had already been sacrificed to that pursuit tonight, and boats were not something she knew anything about.

"Any idea where Ferguson may be?" The question was for them all – Ian, Finn, and Ben.

"Sorry, no." They chorused.

"He can't get far," Ian said. "There are only a few roads that lead anywhere on this island."

"There's only one that leads off." Finn turned from looking out at the water.

"You're right."

"Bad weather for a road chase," Murdo observed.

"Never mind," said Jamieson. "I've got it. You keep an eye on Ian in case the bastard comes back. We could have a killer on the loose."

"Watch those roads." Finn's voice was full of concern. It

touched her, but, after a brief pause, she was back to business.

"I'll be fine." She turned and stalked out into the rain, got in the cruiser, and fired it up.

The passenger door opened, and Finn slipped in beside her.

She opened her mouth to object. He leaned over and closed it with a kiss.

"Now let's get moving," he said, when it ended.

It was wrong in every way, she thought, but she was silent. Silenced by desire, a feeling alien to her body and mind.

"Right." She engaged reverse, her porcelain cheeks flaming red.

The rain hammered down on the car, a fresh blast of a storm that had not given up yet.

Not quite yet.

***

Like a child gnawing on the details of a bedtime story, Hy questioned Dot over and over about her pursuit of Abel.

"You must have wanted to stop him?"

"No. I thought I could stop him – maybe – but I didn't think I should. He needed to do this. At ninety-two, why not? If he died trying to fulfill a lifelong dream, what harm was there in it? But I did want to keep him out of danger."

"That ship has sailed."

Dot winced. At both Hy's comment and the fact that she'd just put pressure on her elbow, trying to shift her position. She hadn't broken any bones, but she was badly bruised.

"Not much I can do now."

"Even if we knew where he was."

Dot motioned toward the north shore.

"Out there somewhere is my guess. I hope he's safe. That he's weathered the storm."

"Better than you, anyway. Maybe he's tackling that fish, as we speak."

Dot grinned. "Yup. One more round." She lay back and covered her eyes with her good arm. In a few seconds, she was breathing deeply, fast asleep.

Hy lay back, staring at the ceiling, listening to the rumbling, the edge of the storm pouring down sheets of rain in some places but clearing in other places, clearing of thunderclouds and of that oppressive smoke that had ruined these last weeks of summer. Maybe it was gone for good.

Dot had woken as easily and instantly as she had fallen asleep. She was staring at Hy, who was staring out the window into a black dawn.

"Penny for your thoughts," said Dot.

Hy smiled as she met cliché with cliché. "Let's blow this pop stand."

***

At Big Bay, a fat wave flowed over the sandbar, and the *Cape Islander* came unstuck. Like a trained horse that knows its way back to the barn, she rode the waves into the harbour and slipped into her berth. Her rope wound itself around the structure of the pier. Will Fairweather would never know she'd been out to sea without him, nor the adventures she'd had.

The *Annaben* would not return so gracefully to harbour. She'd be hauled off the beach later in the day by Ben, in another boat borrowed from a buddy. Like Dot, she'd been badly bruised, but nothing was broken.

***

Abel.

Gus could sense him all around her, as if he were there. Did that mean he was alive, or did it mean he was dead?

She glided back and forth on the purple recliner and felt herself floating toward him, in the grey smoke descending over The

Shores like a shroud. She was drifting…drifting…

⁂

He was there.
All of him.
Naked.
The waves were pushing the boat into shore. He was standing in the back, the big fish splayed across the bow of the dory with its bright yellow and red stripes. His big yellow mac was flying open in the wind, the fasteners ripped off by the gale. Where were his long johns? His Tilley hat obscured his face, clinging to his head, the wind cord tied tight.

It was Abel, bowlegged and stubborn, Abel.

The boat was low in the bow from the weight of the fish. He stood, legs astride, arms raised up, and two fingers on each hand in the victory sign.

The boat hit the sandbar, and he pitched forward. He went flying out.

The weight gone from the back, the big fish slid into the water. Abel struggled to grab it, but the coat got in the way. He pulled it off, and flung it over the cod, trying to slow it down.

⁂

Ferguson couldn't believe what his life had come to. Vandalism. He was bound to be charged with vandalism for what he'd done to Ian's house. Vandalism and worse, far worse. The murder of Letitia. He was sorry about that. He kept telling himself he was sorry about it. She didn't deserve it. Now he'd as good as confessed to killing her. He'd been so vicious about the bird, the bird confessing murder in his voice; they'd be bound to put two and two together. Crab asthma wasn't as well known on this particular patch as in Newfoundland, but someone would know, Ben would blab about the lobster and the crab.

He pressed his foot on the accelerator. The needle on the speedometer edged up, until he was going two hundred kilometres an hour. Ferguson was setting a record and didn't know it.

He was going too fast on the rain-slicked road rutted by heavy farm equipment and transformed into an ideal surface for hydroplaning. Add a curve and a swerve, a cat streaking across the road, a truck hauling a trailer transporting a hay baler ripping down the opposite lane, and he didn't stand a chance. His vehicle slammed into the baler and went off the road, upended, its wheels spinning in the air. Ferguson's last thought as the airbags exploded was *who will feed the fish?* The hay baler pointed to the sky. It looked like it was giving the finger. The trucker was. Once he got over the shock, he jumped down from his vehicle. He peered inside the driver's window of the SUV, and felt more compassionate. The roof was crushed flat. There was an unending *beep, beep, beep* sounding from the dashboard.

Chapter 38

Jamieson hadn't expected Ferguson to die on her.

She hadn't expected to be the one to kill him.

She and Finn had been driving through the dark dawning of the day, windshield wipers unable to keep up with the water sheeting from above and splashing up by the bucketful from the ground. They tore along, bumping and scraping, on muddy clay lanes rutted with holes, crossing the island in a zigzag, the shortcut to the train tunnel.

They caught up with him, barrelling down the main highway. Jamieson put the pedal to the floor, and the needle of the speedometer climbed up into the red zone – 180, 190, 200. She didn't hesitate, not for a moment, strong and sure behind the wheel.

On his ass, her siren sounding through the night.

It was a shock when Ferguson hit the trailer and went cartwheeling into the ditch. Jamieson slammed on the brakes. The police cruiser hydroplaned across the road and screeched to a halt within inches of being the third vehicle involved in the collision. That it wasn't was sheer luck.

Jamieson was paler than usual as she emerged from the cruiser. Finn was so unnerved, he tried to get out without undoing his seatbelt.

Jamieson gave the trucker a curt check to see that he was okay. She walked over to the upended SUV.

It was clear that no one could have survived. She called in the accident.

"Two-vehicle collision. Possible fatality." That's what she said, although the driver was clearly dead.

Ferguson.

Finn came up behind her and put an arm on her shoulder. She turned around.

"I killed him." Nothing like this had ever happened to her in years of police work.

He pulled her close to him.

"I killed him." Her tone was flat, without emotion.

"You're not responsible." He stroked her hair.

She buried her face in his chest, like a reluctant cat surrendering her affection. He put a finger under her chin and lifted it up. The rain streamed down on them, so he didn't detect the tears on her face. If he had, he would have been the only one who had ever seen her cry, other than her parents when she was very young. They were dead. That was the last time she had cried.

She wasn't safe in this world of emotions.

But in Finn's arms, it felt as if she might be.

Some of her distress was uncharitable.

So many of her murderers ended up dead. It bothered her. That's how they got away. Not from justice maybe, but from her. This one hadn't got away from either.

***

Gus stirred in her chair. Her chair? She had thought she was in bed. She wasn't sure if she was asleep or awake.

She didn't know what was real and what wasn't anymore.

A stream of villagers flocked down the Shore Lane, across the bridge, over the pond, and onto the beach, Jamieson and Finn in the lead. Behind them, Gladys Fraser leading the ladies of the Institute, with Estelle Joudry bringing up the rear, reluctant to confront her second dead body in a week.

Well behind was Gus, aided by Hy, scurrying to catch up.

From the other side of the run, a flock of cats, led by Jasmine, undulated over the landscape. Somehow, the parrot had managed to interfere with the litter system to free the felines. And somehow, they all looked like Ralphie. Exactly like Ralphie. A column of big, fat, self-satisfied ginger cats following the smell of fish. Their meows rivalled the squawking of the gulls, flapping into the sky as the cats cascaded down the cape.

Humans in one flowing stream; cats in another. Two columns of movement, streaking forward down to the water in a V-shape, like Canada geese.

At the point of the "V," where the humans and cats were both headed, was a big lump, shrouded in a bright yellow fisherman's mackintosh.

For the second time in these long days of wondering where he was, Gus was struck with fear, fear for Abel. She stopped walking. Stopped and stared.

Was Abel the lump lying there? Unmoving? Dead?

The cats had reached the lump before the humans. Jasmine pulled at the mackintosh and slipped it off to reveal a fish, a cod, a three-hundred-pounder at least. It bore a long stripe down one side, smudged in the middle.

The fish flipped. It wasn't dead.

Nor was Abel.

He sat up, slapped his trophy, and got to his feet.

***

On the way back to The Shores, Jamieson had followed the ambulance into Winterside. Like a border collie rounding up its sheep, Jamieson gave in to the impulse to go to the hospital to see if she could bring Hy, and maybe Dot, home.

They were standing outside the entrance to Emergency,

Dot clinging to the Tilley hat. Jamieson pulled up and opened her window.

"Have you been discharged?"

They both nodded, unwilling to put a sound to the lie.

"Get in then."

It was an awkward moment. There was Finn, sitting in front with Jamieson. Dot and Hy climbed into the back.

It was a silent ride to the village. Dot finally broke the silence with the question that should have been on their minds, rather than the awkward position in which they found themselves.

"Any sign of Abel?"

***

The hush created by the sight of him was loud enough to drown out the waves.

Such a silence had never been heard before in The Shores.

It was as if the sea had stopped swelling, the waves no longer rushing to the shore.

The gulls had ceased to squawk, the wind to blow, the rippling of the grasses stilled. All that could be heard was one big silence that drowned out all the other sounds, drew into it the shore, the village, and the villagers, and halted time.

The silence was broken by some of the women giggling, clutching their hands to their mouths. Gladys Fraser was frowning and darting dirty looks at the Institute women. April Dewey was trying to cover the eyes of her six children with two hands, while nudging her partner Murdo Black to do the same. Murdo was too busy grinning to pay attention.

Abel Mack. Round-bellied, bowlegged, and hairy everywhere except on the top of his head, Abel Mack appeared clearly before the villagers for the first time in decades. It had been his failure to land the fish – the original big cod – that had sent him underground in his own life.

Gus was mortified at the naked Abel, his hands covering the

part of him that had produced eight children. "The Big One,"
Wally Fraser whispered behind his wife's back and winked at
Germaine, so he'd know he didn't mean the fish.

Gus elbowed her way through the crowd and threw a blanket
over Abel's shoulders.

"I told you he wasn't dead," she said, looking straight at
Jamieson.

She must have spoken out loud, because she woke to the trace
of the words on her lips and in her ears.

She had a fleeting image of herself and Abel, arm in arm,
plodding up the lane, while, behind them, the pond sparkled
with the tropical colours of hundreds of fish – turquoise, brilliant
orange, deep reds, greens, blacks, and electric blue.

She'd only ever seen them on her computer screen. Never
before in her dreams.

***

Gus woke up as dawn was streaking the sky with fierce flashes
of fire red. Red sky in the morning.

She was in her chair.

In her chair.

She must've fallen asleep after supper, for she remembered
nothing between then and waking. But she remembered
everything from the dream, the dream that had seemed so real.

She flushed. She'd seen Abel naked in the dream. All of him.
She'd never seen him that way in life, not in over sixty years of
marriage. He always wore his pyjamas over his boxers.

She eased herself up from the chair, every part of her aching.
Not just joints and bones and muscles. Every part of her. Skin
sensitive to the slightest touch. Blood racing through her body,
her heart thumping as if it wanted to escape from her body.
Her breath hurt, too – the breathing was ragged, shallow. She
became dizzy and almost fell but righted herself. Hanging
onto the chair, she managed to slide her feet into her slippers,

fallen off in the night.

The red streaks in the sky pointed the way to the back room, the room with the view of the shore. She was fully expecting her dream to be realized, to see Abel thrown from the boat, the big fish up on the shore, being eaten by the cats.

***

She should have known it would not be like the dream.

It was not at all like the dream.

Gus gazed down from the back room, her eyes following the curve of the run from the pond across the stretch of sand and to the water.

Not at all like the dream.

There was no stream of villagers heading for the shore. No cats flowing down the cape. Nor Jamieson. Nor Hy. She, Gus, was not there either. She was here in the back room, a smile growing on her face, tears streaming from her eyes.

One thing was the same.

Abel.

No. Two things.

Abel and the fish.

Not the conquering hero giving the victory sign and baring his flesh to the world. No. Abel, in his yellow coat and tattered long johns, a pink knapsack slung across his chest. No Tilley hat.

There he was, kneeling in the inflatable boat, perched atop the biggest cod Gus had ever seen. The fish was headed, with Abel and the boat on his back, down the deep run toward the open sluice gate and the pond. Abel was smiling up at the house as if he could see her looking down. He could not, not from that angle. Still she felt as if he could. If she were younger, she would have run down to him, but she couldn't. She was used to waiting for Abel. A few more minutes didn't matter in a long life together.

Gus went back to the kitchen and lowered herself into

her chair. To wait.

***

Jamieson dropped off Hy at her place, but Finn didn't get out there. She drove Dot to Gus's, and he didn't get out there either. He stayed with Jamieson, his only word "goodbye."

Dot looked in his eyes.

Goodbye goodbye.

"He's back," Gus said, when Dot came in the door.

"Where?" She looked around her.

"He'll be at the pond. With the fish."

"He got the fish?"

Gus nodded. "'Spect he did."

Dot wanted to dash down to the pond to see her father, but Gus had other ideas for her.

"Why don't you phone Estelle for me, let her know Abel's back?" Gus knew that if Estelle knew, the whole village would know soon.

"Abel?"

"Abel?"

"Abel?"

The one word that everyone said on hearing that Abel had returned. Their surprise gave Estelle a satisfaction she hadn't felt since she'd told people decades ago that she and Germaine were getting married. Then it had been:

"Germaine?"

"Germaine?"

"Germaine?"

Estelle had thought it meant they were surprised she'd made such a catch, when actually they couldn't believe the pair had ever hooked up. He spoke only French at the time, and she only English. How had he communicated his desire to marry her? Maybe the marriage had been a misunderstanding.

Estelle was so excited to be the bearer of the news that Abel was home, she even phoned Jamieson, something she'd never done before.

Jamieson was puzzled by Abel's so-called reappearance.

"I went over to see him" she told Hy later, "but he couldn't be found."

"Does that surprise you?"

"I suppose not, but –"

"It means everything's back to normal. Gus didn't say he was missing again, did she?"

"No, just that he was around somewhere."

"Then I think you'd better accept it. Whatever it means. Things are back to normal. Abel isn't missing anymore. Wherever he is. I'd say that fish is the visible proof of it."

They were at the pond, the immense fish making frustrated circles in the water. The sluice gate had closed automatically behind him, keeping him captive. The cod appeared to have tried to eat the inflatable boat; it was punctured in several places and losing air fast. Hy had brought a crate of lobsters and was tossing them in. The big cod was swallowing them whole in one gulp.

Finn joined them.

"Ian's trying to get up on his feet," he reported.

"Bad idea." Hy tossed in the last lobster. "He's done that before, and it makes it worse. I better go talk some sense into him."

She looked at the fish again. It appeared to be making love to the rubber boat.

It was grunting, so maybe it was.

The cod was trapped, thought Hy. So was Ian. She knew he would be feeling put out by being left out of the action, sidelined by his injured back. She'd better pay him some attention.

***

Dot felt trapped, too, staring down at the pond from the back room of the house, deciding whether to go or to stay in the village. She had to make a decision soon. Little Dottie would be missing her. Dot hadn't actually seen her father but was satisfied he was home, if Gus said he was. She hadn't rescued him, but she had somehow done her duty by him, but, in the doing, she had come face to face with her own wanderlust. Burst from the cocoon of The Shores by her father's adventure, or misadventure, she didn't want to get back inside.

Not even for Finn?

No, she thought. No.

She never did get down to the pond for a close look at the famous fish that had caused all the trouble. Hy had left, but Dot watched Finn and Jamieson crossing the bridge over the run, side by side, hands held, heads inclined toward one another, talking. They were peas in a pod. Tall, lanky, pale skin, and an abundance of jet-black hair. Mirror images. Male and female made in the same mold. Waiting for the moment when they would meet and meld.

At least, that's what it seemed like to Dot. Oddly, she felt released. She was free. It was time to go.

***

Hy was going to do it. Abel had been granted his catch, and now it was time to release.

Hy crept out of the house, although there was no one to wake. Finn had found somewhere else to sleep. Jamieson's? Would she allow that sort of thing in the police house? Jamieson five years before wouldn't have, but now…Hy picked up her pace and ran across the backyard, taking the shortcut to the Shore Lane.

The sun was barely visible on the horizon, streaking a thin line of gold, the promise of a new and glorious day, through a bank of black cloud moving off the shore. The clean beginning after a dirty season. The air was clear. The smoke from Quebec was gone.

She was carrying a crowbar.

The sky began to lighten and she became energized, swinging the crowbar at her side and striding with purpose, anxious to do the deed.

To set the fish free. To let him go to his happy grunting grounds, she thought with the twist of a smile.

Down she went. Down the Shore Lane. Down Wild Rose Lane. Down to the tip of the run where Ferguson had installed the sluice gate. She reached with the crowbar and tipped open the latch, then grabbed at the gate with the hook and yanked it open.

The fish came streaking out, its tail splashing water, drenching Hy as it raced by. Out. Out into the ocean. Out where it belonged. The one that got away. Twice.

A three-hundred-pound cod should not be held in captivity. Nor eaten.

It was gone.

Not missing.

Neither was Abel.

***

Dot slipped out at first light the next morning. She hung the Tilley hat on a hook in the mudroom – the battered old hat with its traces of seagull shit, next to the one that had never been worn. She spied Dottie's pink knapsack on the floor by the table. She'd forgotten it last time. She picked it up. There was something inside.

She pulled out a ducky mug and placed it on the table, next to a white envelope – her goodbye – clearly visible in the clutter.

Bright as it was, the envelope wasn't the first thing Gus saw when she shuffled into the room a few hours later.

It was the ducky mug. The ducky mug was where it should be on the table.

That meant Abel was where he should be, too.

Around somewhere.

My gratitude, as always, for the great support of
Acorn Press publisher Terrilee Bulger and the talented
people she draws around her, including copy editor
Laurie Brinklow and artist Matt Reid, who has
delivered another stunning cover.

I owe more than I can express to Jane Ledwell,
who edited the manuscript so carefully, critically and
supportively and truly made of it a better book. Truly.

I am very thankful to my first readers for their assessment
of flaws in the book: my only-slightly prejudiced daughter
Kirsten MacLeod; Margo MacNaughton (Queen of the
Comma among other points of grammar); and Henry Mead,
one of two great friends to whom this book is dedicated and
who possesses a keen sense of what works and what doesn't.

Thanks to Dr. Ian Feltham for telling me about
crab asthma. You find out the most unexpected
things during a medical checkup.

www.ingramcontent.com/pod-product-compliance
Lightning Source LLC
Chambersburg PA
CBHW061517020726
47502CB00006B/2106